PEACOCK BOOKS

Editor: Kaye Webb

One More River

Everybody thought that Lesley Shelby was the luckiest girl in town. At fourteen, she was not only pretty but rich and clever as well, and had a boy-friend who was in his third year of high school. She lived in a beautiful great house on the banks of the Saskatchewan River in the Canadian Prairies, and had parents who loved and spoiled her. In fact, Lesley seemed to have everything – until one beautiful September day in 1966 when her father calmly announced that they were giving up their safe happy life in Canada and going to live in Israel.

This is the story of their new life in Israel. At first, everything seemed intolerably hard and difficult. Their kibbutz, on the banks of the River Jordan, which marked the boundary between Israel and enemy Arab territory, was bare and bleak, the work was exhausting and the heat unbearable. But Lesley is determined not to give in. Gradually and painfully she won a place for herself in the heart of the kibbutz, and through her strange, secret friendship with an Arab boy she came to understand something of the mysterious conflicts raging between love and hatred, friends and enemies.

As well as being the perceptive story of a girl growing up and learning what is important in life, it is a lucid and living picture of the agonies and confusions which accompany divided loyalties.

Lynne Reid Banks

One More River

Penguin Books

Penguin Books Ltd,
Harmondsworth, Middlesex, England
Penguin Books, 625 Madison Avenue,
New York, New York 10022, U.S.A.
Penguin Books Australia Ltd,
Ringwood, Victoria, Australia
Penguin Books Canada Ltd,
41 Steelcase Road West, Markham, Ontario, Canada
Penguin Books (N.Z.) Ltd,
182–190 Wairau Road, Auckland 10, New Zealand

First published by Valentine, Mitchell, 1973
Published in Peacock Books 1975
Reprinted 1976

Made and printed in Great Britain by
C. Nicholls & Company Ltd
Set in Linotype Juliana

To Arava, Oren, Shikma-Livne,
Lahav and Nitzanim, this book
is affectionately dedicated.

Acknowledgements

My grateful thanks are due to Hana Raz; the staff of the Press Office in the Israeli Embassy, London; Gid'on Telsch and Yoav Bryn of Rex House; and my husband, Chaim Stephenson, who have all helped me with the background of this book. Also to Tirza Lavi for allowing me to use her poem which appears on pages 213–14.

A glossary of Hebrew (and Yiddish) words and terms used in this story will be found on pages 251–30

Author's Note

This book is fictional. The characters, the story, and the kibbutz are all imaginary. The historical facts alone are true.

One more river,
And that's the river of Jordan.
One more river,
Just one more river to cross.

NEGRO SPIRITUAL

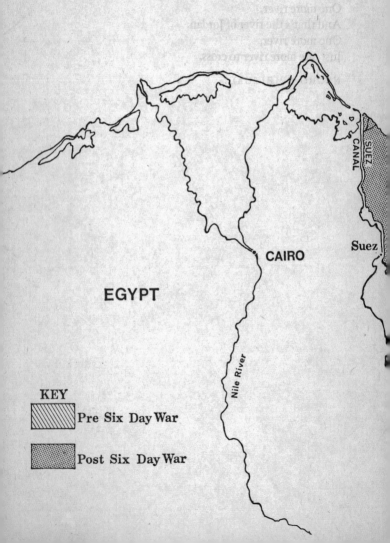

MEDITERRANEAN SEA

CANAL

SUEZ

CAIRO

Suez

EGYPT

Nile River

KEY

Pre Six Day War

Post Six Day War

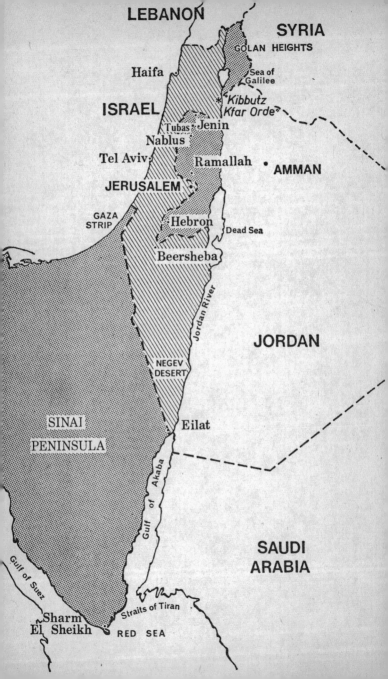

Introduction

If you'd asked any of the kids in her class what they thought of Lesley Shelby, you'd probably have got the answer: 'She's the luckiest girl in Saskatoon.' If you'd pressed them to explain, they might have said that there are rich girls, and pretty girls, and clever girls, but not many who are all three. And if you'd gone on asking, somebody might have said, 'Well, did you get invited to her birthday party?' – as if whatever you might have seen there would have proved Lesley's luckiness without further question.

It was her fourteenth birthday party they meant. Her mother cleared the whole ground floor of their great beautiful house which stood (and may still stand, for all I know) on the banks of the Saskatchewan River in the city of Saskatoon, which is in the Canadian Prairies. She decorated one room like a discotheque, with darkly coloured lights and a bar for soft drinks and a little band. Another room was done up like a marquee, with blue, green and purple streamers hanging from a vast bunch of balloons of the same colours, which were Lesley's favourites, in the centre of the ceiling. The floor was covered with little round tables, each one beautifully arranged with flowers, candles, and little dishes of nibbly things to eat. The guests (there were over 100 of them) could help themselves from a big buffet at the end of the room, spread with a feast that would have done no discredit to a princess's banquet.

There was dancing, of course, and little 'grottos' in the garden for sitting out. There were even table-games in another room, if you felt like it, with terrific prizes, and –

But really, that's quite enough about it.

Lesley certainly was a girl who had everything – apparently. Rich and indulgent parents, to start with. Her father, Nat Shelby, owned the best store in town, and was very important in civic affairs. Lesley had grown up knowing that she was the daughter of a highly successful and popular man. As for her mother, she was all a mother should be – youthful, warm-hearted, sympathetic and devoted to her husband and daughter. It was lovely to be doted on by such parents.

Although Lesley appeared to be an only child, there was once another, a son called Noah, some eight years older than Lesley. But he was not living at home. He wasn't even considered part of the Shelby family any longer. They never mentioned him. It was as if he had never existed. There was only Lesley for the Shelbys to love and devote themselves to.

She was a pretty girl. Tall, with the beginnings of a good figure; hair almost black, and worn in a way which her mother thought too sophisticated, but which was much envied by other girls and admired by boys. Her face I've left till last, being the most difficult to describe. She had good bones and eyes that were on the verge of being beautiful, but missed because they lacked depth. Her face, too, had a certain softness, that was not just the extra fat that might slim away as she grew older – her mouth tended to droop at the corners, to pout almost, at the slightest set-back, and her chin was on the weak side. But her nose was big (too big, she always thought) and her eyebrows dark and straight, giving her whole face a look of strength if you didn't look too closely. The effect if you did, if you examined her features carefully, was that you couldn't really decide if you were looking at a weak person or a strong person. She certainly had a very definite *personality*, but that's not the same, of course, as having strength of character.

It goes without saying that she dressed beautifully. Her

mother's taste guided her until her own developed, and her father's store, the most elegant and expensive in Saskatoon, supplied her. It was with some difficulty that her mother could persuade her to wear the same party dress twice.

At school she did well, but not too well. Girls who do too well academically in Canada are apt to lose a little of their popularity, especially with the boys. And Lesley had just begun to be interested in boys. She had a boy-friend called Lee Tate who was in his third year of high school. Lesley was only a first-year. It was most unusual for third-year boys to make dates with freshie girls. It hardly ever happened. It was a mark of social triumph for Lesley that it had happened to her – the seal on her 'title' of uncrowned queen of her set.

And with all this, of course, Lesley was spoilt. You can hardly blame her for that. To be honest, nobody (except possibly her mother) noticed it. Because what, actually, does 'spoilt' mean? Just that you become used to having everything you want, to getting your own way, to your life and all the people around you conforming to your wishes almost as soon as you make them. And as long as it goes on being like that, there's no reason ever to be jealous, or mean, or malicious, or bad-tempered.

Lesley, like anyone else, could be all these things, but it was so seldom necessary – what reason could she have? – that hardly anybody realized she had another side to her nature.

But what 'spoilt' really means is that somehow your character is too weak, too petted, to stand up to any stiff challenge or trouble. As long as there aren't any of these, you're fine; everyone thinks what a pleasant, as well as lucky, person you are, and you can bask in self-confidence and have never a doubt about yourself.

The thing is, though, that life doesn't allow such people to get away with it for ever. And if you haven't had a chance to strengthen your character with small disappointments and difficulties, then what do you do, and how do you reveal your real, weak, untried self, when something really bad happens – something that would take all the strength of character you had – if you had any – to cope with it bravely?

It's late afternoon on a September day in 1966. And what is the luckiest girl in Saskatoon doing? Not drinking Coke with her best friend Sonia in the corner drug-store, or racing through her homework so she can go out with the kids on her new bike, or choosing clothes in Shelby's Junior Miss department. She's not even sitting at home with her parents watching TV or telling them about her day at school, how she scored in basketball or got into trouble from her French teacher again about her verbs. Nor is she pinning up her hair for a date tonight with Lee, though that's what she *was* doing when her father called her down from her room half an hour ago to speak to her.

No. What she's doing, in fact, is lying on the river-bank of the great South Saskatchewan River, hidden by some very beautifully coloured bushes (it's autumn and the leaves are turning). She's wearing her old jeans and a sweater with a white shirt under it, only it's all rucked up and the white tail of the shirt is dangling out. Her dark hair is half pinned up and half loose, and full of fire-coloured leaves. Her knees are drawn up to her chest and her hand is covering her face. She's crying and sobbing as if the end of summer were the end of the world.

CHAPTER 1

A Terrible Announcement

The story really begins half-an-hour earlier, when Nat Shelby called Lesley down from her room. When she came into the great elegant lounge, still making pin-curls and her mouth bristling with bobby-pins, he put out his hand and drew her towards him.

'Les,' he said, his dark eyes watching her closely, 'your mother and I have something to tell you.' He didn't add, '– and I want you to be a strong, brave girl and take it like a *mensch*,' but Lesley saw those thoughts in his eyes and felt instantly alarmed.

She sat down on the brocaded arm of his chair and cuddled up to him as always. His short, curly grey hair was soft and rich-smelling against her cheek; his perfectly-cut jacket was thrown open on a French silk tie and matching shirt Lesley had bought him for his birthday. His soft, well-manicured hand toyed with hers as it dangled over his shoulder. Lesley thought her father the most handsome, well-dressed and altogether marvellous man imaginable. She adored him, hung on his praise, dreaded his criticism. Not that he offered much of that. But she had always sensed in him a strangeness, something hidden and possibly dangerous – a quality of unpredictability. Deep down this feeling made her uneasy – even a little afraid of him sometimes, much as she loved him.

Across the room sat her mother. Lesley was not quite so close to her mother as to her father. Her mother knew her better than anyone in the world. They had had scenes, when her mother had crossed her, that Lesley hated to remember. It is not very pleasant, when everyone else around you thinks you are practically perfect, to have your mother know – and sometimes remind you – that you are not.

Now Miriam Shelby was smiling, but tentatively, blinking and working her bright lips nervously. This was another bad sign; she was normally so calm.

What could be wrong? Lesley tried to stiffen her inner self to receive bad news, but there wasn't much there to stiffen. In the few seconds it took her father to clear his throat and begin, Lesley's quick brain had run through several dire possibilities.

Maybe they'd decided she was too young to go to the Junior Dance with Lee? He had asked her three days ago (excitement unparalleled!) and she had asked their permission as a matter of form; she'd had to admit – not without pride – that no other girl in her year had been invited.

But it was unlikely that they would change their minds on that. Though very firm in certain ways, they seldom refused her anything.

Another, more sinister possibility was that they'd somehow found out about Sonia's pot-smoking and were going to forbid Lesley to go around with her any more. They almost certainly would do so, if they knew – but how could they know? Sonia only ever did it with her cousin from Montreal, and had confided in a very shocked Lesley under a vow of utter secrecy.

The only other notion that occurred to her was that perhaps her parents had decided not to go skiing in the Rockies this Christmas. That would be awful, having to stay home for Christmas, especially as her family, being Jewish, didn't celebrate it. Most of the other Jewish families in the town made some concessions to the season, but Lesley's parents had always been very strict – ridiculously so, she thought. No party, unless she was prepared to call it a 'Hannuka Party', which would have made her feel too silly. No tree, of course, and the presents were only little Hannuka presents which didn't count (she chose to forget the big ones she got at the Jewish New Year). They did allow her to go to parties, as long as she promised not to sing carols or do anything obviously Christian.

Naturally as soon as she was out of their sight she did everything everybody else did; but she always felt bad about it, and resented feeling bad. But then after all that awful *business* about her brother, her father had started taking her skiing every Christmas holiday, to a Jewish resort, and that made it possible to face Christmas cheerfully.

But somehow none of these possibilities seemed likely. And indeed, all of them fell far short of the really shocking awfulness of the reality.

'Listen,' her father said at last, 'I want you to understand what I'm going to tell you.' Lesley felt a sudden coldness prickle the base of her spine. The last time he had used those words was three years ago when he had told her she must never mention her older brother's name in their family again. She sat up and took her cheek away from her father's hair.

'We're Jews,' he said (and this, too, was like that other time). 'And we're Canadians. It's becoming harder and harder to remember which should come first. My father knew, because he came from the Old Country.' The Old Country, Lesley knew, was the Ukraine. Daddy's name had once been Stupinsky, but he had changed it. 'And your mother's mother – she knew. If your mother and I had been the sort of parents *they* were to us, if we had kept the right sort of home for you, then what happened –' and here her father hesitated and seemed to speak with difficulty – 'What happened three years ago, wouldn't have happened.'

This was the nearest reference to Noah that had crossed either of her parents' lips since he left the house. It gave Lesley a jolt. Noah had been like one not only disgraced, but dead, and to hear her father mention him, however indirectly, was like hearing ghostly footsteps in the next room. Only a matter of the gravest importance and seriousness could make him speak like this. Lesley felt apprehension swelling in her throat; she could hardly breathe past it.

'But Daddy, you do keep a Jewish home for me! Mom cooks kosher and all that, and you're forever telling me –'

'And you, my love, are forever shutting your ears. Jewishness is not a matter of what you're *told*. It's in your blood and bones. If we were doing our job right as Jewish parents, you'd be incapable of doing – a lot of the things we know very well you do.'

Lesley flushed. She was thinking guiltily of a bacon sandwich she'd eaten yesterday at Sonia's. It's hard, one of the hardest things in the world, to be different! And it's hard to accept second-hand rules, specially the food ones, like not eating pig-meat. Sometimes Lesley broke them out of sheer rebelliousness.

But clearly her father was leading up to something far more serious than bacon sandwiches.

'There's a lot more to our decision than just trying to keep you kosher,' he went on. 'Kosher's not the real point at all. I'd be prepared to give up kosher.' Lesley's mother gave a gasp of astonishment, and so did Lesley. It was as if her father had said he was prepared to give up being Nat Shelby. 'Keeping kosher is just a symbol, sometimes of something Jews forget to feel – Jews like us who live in other people's countries.'

Lesley's bewilderment grew. 'Other people's countries? Isn't Canada our country?'

'No. Not deeply and truly. How could a Christian country be our country?'

'But there aren't any Jewish countries! Except –'

'Except Israel. And that's where we're going.'

Lesley simply couldn't take it in at first. It just wasn't possible. She gaped at her father, then turned to look at her mother. She was smiling gently and nodding, in a soothing, now-don't-get-excited way, but her own eyes were wide with a sort of muffled panic. Was she afraid of what Lesley would now do or say, or was she – could she be afraid for herself?

Israel!

Suddenly Lesley's mind began to thaw out of its shock and look at this – this – could it be a *fact*? Could her father and mother, whom she'd always loved, trusted, and – within her limits – obeyed, really be planning to uproot them all from this safe, comfortable, happy life, and drag them all off to that outlandish place the papers were always full of? She knew very little about it, but enough to know quite definitely that it was about the last place on earth she wanted to live in. Her lip curled into an automatic grimace at the very idea.

'But – but – I was *born* here! It's my *home*!' she burst out. 'You can't expect me to leave – this house, this street, all my friends – Sonia – school – Lee –' Each word took her deeper into strange, untrodden realms of despair, and she began to cry, her voice rising and rising. Her father tried to pull her down into his lap, but she tore away and ran to the window, keeping her back turned on them.

But the view outside of the garden, with its beautiful fiery maple tree, the hedge she often hid behind for fun when her father came home, the trim lawn where the couples had sat and held hands on her birthday ... not to mention the wide street beyond, down which, even as she looked, two of her friends came walking arm in arm, giggling over some secret – all these and a hundred other minute details so struck her to the heart that she felt she would fall to the floor and cling to the legs of the piano and defy them to tear her away.

Instead she turned again to face her parents. They were watching her quietly, the way you might watch a person having some kind of a fit, when you can't help them, but must just wait for them to get over it. Lesley couldn't stand their calmness.

'I'll die if you make me go!' she shouted, half-hysterically. 'You can't do things like this to people!' And when her father moved tenderly towards her to comfort her, she struck down his arm and cried: 'You've cut a bit off this family already because of all this crazy stupid Jewishness! Well, I don't want to be a Jew if this is what it means! I'm Canadian, do you hear me? I'm *Canadian*!'

Her father's face, as she turned to it, gave her a new sort of shock. It had turned hard, as hard as marble, and as cold. His eyebrows had risen at the corners and his hooded eyes had narrowed themselves. It was not a face full of love any more, but a face full of grim, implacable determination.

'Nevertheless,' he said 'you're coming to Israel. And I'd better tell you something else –'

But Lesley didn't wait to hear more. What more, what worse could there be?

'I won't!' she screamed passionately. 'I won't, I won't, I won't!' She heard how it sounded, like the shrill abuse of a street-child, and saw her mother jump up, but she was beyond her own control. A moment later, she was slamming the door of the room so hard she felt the vibrations all the way up her arm to her shoulder. She ran across the main road without looking, flung herself down the river-bank to her own secret place, where she lay, crying with bitter incomprehension, rage and fear.

And there was something else. She didn't love her parents in that moment. She had never learned how to go on loving people even when she was very angry with them. This feel-

ing of being cut off from her love for them made her feel sick
and frightened and ashamed.

After a while, the tears stopped, not because she felt better
in any way but because she couldn't cry any more. Her need
now was for someone to talk to, somebody sympathetic and
understanding who would agree with her that nothing worse
could happen in this world. She thought of Lee, but he was
too remote, too romantic a figure in her life to confide in —
certainly not looking like this, she thought, with a flash of
practical feminine sense. No, it had to be Sonia. Sonia was
her best friend, after all, even if sometimes she did things
Lesley couldn't quite approve of, like the smoking ... She
stood up slowly, brushed herself down, tucked in her shirt
and climbed slowly back on to the road.

CHAPTER 2

First Reactions

'And it's not even as if it's *necessary* !'

Lesley and Sonia were sitting outside Sonia's house, on her back porch to be exact. They were eating peanut butter sandwiches, at least Sonia was, and drinking Coke, only after one sip the taste struck Lesley as being so much a part of the life she was going to leave that she choked and could drink no more.

Lesley had lain on the river-bank for quite some time. She didn't want to go home. To tell the truth, she even thought of running away, but she knew that was babyish and impractical.

'What do you mean, necessary? Your dad thinks it is.'

'I mean, really necessary. Like, if I'd been my Aunt Thalia in Poland when the Russians came. You know they looted their lovely house and put my aunt's whole family on a cattle-train for six weeks and took them to Siberia. She was only twelve, and Daddy always tells me stories about how brave she was. I could be brave too, if it was the Russians, if it was an enemy ! But it's Daddy !' She would have begun to cry again, only she'd cried as much as anyone can cry in one day, and no tears were left.

'Well,' said Sonia, a practical and not very imaginative girl, 'I don't know what you're getting so upset about. I think it's very exciting. I'd love to be going abroad !' Lesley could only stare. 'No, honest ! I mean it. Saskatoon !' She put all her scorn into the name of her home-town. 'Stupid, boring, *provincial!*' (Her latest grown-up word.) 'It's a hick-town for Bohunks. You wouldn't catch me bawling my eyes out if I was going to the Mystic East. I'd be crazy with excitement!'

'The Mystic East!' Lesley couldn't keep scorn out of her own voice, and all of a sudden her fondness for Sonia took a downward plunge. 'It's the *Middle* East, and it's not mystic, it's just dirty and noisy and smelly and germy and *ghastly*!' She was on her feet. 'I suppose you think it's next-door to Japan somewhere, with everybody being slant-eyed and exotic! You're just ignorant!'

'Don't you call me ignorant! I'm only trying to make you feel better.'

'Well, cut it out! I don't want to feel better. If I stop feeling bad it'll be like saying I don't mind leaving my home and everything. I'd be a *traitor*!' She started to go, and had actually got out on to the porch steps with the screen-door in her hand ready to let it squeak and bang back in the face of the insensitive, unhelpful Sonia. 'If you think Saskatoon's a hick-town then all I can say is you don't deserve to live here. You don't realize how goldarned *lucky* you are!'

With that she let the door swing to, and ran as hard as she could down the familiar path to the familiar gate for the last time.

Lee was even worse.

She intercepted him on his way to her house to pick her up for their date. She knew she looked a mess, with her hair in rats' tails and her face all dirty, but for once she didn't care – at the back of her mind was the thought that if he saw her like this he would realize how desperate she felt and give her the comfort of some real sympathy. Sonia! How could a spoilt, pampered girl like that talk about going to Israel as if it were some kind of glorious adventure? She'd fall down in a dead faint if she *really* had to face going.

Here came Lee, along the road. He hadn't got his own car yet, but next month, when he was seventeen, his father was going to let him buy his own jalopy. A sudden memory came to Lesley as she thought of this. Her brother, too, got an old car when he was seventeen, and he used to let her help him paint and clean it and even take her out for rides, when he wasn't taking his girl-friend Donna . . .

Watching Lee's approach, it was suddenly Noah's face that she saw. She was conscious, for the first time, oddly enough, in three years, of truly missing him. Why hadn't she missed him till now? Maybe because it was her darling father who had told her she must put him out of her thoughts for ever. She was only just eleven then, and whatever her father said, she accepted as if it came from God. She cried on and off for about a week, and then she did as she'd been told.

But now it was different. Now her father was not God any more; he'd stepped down from his pedestal and done something wholly unreasonable, cruel, incomprehensible. She didn't accept everything – or even anything – from him. And suddenly the biggest pill she had ever swallowed in her life – the loss of her brother – rose in her throat to choke her. Had Noah, in his time, felt as she did now, as if everything familiar and loved had turned traitor? As if the whole world were upside down and out of joint?

But now Lee had seen her and came hurrying up to her, looking in amazement at her dishevelled and grubby appearance. Not he, nor anybody else, had ever seen her looking like that, and he was shocked. Shocked, too, as he got close to her, to see she'd been crying.

'What is it, Lesley, what's happened? You look a mess!'

He looked so worried and tender, her spirits lifted a little. She clutched his hand and felt that perhaps she might be able to cry again after all. Seeing that anxious, fond look in his eyes made her feel so desperately sorry for herself. To get a boy-friend like Lee, and then to have to leave him!

'Lee! It's so ghastly! Mom and Daddy are taking me

away – to Israel!' Into the name she put so much negative feeling that she might as well have been saying 'to hell'.

Lee dropped her hand and looked over her head. His eyes took on a strange look, as if something she'd said had touched some deep secret place in his heart. 'To Israel!' he breathed. She forgot about crying and looked up at him sharply. And she saw a slow, dreaming smile playing over his face like a sudden flare of torchlight.

And quite unexpectedly, quite abruptly, he grabbed her shoulders and gave her a little shake. His eyes were sparkling with excitement.

'Les – you're going to Israel! Gosh! Israel! That's great! Gee, you're so lucky – you're so lucky I could die of envy!'

She gaped at him, and with a quick wrench, pulled back and away from his hands. He looked almost crazy, like one of these fanatics in the movies. Of course Lee was Jewish too, but still ...

'Why am I so lucky, pray tell?' she asked sarcastically, her voice cracking upward.

'To be going there! To help build it! You'll be a pioneer, Les, just think! Gosh, I envy you. I'd give anything, but my old man won't hear of it, he likes his comforts too much. Gee! I always admired your dad, but now! Just imagine, leaving Shelby's and all he's built up here, just giving it all up and emigrating, like our grandparents did in the old days!'

'That was completely different! They were running away from horrible persecutions in their countries! There's nothing to run away from here.'

'Oh, you don't understand! He's not running away from anything, he's running towards something, something exciting, something that'll – that'll test his manhood. There's nothing to make you feel a mensch here. How can you feel like a mensch when you go into your old man's business and spend your whole life going through a routine like a squirrel in a cage? I'd give anything –'

But Lesley wouldn't listen to another word.

'If one more person tells me how lucky I am, instead of trying to figure how sick and miserable I feel, I'm going to scream so long and so loud I'll make their ears ache for a week!' she cried. 'You just can't understand a person's feelings! I don't know why I ever liked you. You're just a stupid, insensitive ox!' And with that she pushed past him and ran into the house.

She went straight up to her bedroom, shut herself in and stayed there all evening, only venturing down when her parents had gone to bed (after repeatedly knocking at her door, which she ignored) to get herself a sandwich and a glass of milk. She'd been doing a lot of thinking. What if all the kids at school felt the way Lee and Sonia did – what if they were all so dumb? If the two kids closest to her couldn't understand, why should any of the others? And if they couldn't see what an awful fate her parents had prepared for her, they might – they might even laugh at her, say she was making a drama of things ... But even if they didn't, just a lack of sufficient sympathy would be bad enough.

She decided not to go to school any more.

The next morning, when her mother came to wake her for school, she just kept the door locked and wouldn't answer. Her mother coaxed, and then her father came up and pleaded with her through the door. She sat on her bed, fully dressed, holding her hands clenched into fists, and her teeth gritted together, and would not reply.

She heard her mother and father conferring together in whispers. Then they went away and left her. The battle was won; but it didn't give her much satisfaction, and she didn't know quite how to take it from there. She couldn't *live* up in her room, for heaven's sake, creeping out like a mouse to

eat when the household was asleep. She'd die of boredom.
She decided to wait till her father went out to the store and
then just stroll down to breakfast casually. She felt she could
deal with her mother alone; she loved her and was afraid of
her 'hurt' moods when Lesley misbehaved, but her father
she deeply respected and even feared a little, deep down; she
knew he had a temper, though he had seldom used it on her.
Again she remembered Noah . . .

However, it didn't work out quite as she'd planned. She
waited and waited for her father to leave; her bedroom window overlooked the front drive, and she could have seen him
go to the garage and drive away. Nothing happened. She
could hear household noises in the kitchen and then the vac-
uum in the living-room and at last her hunger, her desire
for normality, drove her out of her room and down the
stairs. She could go into the kitchen for food while her mother was in the living-room, and perhaps get back up unseen,
if her father was in his study . . .

But he wasn't. He was sitting in the kitchen waiting for her.

She stopped dead in the doorway like a guilty criminal
when she saw him, and then, furious with herself, and with
him, tossed her head and made straight for the fridge as if
he weren't there. But his voice stopped her.

'Lesley.'

It was a very cold voice, colder than she remembered it
ever being. Instinctively she paused for a second, and then
ignored him and opened the fridge door. She had a moment-
ary glimpse of all the delicious foods that always filled it
before it was roughly slammed.

She whirled round, on the verge of breaking her vow of
silence to ask her father how he dared treat her like that . . .
but a flash of cold fire in his eyes froze the words in her
mouth.

'Now just you listen to me, miss,' he said, biting out the

words in a way that made her shiver. 'We've spoilt you rotten all your life, and that's our fault, but no daughter of mine is going to behave like a weak-kneed baby. I'd have helped you and been sympathetic if you'd let me, but if you want to play it rough, I can play it rougher. Now you go and sit down over there.'

When she didn't move, he took her by the shoulder and forced her into one of the kitchen chairs. She was simply trembling with rage, but so, she felt through his hard hand, was he. She stared into his eyes to show him she wasn't afraid, although she was.

'You've had it soft, and so have I, these last years. Difference is, I've earned it and you just got it given you a present.' (Sometimes he talked the way his mother had, even with a Yiddish accent.) 'But where we're going, kid, nobody's going to spoil either one of us. This soft, sick life is over, beginning as of now. No, now you just shut up and listen ! You know what your grandfather used to say, in the old days? He who doesn't work, doesn't eat. Your work is school. Now you get your books and brush your messy hair and get into the car and I'll take you there, because if not you're going to be a mighty empty little girl by tomorrow morning when you'll get your next chance.'

Speechless, stunned, Lesley slowly stood up and went upstairs to her room. In a daze of shock and amazement she ran a brush through her hair and put her day's books into her schoolbag. It was already 10.30, the school morning was half over; she had missed two lessons and would have to walk into the middle of the third. All these thoughts ran through her mind in a far-away fashion, not really horrifying her as they would have done normally; she was far too appalled by her father's sudden, brutal show of authority.

Appalled, and, in some extraordinary way, admiring and relieved.

CHAPTER 3

A Dangerous Idea

So Lesley went to school, that day and the following days of September and October until it was time to leave it forever.

It was not as bad as she'd expected. Lots of the kids really were sympathetic and there was a feeling around as if they would be truly sorry to say goodbye to her – even some of her favourite teachers expressed regret, and this was balm to her wounded feelings.

But to make up for that, life at home was ghastly, and seemed to get worse and worse. Her father never spoke to her in that awful way again – she made good and sure he never had reason to, because it had given her the shock of her life; but he always seemed to be watching her, as if just waiting for her to step out of line and give him the chance to jump on her again. They spoke to each other only when it was necessary – politely, but without any warmth at all. As for her mother, she was going through some private crisis of her own, and, although she was not cold to Lesley, she seemed somehow distant, as if preoccupied with her own thoughts and worries. Lesley, when she could stop thinking about her own feelings of despair, occasionally wondered whether her mother, too, might not be exactly looking forward to leaving her home and flying off into the unknown. Lesley might have felt a shared sympathy for her, and treated her much more lovingly, if only she could have spared the pity that was all going on herself.

One thing she wouldn't do, was show the slightest interest in their enterprise. Once or twice her mother gently suggested that it would be a good idea if she read some books about Israel, or, more important still, tried to study Hebrew in preparation for their new life. She simply wouldn't listen. She turned her back, she turned her *mind* completely away. Anything like that would be the same as agreeing to go. She saw now that it was inevitable, but for the sake of her pride – and of her patriotism – at least she would not co-operate. Let them drag her. She wouldn't help them, not in any way at all.

But at one point, where her wall of defence was at its weakest, her clever mother finally made a breach.

One day she got home from school to find a big dress-box with the name of the family store on it. She knew these boxes very well indeed. A box like this lying on her bed when she got home always gave her a wonderful, excited lift, because it meant that her father had brought home some of his latest stock for her to choose from – a new dress, a pile of bright sweaters, or perhaps some pretty undies or shoes. She looked at it now with a flash of automatic excitement which was instantly spoiled by suspicion.

She left it there untouched while she did her homework. But curiosity overcame her at last and she had a peep.

A minute later she was running downstairs with the box. She threw it on the living-room sofa next to her mother, who was sitting there sewing placidly, as if butter wouldn't melt in her mouth.

'I wouldn't be caught *dead* in any of this junk!' she said shrilly.

'Oh, darling, have I chosen the wrong things?' exclaimed her mother innocently. 'Well, but you wouldn't come with me, would you? Never mind. Why don't you go down with Daddy in the morning and choose what you like?'

'My old things will do well enough. The oldest *shmatter* I've got will be ten times nicer than anything *there*, I bet!'

Her mother seemed about to speak, then changed her

mind. 'Oh, okay, honey. You must do as you think best. You've certainly got plenty of pretty things already.'

Lesley's mouth opened automatically to contradict this – what girl will ever admit she has enough pretty clothes? – and stayed open in admiration of her mother's shrewdness. Trapped! Not that it matters, she told herself sharply. Not that anything in the world matters any more. She walked out, slamming the door.

But vanity was her weakness. The next morning, after a long and losing battle with herself in the night, she put on her coat after breakfast and left the house without a word. Her father, going out to his car, found her already sitting in it. The big dress-box was on the back seat.

His eyebrows went up in a way that made her squirm.

'Coming into town with me?'

'Mother told me I had to get some new clothes,' said Lesley, aware not only of the lie, but of the irony – her mother had never had to order her to get clothes. Her father smiled.

Once that smile would have made her ask him rather rudely what was so funny. Now she had to hold her peace because their new relationship wouldn't allow her to take risks with his temper.

On the way into the town centre, they didn't talk. It was painful for them both, because in the old days she would have hugged his arm affectionately and chattered away about everything, and now – nothing. Coldness and silence. But when they were nearly there, Nat Shelby said, 'Well, Lesley. Time's getting short. Apart from choosing clothes, are you doing anything to prepare yourself?'

'No,' she replied, with more sharpness than she really dared, so that she had a pang of alarm. But he didn't bark at her, and she was emboldened to go on: 'There's no need to be sarcastic about the clothes, either. Here in Saskatoon I'm *somebody*, and I have to dress like somebody, but *there* I'll be a nobody. Well then, at least I'll be a well-dressed nobody.'

'Protective colouring, eh?' remarked her father. She didn't understand that, so she said nothing. 'And why are you a somebody in Saskatoon, Lesley? Have you ever thought about that?'

Honesty compelled her to answer, after a moment's hesitation, 'Because I'm your daughter, I suppose.' And then she added defensively, 'But I'm popular in my own right at school. Being Nat Shelby's daughter wouldn't help me there if I was no good.'

'True enough,' he said soberly. 'And in Israel, to begin with at least, you'll be – as you said – a nobody. A nobody's nobody.' He swung into the executive's car park and switched off the engine of his powerful car. He sat still for a moment. 'A nobody's nobody,' he said softly.

A wild hope sprang alive in her. She turned to him. 'It doesn't have to be that way, Daddy! It's not too late! We could still – not go – couldn't we?'

He shook his head slowly, narrowing his eyes. 'No, daughter,' he said quietly. 'There's no turning back. The store is sold.' She drew back, staggered. She hadn't thought of that. Shelby's, sold! 'Daddy!'

'Oh, it'll still be called Shelby's,' he said, stirring himself as if a weight lay on him. 'And the new owner's keeping all my staff on. I had to make that part of the deal. I want to – to leave something behind me.'

Lesley was shocked by the sadness, the heaviness in her father's tone. This whole business was making her grow up a little faster than she would normally have had to, and some newly-developed wisdom made her understand that her father's heaviness of heart had something to do with his son, Noah. Once, she knew, it had been his dream to add 'And Son' to the twirly gold lettering on the front of the store.

Now he had to sell it into the hands of strangers, leaving only the name and some men and women who had worked for him and would remember him with gratitude because he had secured their jobs.

Some sort of desperation made her, abruptly and briefly, incredibly brave.

'Daddy, where's Noah?'

Without actually moving, her father seemed to go rigid all over until he became a statue, sitting in profile. She forced herself to go on, despite a quaking certainty that she was now playing with fire a great deal hotter than her father's mere anger.

'Has it got anything to do with Noah – all this? Are we leaving Saskatoon and everything, so you can get right away from – him?'

Her father turned his face to her very, very slowly and stared at her woodenly. It was a stranger's face, cold, calm, almost empty. At last the statue of her father opened its mouth and some words dropped out like chunks of ice.

'Nothing I do now could have any connection with your brother.' She noticed he neither named Noah directly nor said 'my son'.

'But Daddy –'

'Not another word, Lesley. I beg you. Not another word.'

He turned away from her abruptly, got out of the car, and, as always, came round to her side to open her door and help her out. He had done this from the time she was a very little girl, and she had grown up with the understanding that this was the way men should treat women – pampering them and making them feel feminine with innumerable little courtesies. She had sent her first boy-friend about his business because he had not known this way of behaving. Now she got out and she was shaky on her legs. She felt as if they had passed very close to some great danger, and only just managed to avoid it. Her father's hand on her arm was trembling too.

He carried the dress-box into the store for her. The doorman saluted them both, and Lesley was aware of the deferential nods and smiles of the staff as they passed through the ground-floor departments to the private lift. The sudden awful realization that this might be the very last time she would walk through Shelby's in this way, bowed to and respected like a royal personage, made her want to weep, but she didn't. She put her head up and smiled back with far more than her usual warmth. Dear people, she thought suddenly. Dear Canadian people who admire and love my father and give me a place in the world! Going up in the lift, her father unexpectedly spoke to her again.

'I know you're having a bad time,' he said abruptly. 'But I find it hard to take your suffering very seriously when all it does is make you more and more childish and unpleasant. And cruel,' he added. They reached the floor she wanted and the doors opened, but her father pressed the button that closed them again. 'You're making everything much harder for your mother and me.'

She felt subdued by the recent danger, and tried to speak quietly and reasonably. 'But it's not hard for you. You want to go.'

'We feel it's right to go. That doesn't mean it's easy.'

He opened the door again as a sign that he'd finished. He handed her the box, nodded to her distantly, and in a moment she was outside in the dress department and the lift doors had closed. Her father was on his way up to his office to complete the sad task of winding up the business he had spent all his life building up. Lesley imagined him going about this and her brows contracted for a moment as if she felt his pain.

However, there followed a not wholly unpleasant morning. Choosing clothes is a delight which has comforted many an older and sadder woman than Lesley. She emerged after two hours in which her only thoughts about going *there* had been the impression she would make on the primitive inhabitants. She didn't realize it, but the reason she was choosing so many things – far more than she strictly needed – was not just to console herself, but to spite the Israelis, the people of her own age among whom she was to be thrown willy-nilly, a nobody's nobody. She would show them! She would dazzle them. She would march in among them like a knight in full armour, and force them to give her the admiration which was her due.

On her way out, the doorman who had bowed her in earlier asked if she wanted him to call her a taxi.

'No thanks, Bob,' she answered automatically. Nobody in her crowd at school took taxis, however rich their parents were; it was considered show-off. But suddenly she changed her mind. 'Oh – well, perhaps I will, today. I've got such a lot to carry.'

He stepped to the kerb and waited for a cab to come round the corner. She stood by him. He cleared his throat.

'So you're leaving us, Miss.'

'It looks like it.'

'And Shelby's sold!' The man shook his head. 'Saskatoon won't seem the same without your father. I don't speak against the new boss, but I can't think he'll be as good as Mr Shelby, by many a long mile.'

Lesley felt warm with pleasure at hearing her father praised, but at the same time angry. Kind enough to his staff, perhaps – but to his family?

'And how's the family, Bob? How's your son these days?'

The man's face lit up with pride. 'Great, Miss, just great.

You know he graduated from the University? Oh, but of course you know! He took his degree on the same day as your –'

And there he stopped.

No man, thought Lesley, ever looked more uncomfortable. And it gave her an unpleasant feeling, to realize for the first time that naturally all the staff of Shelby's, all the people they knew, probably the whole of Saskatoon, knew the full story of Noah's banishment.

And quite suddenly, standing there waiting for a cab, a most daring and fantastic idea came into her head. It was born of her first feeling of separateness and hostility towards her father. As she had no way of fighting his plans, she had a rebellious longing to do something else against him. Nothing she could do, nothing in the world, would be a greater act of courage and rebellion than to seek out Noah and see him again.

But there was more to it than that. She had recently begun to miss Noah seriously, to want to see him for her own sake. After all, he was her brother, her only brother. He had done something unforgivable in their father's eyes when he converted to Catholicism to marry Donna; and Lesley, at the time, had taken her father's word for it that this was a crime sufficient to justify her parents disowning him and exiling him from the family forever.

But now Lesley was growing up and developing a mind and a judgment of her own. A girl in her school had a Jewish father and a Christian mother. Lesley had been to her house and felt good there. She knew that lots of Jews in her town had 'married out'. Was it really so terrible? Or had her father acted irrationally, even tyrannically? Now she thought about it, hadn't she heard other people, grown-ups, members of her family even, whispering similar ideas when it first happened?

Aunt Hannah hadn't even whispered. 'You're a pig-headed fanatic, Nat! You'll regret it! Look around you. Times are changing. If you send your boy to school with non-Jewish girls, what do you want from his life? Well, don't expect *me* to abide by this ban of yours. He'll need somebody to turn to, poor boy!' Daddy's very own only sister! He had never asked her to the house, nor spoken to her again, not in three years.

And now Lesley made up her mind. She turned to Bob the doorman with abrupt determination.

'Is your son still friends with my brother Noah?'

'Now then, Miss Lesley, it's not fair you putting me on the spot that way. Ah!' It was an exclamation of relief as a taxi came in sight and he stepped into the road to flag it down. Lesley put her hand on his sleeve.

'Bob.'

'Now then, Miss, here's your cab. Off you go.'

Lesley felt anger and stubbornness rise in her together, because now he was treating her like a child.

'Bob, I want to know where to find him. I want to see him before we go away.'

'I'm sorry, Miss. I know what your father –' The cab-door was open and she was still standing there, her eyes fixed on him. She was her father's daughter. She knew instinctively how to fix a subordinate with an eye of command, how to get her own way simply by expecting to. She saw Bob's resolute look falter.

'Bob, I want his address.'

'You'd better talk to my boy about it,' he muttered.

Lesley briskly took pencil and notepad out of her pocket.

'How do I get in touch with him?'

'At work.' He reluctantly gave the name of a big engineering firm. She thanked him and got into the cab. Just before it pulled away, Bob leant down to the window. 'I might as well tell you, your brother works there too. Only, look, Miss, if you tell your father I told you –'

'What do you think I am, Bob?'

He didn't reply and she felt him standing there dumbly, no doubt wondering what had possessed him. And she, meanwhile, burning with a fierce excitement, was inwardly echoing her own words and asking herself, 'What do I think I am?' Not a very good or a very loyal or obedient girl, that was clear. But this visit she intended to pay to her brother was something no conscience in the world could have kept her from, now.

CHAPTER 4

Noah

She found Noah. She found him that very same day, by the simple method of directing the taxi to the big firm of engineers that the doorman had given her the name of. Trembling with terror at her own wickedness, and also with sudden great nostalgia and longing to see Noah again, she asked for him at the desk. She was sent up to an office high above the city, and there on the door she saw his name, Noah Shelby, and his degree, and the words 'Junior Engineer'. The name of Bob's son was there too.

She stood outside the door, shaking all over. It was not too late. She could still turn round and go home and no one would ever know how close to treachery she had come. But suddenly she heard Noah's voice inside and without hesitating her hand went out and opened the door, and she walked in.

He hadn't changed much. He had been eighteen when he left and he was now nearly twenty-two, still the same gangling tall body, but filled out a little with hard, masculine muscle, and the same long, not good-looking but nice-looking face, dark hair, like hers, falling over his forehead and black-rimmed glasses.

She remembered in that split second before he saw her, how he had fooled around with those glasses when he first got them, at the age of sixteen, saying there was nothing wrong with his eyes but that he needed them to look like a big executive – taking them off wearily to show how much paperwork he did, or snatching them off and pointing them at some unlucky underling ... How they'd laughed together, what fun he had been ! Oh, she had loved him !

And there he was, really sitting at his desk hard at work,

an executive at last, if not a very important one yet, and lo and behold he actually took his glasses off and rubbed his tired eyes just as he had done in the game. It took her right back six years and she burst out laughing, and then he looked up suddenly and saw her and the glasses dropped on the desk.

'Les – Sis, can it really be you?'

'Sure it is!'

He jumped to his feet and they rushed into each other's arms. He hugged her until she had no breath left. He kept making silly noises and saying things like 'Gee, Les – Gosh, you came – Gee-whiz, let's look at you –' And he held her away and looked at her as if she were a revelation from heaven and then he grabbed her and hugged her again and they were both laughing and neither of them really could think of anything to say.

At last he seemed to sober up and stood away from her, looking at her slowly and carefully.

'Don't say it,' she warned. 'Don't say "How you've grown!" I'll hit you if you do.'

'I can't help it,' he said softly. 'You've grown real pretty too – you little monkey-face – you're real cute these days. I bet the boys are coming around already, eh? I bet you're fighting 'em off.'

'Ah, don't be crazy, Noah!'

'You need a big brother around to –'

And then suddenly it wasn't fooling any more and he looked at her for only a second and then turned away very quickly. But she had seen. Actual tears. The sight of them broke down her own thin shell of bravado and she caught her breath on a great sob.

'Oh, Noah! Why does it have to be this way? It's so good to see you and I love you and I feel so *crummy*! Dad'd kill me if he knew I was here!'

Noah took out a handkerchief and wiped her eyes and then, with one arm round her, he blew a trumpet-blast on his own nose that made them both laugh at least a little, and then he led her to a sofa and sat her down on it.

'Now look here, Sis. First of all you tell me why you came. Then I'll tell you why it's okay.'

She tried to tell him. She told him first about her parents' decision to take her to Israel. When she'd told him that, she had to stop talking awhile and give him time to recover. She'd half-expected him to have heard about it, but clearly he hadn't, and clearly he was deeply shaken by the news.

When he'd got over the first shock, he sat down beside her again and held her hands so tightly in his that the bones cracked, and pumped questions at her one after the other:

'When did they decide? What made them decide? What about the store? Is Mom happy about it? What'll Dad do over there? Is it for ever or is he bringing you back? How do you feel about it?' She answered as well as she could, the words hardly out of her mouth before he was firing the next one at her. But then suddenly he stopped and was silent for a long moment, staring at her, and then he asked, 'Does he ever, ever mention me?' And she had to say no, and he lowered his head and sat there, only one thumb moving a little, stroking the back of her hand.

She put her arms round him and said quickly, 'But Noah, he thinks about you. An awful lot. I just know he does! I know it!' He didn't reply. 'And Mom cried for *months* after you left. I'll never forget it. Surely it's a sign that they still love you, that they're so rigid about never mentioning you?' Where this bit of grown-up understanding came from, she didn't stop to wonder. She told him instead what had happened in the car, only that morning. 'If he was over it, if he was sure he'd been right, wouldn't he be more – quiet about it inside, after such a long time?'

After another long silence. Noah stood up again slowly and walked to the other side of the room, rubbing his fingers through his hair the way he used to. His hair had grown at the back, she noticed. Dad wouldn't like that, he thought long-haired boys were all weirdies. But Lesley thought it suited him. The truth is that as soon as she saw him again, she loved him so much that anything he did, said or wore would have been all right with her, just because it was him.

He came back to her when he was ready. She had never stopped to ask herself how *he* had reacted to being thrown out of the family. Now, without him telling her anything directly, she realized that he had suffered fully as much as her father, and was not over it yet by any means. She began to wonder all sorts of new things about him, inward things and outward things that had never occurred to her before. Suddenly she sat bolt upright.

'Noah! Am I – an aunt?'

He grinned slowly through his confused, heavy thoughts, and shook his head. 'Not yet, Sis. We're working on it.'

'How is she – Donna?'

'Great,' he said absently.

'And you're happy, you and her?'

'Sure. Sure we are.'

'So you're not sorry?'

'Sorry?'

'That you – you know – converted.'

He looked at her oddly through his glasses and didn't answer.

'Why did you, Noah? I've found out you don't have to. I mean, lots of non-Catholics marry Catholics. They only have to promise to bring the children up as Catholics.' Still he didn't speak, and she pressed him reproachfully, 'You must have known what it would mean to Daddy and Mom.'

'Well, do you know, I guess I didn't. I mean I knew they'd be against it, that's why I didn't tell them till I'd done it. I see now I made a big mistake about that. I just didn't dream they'd care that much. The trouble was I was so darned young. We both were. There was Donna, barely seventeen, and her folks wouldn't hear of our marrying unless...' He sat still for a long moment. 'I remember the priest asking me, "You're not just doing this because of outside pressure, young man, I trust?" I lied. It all began with that lie. All of it ... But I loved her so much, and she was so unhappy ... And I didn't care for myself. You know I wasn't especially Jewish. At least, that was what I thought then ...'

Lesley digested all this with a deep frown. 'What do you mean, "that was what you thought then"?'

But Noah's mood suddenly seemed to change. He grabbed her hand and jumped up.

'Look, this is a great occasion! Do you have to go home right away? Because it's lunchtime and I've got a whole hour to do what I like in. And what I'd like is to take you to the Bessborough Hotel and give you the biggest slap-up lunch you ever had in all your life.'

'Gosh, Noah! I'd just love it! But I'm not grand enough in these *shmatters*.'

'Well, what's with the boxes? I bet you've bought yourself something good enough for the "Boozeborough" if not for the London Ritz.'

They rummaged through the things she'd bought and he chose a sharp pants-suit in his favourite colour, yellow. Then she changed into it while he washed and she said she wished she'd thought to have her hair done that morning and he said nuts to that, he liked his women to look natural. So they talked nonsense instead of telling about the deep, confused feelings that were upsetting both of them underneath, because they didn't know how to express them, and besides, they weren't sure of each other yet.

Outside, Noah hailed another cab in a very worldly way; they piled Lesley's things inside it and Noah said grandly, 'To the Bessborough,' which was the best place in town, and added to her, 'Have you ever drunk champagne? That's what all the really wicked women drink. We'll have some to celebrate the coming of your independence.' Lesley secretly thought she'd rather not – she'd tasted wine from time to time but she only liked the very syrupy, ceremonial wine they drank at Passover. But she just giggled and said he was the boss.

However, when the cab put them down outside the main entrance of the hotel, and Noah was in the middle of paying him, he stopped and glanced at Lesley and then around at the people who were coming and going through the entrance. 'Hell, what are we thinking about?' he muttered. 'Anyone could see us here together! C'mon, let's get out of here!' And they climbed ignominiously back into the cab and got it to drive them to a little Chinese chop-shop over on the far side of town, where none of their father's friends or business associates ever came. There they sat down in a booth and ordered chicken chopsuey and chips, and Cokes instead of champagne.

'Sorry, Sis. I guess I must have had a moment of madness.'

'Gosh, don't give it another thought! I like it better here anyhow.'

He took her hand and gave it a squeeze and they smiled into each other's eyes. She thought she could see tiny little lines beginning to show around his, behind the glasses. Did you begin to get old at twenty-two? Only if you were very worried or sad, perhaps. Worry and sadness aged people earlier. She squeezed back, feeling quite suddenly as if Noah were not just her beloved brother, but her dearest friend. She couldn't imagine how she had lived all these years without him.

'You don't know what it means to me to see you. You just don't know.' It was Noah who had spoken, voicing her thoughts.

'Have you missed us?'

He frowned, dropping her hand, and went on playing with his chop-sticks. He wasn't really eating, she noticed. 'You could put it like that,' he said. 'We're very tied to our families.'

'We?'

'Jews.'

'But you're not a Jew any more,' she said unthinkingly.

He looked up at her quickly, then down again.

'Oh yes I am,' he said.

'But you – you know.'

'I turned Catholic. Oh yes, I went through the rig-marole. Don't let anyone kid you, Sis. You're born a Jew, you stay a Jew. Nothing you can do will ever change it. If you try to forget it, there're always people who'll remind you. The German Jews, for instance, before the War. They thought they were Germans. But the Germans didn't think so.'

Lesley wriggled uncomfortably. 'Oh, shut up about all that! I hate thinking about it.'

'You have to think about it sometimes. Otherwise how can you understand?'

'Understand what, for gosh sakes? What's all that junk about the past got to do with us now?'

'The past is what makes the present. Don't they teach you kids anything nowadays?' He said this last sentence in their father's voice, and they both laughed. Then his face grew serious again. 'Going to Israel, for instance. How can you understand what's making Dad act this way, unless you know what's been happening with the Jews all the way back for 4,000 years?'

She looked at him with her mouth open. 'Gee, Noah, 4,000 *years*? We've only got back as far as the Battle of the Plains of Abraham !'

'Well, you'll have to go back to the original Abraham to figure out what's motivating our old man.'

'Do *you* know history all that way back?'

'Jewish history, yes.'

'When did you learn it?'

'I've been reading it up. These last years, since . . .'

'Since you were *supposed* to've stopped being a Jew.'

'That's right.'

'I don't get it, Noah.'

'No, of course you don't. How could you?' He picked up a crispy noodle between his fingers and crumbled it slowly to fragments. 'Look. Would you read some books if I gave them to you?'

'What kind of books?' she asked warily. This was beginning to have a smell of homework.

'Don't sound like that, Les. Listen, will you? Now we've like found each other again, what's the use if we don't try to help each other? Life's kind of strange, don't you think? Here's you, going off to Israel against your will –'

'I'll say !'

'While I'm staying here, when I –' He stopped. 'Anyhow, if you gotta go, you gotta go, as they say. The thing is to accept it and start getting your mind in shape for the journey. I bet you don't know from nothing about Israel. I bet you think it's all camels and *gefilte* fish. Will you let me wise you up a little? I can, you know. I can even give you a Teach Yourself Hebrew book, if you promise not to tell anyone where you got it.'

'Especially Donna.'

'What?' he asked sharply.

'I said, especially I shouldn't tell Donna.'

Now it was his turn to stare. 'You may be weak on history, kid,' he said at last, 'but you're sure no slouch on psychology.'

'I don't know what you're getting at. It's obvious if you turned Catholic for Donna's sake and here you've been boning up on Judaism, you wouldn't want her to know about it.'

He stared at her some more, then slowly shook his head. 'Listen, Sis, don't work too hard on me, will you? I mean, just do me a favour and point your crystal ball the other way. You see too much, much more than you're grown-up enough to understand properly. So just let me be the wise-guy around here, okay?'

'Okay, Noah,' she said, feeling quite bewildered, but willing to do almost anything he asked.

'And will you let me feed you a little reading matter?'

'I guess so,' she said doubtfully. 'As long as –'

'What?'

'As long as Mom and Dad don't find out.'

'They'd be pleased. Don't you know that?'

'Sure I know it, stupid! And I don't want to please them that way just now! Don't you know *that*?'

'Are you being a cow-face about all this?'

'What if I am?'

'Nothing, I guess. Except you may be sorry later.'

'Why should I be? They deserve it.'

'You won't always think that way.'

She set her face in a scowl. 'They're tearing me up by the roots. Like they did you, only worse – in a way, I mean. I mean, they're not throwing me out or anything, like they did you, but at least you're still here, you're still living in our home-town with your friends around you ... Just think of it, Noah! In a couple of weeks I'll be in a strange country, full of foreigners –'

'Full of Jews like you.'

'They won't be like me! How could they be? They come from all the countries of the world. I'll be lucky if I find one Canadian! The people I meet'll probably all be a bunch of Bohunks from North Africa –'

'Shut up!'

'What?' she asked, startled and shocked by his sharp tone.

'Those are Jews you're talking about. If you go over there with a built-in snobbery about the dark Jews you'll be a traitor before you start.'

'I'd be a traitor to Canada if I liked one single thing about it!' she returned hotly. She didn't like him being angry, but it was great to be able to argue and fight with someone who knew what you were feeling and wouldn't be too hurt or offended. Even having a sort of row with Noah made her feel closer to him.

'I never heard such bushwah in all my life! Part of you will always belong to Canada. That's no reason for not trying to enjoy another country, and be a good citizen there. I think you're just looking for excuses for not doing a bit of work in advance.'

'I am not!'

'You are, too! You always were lazy.'

'ME? Let me tell you I get straight A's, except maybe in French –'

'So what? You can't claim credit for what comes easy. I got straight A's too, we've inherited good brains from our parents, it's nothing to brag about. What's to feel pleased about, IF you've got it, is character. And kid, we ain't got it. Yeh, I include myself. Spoilt to pieces, the pair of us. If you want to blame poor old Dad for anything, blame him for being too kind to us. He should've known nobody else would be able to keep *that* up. We were bound to take knocks. When he threw me out in the cold, believe me I bounced so high I knocked Telstar off course, and don't imagine I landed on my feet, either. I landed right on my little pointed head and kept bouncing till I was bruised all over. I don't want anything like that to happen to my kid sister. I want you all kitted out like an astronaut with protective clothing, built-in reserves, oxygen mask to help you in the new atmosphere, and most of all you've got to be ready *inside*. You know how long those boys train before they actually blast off? If they didn't, they'd be dead pigeons in about two minutes from count-down. You've got to train too. You can't just jump into space and hope to survive in comfort, any more than they can. Is it reasonable to expect to? I ask you.'

She ate five chips slowly, to calm down. What Noah was saying, she fully realized, was only the same as her mother had said when she suggested tentatively that Lesley do some preparation. But it was very different coming from Noah, somehow.

'Well,' she said at last, 'I guess you could be right at that. Okay then. What do I do?'

'How long've you got?'

'Four, five weeks, maybe.'

'Geez, that's short! Can't be helped though. Look, you go on home now. I'm going back to my office, and instead of doing any work I'm going to write you a letter.'

'Don't send it! Dad always looks through the mail. He'd see your writing –'

'Do I look crazy? I'll put it in the old place.'

'The old place?'

'Don't tell me you've forgotten!'

She frowned, thinking back. 'You don't mean ...' She groped slowly. 'Hey! The tree-stump!'

'Is it still there?'

'Sure it is! And it's still got that slit in the back, where we used to keep our treasures and post secret letters to each other. Gee, I'd nearly forgotten! Will you write to me in invisible ink?'

'Heck, no! That takes hours. I'll type it. You just make sure you keep it hidden.'

'You bet I will! My life wouldn't be worth a plugged nickel if Dad found it.'

'Just out of interest, has he ever hit you in your life?'

'No – o, but –'

'Yeh, I know what you mean. He can be pretty high-powered sometimes, even without using his hands. Well, so that's fixed. You run out there before school in the morning and you'll find something waiting for you. I can express it better in writing.' He stood up, and so did she. They faced each other across the table, in among all the lanterns and phoney Chinese pictures and stuff they stuck up for atmosphere. He put his hand out and she took it.

'Let's make a vow,' he said, 'in case we don't see each other again.'

'But we will!' she cried, her heart giving a great painful lurch. 'Won't we?'

'Maybe, but we can't count on it. Anyhow it can't be many times.' He looked at her, his eyes very gentle. 'You're all I've got left of the family. I didn't even know I had you. Let's promise never to forget each other, or lose touch, no matter how far apart we are. Let's swear to be true brother and sister, even though it has to be a secret so as to save Mom and Dad from being hurt.'

'Sure, of course I'll swear that, Noah! And maybe, one day –'

He shook his head sharply. 'No. We mustn't talk about that. Dad knows what he's doing. He knew with me, and he knows now with you. I don't blame him for anything, and you mustn't, either. I'll try to write you what I mean. Maybe we're doing wrong, but I don't think so. I need a sister and you need a brother. If we help each other and do good to each other, I think that's a right which outweighs the wrong we're doing by disobeying Dad.'

They took hands and swore their vow, as they'd sworn vows when they were children. But now Lesley felt it was the most solemn grown-up thing in all her life.

CHAPTER 5

Arrival

'Look, Lesley! Israel!'

Lesley, who was sitting next to the plane window, looked up from her magazine and glanced downward past the huge silver wing. Below stretched a jig-saw country of dark cream and green, dotted with clusters of tiny white boxes which must be buildings. Most of the vast pattern was the misty blue Mediterranean.

'It looks very small.'

'It *is* small,' said her father, in a tone both reverent and thrilled. 'Small and great.'

Lesley went back to her magazine. She was not going to risk letting him notice the surge of sudden excitement that had gone through her, looking down and seeing her new world spread out below her.

Five weeks had passed since Lesley's first meeting with Noah. In those weeks, she had apparently changed very little; she had stayed aloof, refusing to bestow open interest on the family adventure. Yet her father, more alert and sensitive to her inner moods than she knew, had noticed a subtle, but welcome, change.

She was no longer rude, surly or mutinous. She didn't volunteer help, but when asked for it she gave it, ungrudgingly if without obvious enthusiasm. She made no more scenes. It was as if something had made her quietly resigned.

And there was something else. She spent a lot of time reading in her room. She had shelvesful of books up there, and she'd always read a lot, but something in the dedicated regularity of her reading sessions, always behind a closed door, had aroused her father's curiosity. He was still very troubled about her, and was not above doing a little parental spying; and he finally discovered, what she was at great pains to hide, a small pile of books concealed among some old clothes in her wardrobe – books about Israel. Several were novels – *Exodus, New Face in the Mirror, Dust, An End to Running*. But there were more serious books, too, books about the recent history of the State of Israel, about the early immigrants from Russia, about the time when the British were there and how they were driven out, about the time just after the end of the Second World War, when the homeless Jews of Europe were flocking to Israel and being turned away and getting in just the same, about the War of Independence against the millions of Arabs all around Israel, which Israel won, and about the years since, years of tension and trial when nobody expected the State to survive, let alone prosper, but somehow it did.

Nat Shelby was very curious to know where Lesley had got them from. Interestingly enough, nearly every one of these books was in his own collection, because he had spent years buying and reading every book about Israel that came out; but a quick check showed that his own copies were still in their usual places. These books were not new; they weren't library books. Where was she getting them? From school, perhaps? They were not worn enough to be school library books. She must be borrowing them. But who from? And who or what had had sufficient influence on her to persuade her to read them?

There was another change. Lesley no longer showed any special interest in her social life in Saskatoon. When her school friends phoned, she fobbed them off with excuses. When Lee Tate came round, she told her mother to say she was out. She kept to the house more and more. Occasionally she would announce she was going out to the movies; but her description of the films afterwards was strangely vague.

Mr Shelby guessed she didn't go to the movies. He wondered, long and often, where she did go. But short of following her like a detective, he had no way of finding out, and he drew the line at that.

She had parted remarkably calmly from all the places, people and things which, earlier, she'd hysterically declared she couldn't live without. And now, here they were, flying down to Lydda Airport, to begin their new life; and Lesley was puzzling her father more and more. She sat beside him, reading a magazine, as composed as a woman twice her age who travelled back and forth across the Atlantic every month. Watching his daughter's neat, strong profile, Nat Shelby shrugged his shoulders. Time would tell. One thing was sure, though. These weeks of inner conflict had had a lasting effect on Lesley. In some odd way, she no longer seemed to him like a child.

When the Shelbys arrived, they were processed with a lot of other new immigrants and placed temporarily in a big ugly block in Tel Aviv called an Absorption Centre. Lesley had known she had left luxury and ease behind, probably for ever; but the smallness, the comparative crudity of their apartment (if it could be called that – it was only two small rooms) shocked her just the same. She herself had to sleep on a sofa, an ugly, shabby modern one, in the living-room. She had nowhere to hang her clothes, and they lived more or less out of their suitcases for the six weeks they were there.

Those six weeks dragged by with agonizing slowness for Lesley. It was as if they were hanging in space, neither here nor there, neither this nor that. She felt Canadian, yet Canada had been left far behind. She longed – secretly, of course – to begin exploring Israel, about which, thanks to Noah, she had learnt and read so much; yet this was impossible except in a very limited way.

They shared their lives in claustrophobic closeness with some sixty other families who were also new immigrants. Lesley's presumption that she would hardly meet any Canadians was proved false. At least ten of the other families were from different parts of Canada (though none from the Prairies – they mostly came from Toronto, Ottawa and Montreal). There were also some English families, and the majority were from the States. But they were nonetheless strangers at first. They lived a sort of awful communal existence, even eating together in a huge, noisy, crowded canteen, where you helped yourself from a long counter to all sorts of strange foods that Lesley was not used to. For instance, at breakfast-time instead of the cereal, eggs, waffles and maple-syrup she was used to, there was a salad, a sticky bland white cheese (or salty sheep's cheese, which was worse), dill pickles and bread and margarine – a substitute for butter which Lesley had never even tasted before, and hated. Only the coffee was the same, except that it wasn't the same, it was horrible, not a bit like the hot fragrant fresh-ground brew her mother had made at home.

At lunch they ate a lot of rice and spaghetti and goulashy sort of hot stews, with chicken once a week on the eve of sabbath. Sometimes they were served dishes that Lesley had never tasted. Once she was faced with a plate of ridged lumps of rather greyish meat, and, asking what it was, was horrified to be told by an American boy sitting near her that they were 'chickens' belly buttons'. 'They're the gizzards dear,' said her mother. 'Try to eat them, I'm told they're very nourishing.' But Lesley, pushing her plate away in disgust, noticed that her mother wasn't managing very well either.

The day's routine for the inmates of the Centre was quite simple and almost unvarying. They had no actual work to do beyond keeping their own little apartments clean. The work consisted in learning to speak, write and read their new language, Hebrew. The course was intensive, and everyone at the centre, young and old, rich and poor, was expected to attend language classes for six hours a day.

Lesley's father didn't always manage to do this, because, as the head of the family, he was very occupied with trying to make arrangements for their settlement. Lesley presumed that he was trying to find a suitable business to buy, or employment in some big concern which would enable the family to enjoy a standard of living at least comparable to what they'd had in Saskatoon. Obviously this wouldn't be easy – positions worthy of such a man as Nat Shelby must be hard to find.

Her mother did attend the lessons. It gave Lesley a queer sensation of unreality to see her mother bent over the little mass-produced table at night, wrestling with homework. She would as soon have expected to see her sucking her thumb and playing with dolls ! Her mother never complained and neither, in her hearing, did her father, but it was gradually borne in on Lesley that both of them were having a very rough time of it.

As to Lesley herself, something odd was happening to her. She went into the first few lessons after they arrived, with the same fatalistic feeling of acceptance that Noah had instilled in her regarding the books. But she seemed to have a mental block about the language.

It may seem strange that Lesley had obeyed Noah about the reading, but not about beginning her study of Hebrew. She told herself that if she learnt Hebrew it would be like saying 'yes' to the whole project, a 'yes' which would make her an accomplice to the crime of dragging her away from her beloved homeland. But a deeper reason was that she was afraid. She had always failed in languages – it was the only thing she was really bad at. French, Latin – even with private tutoring, she had not been able to do well at them, or master them properly. And this was so important, Noah said, vital. He said everything in her future depended on it, that it was the most essential weapon in her new armoury. She took a look at his 'Teach Yourself' book – one look at the hieroglyphics of the lettering, the words written back to front, the strange throat sounds – it terrified her. 'I'll never do it, never!' she had wailed – and thrust the book back. 'You'll have to,' Noah said grimly. But Lesley wouldn't listen or believe it. Somehow, somehow she would manage without it. Better not to try, than to try and fail.

And even now, when the opportunity, even the necessity of learning was thrust on her, when she sat in the lessons day after day watching all the people around her – even her own mother – bent over their books, hanging on the teacher's words, making painful scribbles in their notebooks, carrying their texts and exercises and newspapers back to their rooms even after six-hour stretches in the classroom to work some more, she just couldn't get to grips with it. It flowed around her and over her, but it wouldn't *go in*. When the teacher asked her a question she just shook her head, infuriated by the look on his face, which clearly said he thought she must be an idiot. This, instead of challenging her, only made her more stubborn.

'What do I care what they think of me?' she thought bitterly. 'I don't want to learn their stinking language anyhow.' And quite soon she stopped going to the lessons.

Her mother and father were dismayed by this. Not since the very beginning had she seen them so worried, distressed and angry. Neither had the same reserves of patience that they had had at home. Her gentle, tolerant mother came back from lessons at lunchtime on the first day Lesley had not attended, and simply flew at her.

'Where have you been all morning? The teacher asked after you and I didn't know what to say!'

'I'm not going any more, Mom.'

'You're *what* did you say? Well, you just think again, miss! If I can drive myself crazy learning a new language at my age, you can get down to work too, and if it doesn't come easy at first, you just think how it feels for someone like me and all those other older people, sitting down to study for the first time in twenty years and being scolded like children by that young teacher when we can't learn quickly enough!'

'Listen, will you please? I –'

'No I will not listen! You're going to say it's too hard. You're telling me! And what about your father? He has to work at night, when he comes home from tramping the streets and waiting around in offices – your father, waiting for a lot of *chutzpahdik* young kids to get around to seeing him! Do you know what that feels like, after running your own business?'

'Nobody told him to come here!' Lesley flared, with the old fire and resentment returning. 'Whatever he's going through, he brought it on himself! And that's more than you can say to me. I know the only language I needed to know for the life I wanted to live. I'm not going to knock myself out learning a new one I don't even want!'

The trouble with family rows here was that there was no place of your own to go to and slam the door. You could go out of the flat and slam *that* door, but then you just found yourself outside in a bare corridor with nowhere to go but the canteen or out. So she just flung herself down and snatched up a magazine. To her utter astonishment, her mother, who had hardly made a violent gesture in her life, grabbed it out of her hands and flung it across the tiny room.

'Don't you dare read when I'm talking to you! You wait till your father gets home!'

Lesley had no intention of doing that. She got up with as much poise as she could and walked out of the apartment, down in the lift and out into the streets of Tel Aviv for a walk and a think.

It was a funny thing about Tel Aviv. It meant 'Hill of Spring', which is a beautiful name, but even Israelis didn't seem to like the city much, and were always urging you to visit Haifa or Jerusalem if you wanted to see beautiful Israeli cities. Lesley had done day-tours with her parents to both, and although you couldn't help seeing that they were much more attractive, there was still something about Tel Aviv that she loved.

Perhaps it was the bustle, for Tel Aviv is a commercial town first and last. All the honking traffic under the bright winter sunshine; the balconies jutting out from every apartment, got up like rooms – real extensions of the homes inside, with furniture and pictures on the walls – made Lesley feel as if the people living there wanted to share their lives with you, or at least didn't mind if you looked in and watched them eating their meals, playing cards, doing their homework in front of your eyes.

But best of all she liked the sidewalk cafés of Dizengoff Street. These made her feel happy and relaxed, because there were so many tourists there, all smartly dressed (not like the people in the Centre who had begun to dress for comfort and casualness) and rather loud-voiced, but at least in English, carrying their transistors and cameras and making music and colour and laughter in little swirling pools and eddies as they passed.

You could sit down outside (although it was December) and drink or eat something which reminded you of home – real coffee, or Coke, or a hamburger or hot-dog. You could buy an American paper and read the baseball scores and listen to American jazz from the radio inside, hear North American accents all round you, watch the passing parade and pretend you were having a glorious holiday in – say – Paris, enjoying the best of both worlds before flying back to your real, dear, familiar world of home.

This was what Lesley did that day. And after she had had some Coke and sat there for a bit, just unwinding, she opened her bag and from a secret zipper-pocket she drew out and unfolded Noah's letter.

It was perhaps the hundredth time she had read it. It was this, plus her very few, stolen meetings with him, which had given her the strength to behave so much better during the last weeks of being in Saskatoon. She didn't fully understand it; but she felt he understood *her*, and her father and mother too, and sympathized with them all, and this helped her to reconcile herself to the situation, and even to them. Some of the time, anyway.

This is what it said:

Hallo, dear Sis,

You asked me to write down some of what I said to you during our meetings, so you could have it with you when you go away. I've arranged it under headings like we had to at school so it'll be easy to remember. But I hope you know that it's not cold and analytical, like school-work.

1. *Background:*

Dad and Mom are Jews, children of Jews who were children of Jews, all the way back 4,000 years or so. You and I are the children of all those Jews right back to Abraham. Maybe we don't feel it, but we are. Since what happened in Germany, *no Jew in the world* feels really safe. Maybe he thinks he does, but deep down he is insecure. Many are also split-personalities, all the more so since 1948 when Israel started. Most Jews support Israel, but they don't go there because they're comfortable where they are. Apparently. But inwardly many of them are not comfortable at all. How can you be loyal to two countries? Mom and Dad don't want to be divided inside themselves any more, and they want you to grow up knowing who you are and where you belong. They also want you to be Jewish, that is, part of the Jewish nation, not just the religion which doesn't mean so much any more without the other.

My opinion (for what it's worth): They're right. It's true: Once a Jew, always a Jew. Officially I'm a Catholic but in my secret heart I'm more Jewish since I converted than I ever was. That's how it is. CROSS YOUR HEART AND HOPE TO DIE AND HAVE TO EAT A DEAD PIG'S EYE you will never reveal this to a LIVING SOUL, especially not to Donna, who might mistakenly think I was sorry I married her.

2. *Present Action:*

Don't go on being a cow-face. Dad and Mom have it tough enough without you making it tougher. You've chosen for the moment to forget you love them, but you'll remember later, and then you're going to feel horrible about having punished them so much. In any case:

(a) *Nothing* you do or say is going to make them change their minds. I know. I tried it once.

(b) You owe it to yourself to be brave now the first shock's over.

(c) This town, school, friends, etc. all seem vitally important to you now, but believe me, THEY ARE REPLACEABLE. Especially your idiot friend Sonia with her doped cigarettes. Has it ever occurred to you that this sort of thing might be a minor reason why Dad wants to get you away? And he's right about that, too. Thousands of kids in this country smoke pot by the time they're in University. It's a lousy dangerous business and it's hard to resist when everybody's doing it.

(d) Israel is a very exciting country and you may well love it if you only give it a chance.

(ii) Try to prepare yourself a bit for the inevitable. Be like a soldier going into battle; arm yourself. Read about it, learn about it. Above all, *start learning the language.* You won't be able to get from A to B without it, and it's a hard one. Only mulishness can stop an intelligent kid like you from seeing the *necessity* of this. Hide the books from the folks if your pride tells you you must, but learn.

3. *Future Prospects:*

(i) When you get there, open up. Take part. Don't be snooty and up-stage – and DON'T talk about how popular, well-dressed, etc. etc. you were in Saskatoon. You're a spoilt rich brat (no offence, so am I) and that's a species that doesn't go down so well with kids who are not, so try to hide it from them and mix with them and be a 'chevraiman'. That's a Hebrew word I learnt, means a good Joe, a sport. You won't gain anything by wrecking all your chances of a good social life.

(ii) Try to forgive Mom and Dad for hiking you out there, just as soon as you possibly can. I don't ask for miracles, but sooner or later you're going to grow up and realize they're doing it mainly for you and then every unkind thing you said and did is going to come back on you like a boomerang. (See 2i above.)

(iii) Don't look backward at Canada and me and everything. We're all lost causes as far as you're concerned. Your watch-word must be *'Tamid Kadimah'* which means 'Ever Onwards'. Sounds gruesomely like Girl Guides or something, and in any case easier said than done, but that should be your aim.

4. *General Observations:*

(i) You are a clever, pretty, and *nice* girl underneath. (Notice that 'underneath'. It's pretty *far* underneath at the moment, but you've let me see it so I know it's there. Anyway I remember you from those happy, lost days when I was a member of the Shelby family and we were proper, non-secret brother and sister, and I – well, I'll save that bit of schmaltz till the end.)

(ii) If you are clever, pretty and nice basically, you can be popular and successful anywhere if you only don't spoil everything.

(iii) If you're popular and successful, you can be happy.

(iv) i, ii and iii are not so easy to come by as they may sound. They will take hard work (*the language*) and courage (facing up to it) and determination (not to show off, look back, etc.). Strength of character, in a word – but the right sort, not stubbornness.

(v) I know what I'm talking about.

(vi) I know what I'm talking about.

(vii) I *do* know what I'm talking about.

(viii) I'm gladder that you came to see me than I am about anything that's happened to me for ages.

(ix) I'm your brother whatever anybody says and I always will be.

(x) I love you. That's the schmaltzy bit. (See also viii and ix)

Kol Tuv. That means 'Good Luck'.

Your outcast brother,

Noah.

CHAPTER 6

A New Disaster

Re-reading Noah's letter had its usual effect of making her feel stronger and better able to cope. It all but convinced her that she must, after all, give way, and return to Hebrew lessons. She walked slowly back to the Centre wrestling with herself, hearing Noah's voice in her head saying, 'You're talking bushwah, and you know it. It's not surrendering, it's picking up the gauntlet, accepting the challenge. Dad'll respect you for it. *I'll* respect you for it.' But then she remembered the look of impatience on the young teacher's face and the awful waves of blank impotence which washed over her whenever she was faced with Hebrew writing in a book or on the blackboard. Could she battle her way through this barrier to something like the success she'd come to take for granted in school at home?

She got back late and tired. Her father was waiting for her. He was tired, too, tired with a deep, fundamental tiredness which comes from tackling new and difficult things when you are already well into your middle-age, from failing when you are used to succeeding. This father and daughter, if they'd only realized it, were facing the same basic problems, and they should have been able to reinforce and help each other, but it isn't always possible even for a grown-up to see things objectively, especially when he's up to his eyes in difficulties of his own.

Nat Shelby was actually a very kind and loving father, but he could make mistakes like anyone else. He made one now. Instead of understanding that Lesley was afraid, just as he was himself, he hid his own fear and allowed himself to throw an angry challenge at her.

'Your mother tells me you've opted out of your Hebrew lessons,' he began the moment she walked in.

Two seconds before, Lesley had been on the point of telling him that she'd decided to go back and try again, but this point-blank attack had the instantaneous effect of changing her mind.

'Yes I have!' she answered him sharply. All the renewed strength Noah's letter had given her was turned to ill-account.

'I see,' he said, obviously seething with rage. 'And how do you propose to spend your time, if I may ask?'

'Reading. Walking. What do you care?'

This was terribly rude, of course. She regretted the words the minute they were out. How had this happened? She had been planning a new start, a return to the old relationship of love, gentleness and understanding. But the words 'What do you care?' had sprung from the depths of her. If he'd cared, would they be here, would she be so afraid, would any of this be happening? She forgot about the Jews of Germany and Russia and all that Noah had told her, and reverted to a child-ish idea that her father was doing this just to be mean to her.

For a moment after she'd spoken, she thought her father might actually slap her, in fact she flinched back as she saw his hand move. Then it dropped, and his head with it, and the angry colour slowly went out of his face. After a long moment, he said, dully, 'Okay. You play it your way. It won't be for much longer anyway.'

'What do you mean? Are we leaving here? Where are we going?' Lesley cried, forgetting everything in her eagerness to leave this place and have a home again.

'You'll be told all you need to know when the right time comes.'

And that was all she could get out of him, or her mother, who closed up like a clam and would hardly speak to her.

Lesley realized her life was changed for ever. But she didn't in the least anticipate that her circumstances would be any less comfortable, in the long run, though it might take time for her father to work up to a position of the first importance. Lesley had seen big houses, rich apartments, here, Socialism or no Socialism. She rather fancied a penthouse in one of the few new high-rise blocks, or, better still, a private house by the sea in the luxury district of Hertzlia, just outside the town. Things might not be so bad, after all . . .

She heard the ghastly news eventually, not from her parents at all, but from a stuck-up English girl at the Centre called Diana. She came up to Lesley one morning after breakfast, smiled at her sweetly, and dropped a bombshell.

'I hear your family's going into a kibbutz.'

Lesley didn't reply. She simply stared at her.

'Oh, didn't you know?' asked Diana innocently. 'Well, it's not everybody's cup of tea, of course. I can hardly imagine someone like you in a kibbutz – I mean, you're such a *city* kind of person. You'll have to put all your posh clothes away. And how will you manage about talking? I know a lot of Hebrew so I don't much mind where we go, but then, I've been going to lessons.' And with that, she stuck her nose in the air and walked off.

Lesley felt all the old rage come flooding back on her like a tidal wave. Without stopping to think, she rushed straight up to her parents' apartment, and threw the door open.

They sat there, frozen into funny positions. It occurred to her that they'd been talking about her. 'What's this I hear!' she cried. 'Going to a kibbutz, and you never even told me!'

They exchanged glances, then both began to talk at once, and both stopped. Suddenly her father's face changed. It became cold and hostile.

'Yes,' he said, 'we're going to live in a kibbutz. I didn't

tell you because you haven't deserved to be treated like an adult member of the family. Your mother and I are too tired for scenes.'

Lesley felt so hurt and furious she could hardly speak. She'd tried so hard, been so much better lately ! At least till the business of the lessons. And never a word of praise, only anger, and shutting her out ! Surprisingly, her mother spoke up for her.

'Nat, she had a right to know –'

'She has *no* rights in the matter !' her father said, too loudly. 'She's a child. She behaves like a child and must be treated like a child. Where we go, she goes, and if she doesn't like it she'll have to lump it. That's all I've got to say !'

There was nowhere for him to walk away to without leaving the flat, so he threw himself down in a chair and picked up a Hebrew paper, which rattled in his tense, angry hand.

Through her own anger, Lesley had a sudden very strong impulse to go over to him and comfort him. She couldn't understand how she could be so angry and yet at the same time feel so sorry for him. It was so unlike him to lose his dignity. But she couldn't bring herself to it, so she stood still and stared at the ground.

'Why a kibbutz?' she got out at last.

It was her mother who answered. 'Lesley, I'd like to take a walk with you.'

Her father looked up quickly, seemed about to protest, and then shook the paper and hid himself behind it. Lesley hesitated, looking from one to the other. Then she nodded shortly. Her mother passed her and went out. Lesley looked once at her father. Again she wanted to go to him, make it up with him, be admired by him again. But she couldn't.

Outside in the warm early January sunshine, she and her

mother walked. They walked a long way without a word.
Then Lesley repeated her question.

'Why a kibbutz, for gosh sakes, Mom? Don't tell me we
can't afford to live in town!'

'Well, Lesley, it's this way. When your father decided to
come out here, he sold the business, as you know. And he
invested the money. The income from that investment comes
to us here – at least, it will, as soon as certain formalities
have been cleared up. Sure, we could be as well-off here as
we were in Saskatoon, but your father doesn't want it that
way.'

'You mean – he doesn't want us to be rich any more?'

'Just that.'

'But why, Mom, why?' It was utterly crazy! Everyone wanted to be rich, it was the most natural thing in the
world. Who ever heard of people who *could* be rich, not
wanting to?

'Lesley, your father is a very – unusual man. I've been
married to him for twenty-four years and I still get surprises.
Like what he said that day about being ready to give up keeping kosher. He meant it literally! – the kibbutz we're going
to is not religious. You uproot yourself and come to Israel,
and then give up the one thing that's kept you feeling Jewish! I don't always understand him myself. Do you know
what he said last night? He said, "Now we're here, we can
forget about being Jewish"!'

'But Mommy, how long will we have to –'

'I'm trying to explain. Your father has been dreaming
about immigrating for many, many years. I don't know myself how many. And now he's here, he wants to make more
changes. In himself, in us, in our whole way of life. We've
been a Jewish-Canadian business family. Now we're no longer Canadian –' Lesley bit her lips – 'we no longer have a
business. Your father seems to want to change everything at

once. It's as if he felt he'd – failed until now, and he wants to start his life again.'

'Daddy – failed? How? He was one of the biggest men in town!'

'He wasn't big with himself, honey. He succeeded with the store, sure, but it didn't give him anything after the first years – other than money, and that meant less and less to him. And then – and then – you see, he feels a failure as a – family man.'

Lesley's heart jumped, with sudden fright, like guilt. 'You mean because of –'

Her mother turned her face away and her voice was muffled. 'Because of him, yes. And for the same reason he feels he's failed as a Jew. You know what I think? I think keeping kosher has become a symbol for him of that failure, just because it was the only Jewish thing we did.'

Lesley brushed this aside, because when people started talking about symbols she always grew impatient.

'But the kibbutz, Mom!'

'Yes, well that's something else again. You know your father's always had what people call "left-wing leanings". In other words, he always held that in theory everybody should have equal opportunities and not be deprived, and he was against exploitation –'

'So what?'

'So everything, apparently. I didn't realize how deep it went with him. Lots of men believe in Socialism without needing to practise it. But your father's not "lots of men". It always troubled him that the business automatically made him an exploiter. That's why he always took such good care of his staff, even when he was leaving. His conscience was uneasy all the time. And now that he's made this great change in our lives, he wants to go the whole way. He wants to be a real, practising Socialist. And the kibbutz, he says, is the only truly Socialist society in the world, where you can still be free, and where you can be a Jew without having to think how to do it.'

'But what about *me*?' cried Lesley, her despair growing with every half-understood word.

The fact was, she couldn't imagine herself in a kibbutz, any more than that uptight English girl could. She knew quite a lot about kibbutzes – kibbutzim, one should say, and none of what she knew made her want to go there.

Kibbutzim, to begin with, were something like very large farms, or farm-villages. They were called 'collective settlements', and 'collective' meant that, incomprehensibly, nobody owned anything, and yet everybody owned everything. Each married couple or grown-up single person had a house, or a flat, or something like that, but there were no kitchens because everybody ate together in a communal dining-hall. Just like the horrible canteen in the Centre! The children were brought up separately. They didn't sleep with their parents, but in children's houses with others of their own age. Everybody worked, and everybody shared the profits that the farm made. But not money – nobody had any money, because the kibbutz gave you what you needed. Nobody was supposed to be better or more important than anybody else.

First of all, then, Lesley had always lived in the town. She had not the slightest wish to go 'back to the land'. Such farms as she'd seen in Saskatchewan (the province of Canada where she'd lived) were isolated clusters of buildings stuck in the middle of hundreds of lonely miles of wheat fields: the farm animals smelt disgusting and needed all sorts of dirty work done for them, work which Lesley would have considered far beneath her if she'd ever thought of it in connection with herself at all. So farms, for her, were desolate, Godforsaken, boring, smelly places.

As for the idea of living seperately from her parents, it gave her cold shivers. It was completely unnatural. She had a fleeting vision of herself being torn from her mother's arms and dragged screaming away by some vaguely Russian-looking peasants with brutal, Mongoloid faces and possibly guns. One part of her recognized that it couldn't happen like that, but she couldn't imagine any other way in which families could be separated. Certainly she wouldn't let herself be taken away from *her* parents without a fight, even if she had often wished she could be free of the restraints of living with them!

Such a concept as having no money and being treated as the equal of everybody else, was completely unacceptable to Lesley, who was used to thinking of herself and her family as being a whole lot better than most other people.

If her father were not superior to the average man, would he have been able to build up a great store from nothing, and make them rich and respected all over town? It was nonsense. And how could normal people manage without money to spend, to buy the things they wanted and which set them apart as individuals, showing other people that they had good taste and were successful? Lesley had never been without money. Even here in Tel Aviv she had not been short of pocket-money, though she hadn't felt like spending much. Was she now, on top of everything else, expected to give up this last element of security?

'It's all right for Daddy. But what about me? I can't live like that! I bet you won't be able to, either. It's not fair to drag us off to live like peasants just because he has some crazy ideas!'

Her mother stopped walking and looked at her.

'Anyway,' went on Lesley, too desperate to care if her mother thought her selfish, 'What's happening to the money? Daddy won't just let it go to waste, I suppose?'

'When people go into a kibbutz,' said her mother slowly, 'they're supposed to give all their money in.'

'What?' Lesley almost screamed. 'Daddy's going to give all our money away to some beastly stinking *farm*?'

'It's not our money, Lesley,' said her mother. 'It's his. He made it and he has the right to decide what to do with it. But he's not giving it all in. Some of it has been invested in a special trust. He won't be able to touch it. Nor will you. But your children, if you have any, will have money for their education. Daddy says we have no right to make decisions for our grandchildren.'

'But he has the right to do anything he likes to *me*.'

'He feels,' said Miriam Shelby slowly, 'that he's failed with you, too. He thinks if you were living close to us but not *with* us – if some other people take a hand in your upbringing –'

She stopped because Lesley's hand had flown to her mouth and her eyes were wide and stark.

'It's not true, Mom, it's not true!' The words tumbled over each other, right there in the street. 'I love Daddy! I know I've been horrible but I couldn't help it! Don't let him punish me like this, don't let him send me away from you!'

She began to cry wildly. Her mother, with anxious looks round at the staring passers-by, put her arm round her and led her into a quieter street. The houses there stood on stilts, and Lesley found herself standing under one of them, hidden from the road by some bushes. She cried on and on; she couldn't stop. Her mother held and petted her, saying comforting, motherly things. At last Lesley grew calmer.

'You won't let him, Mommy?' she asked, pitifully, certain in some deep, experienced part of herself, untouched by her genuine misery, that her outburst would have changed everything.

Her mother looked at her sympathetically and shook her head. But her words blasted Lesley's hopes. 'Lesley, your father is right. You're still a child, and you must go where we go. I'll help you to make the best of it. It won't be easy for me, either.'

But once again, Lesley was back at bedrock, where she could think only of herself.

CHAPTER 7

The New Life
Really Begins

Several more weeks had to pass before they left the Centre
and went to the kibbutz. Lesley was at an all-time-low ebb.
Her father and mother urged her to come with them to visit
a kibbutz near Tel Aviv, which would, they insisted, cheer
her up by giving her a clearer idea of what a kibbutz was
actually like; but she was turning more and more in upon
herself and flatly refused. It was like at the very beginning –
she was rude again, and sulky, and followed a policy of total
non-cooperation. She spent most of her time curled up in a
corner of the apartment, brooding and concocting frightening fantasies about the kind of life she would be forced to live
when the time came to leave for Kfar Orde.

This was the name of their kibbutz. It meant 'Orde's
Village'. Orde was Orde Wingate, one of Israel's English
heroes. Lesley knew no more about him than that. But she
knew the settlement was in one of the hottest parts of the
country. The same American boy who'd told her about the
chickens' belly-buttons gleefully informed her that in summer it was like living in a bowl of soup, but that you had to
keep working or they hated and despised you.

Lesley's horror deepened. Even Saskatoon's summers
had made her fit for nothing but lying around sipping iced
drinks. She imagined herself fainting and falling under a cow
she was painfully trying to milk, and then being kicked into
consciousness, though whether by the cow or the cowman
she wasn't sure.

This was just one of the dramatic day-nightmares with

which she almost enjoyed tormenting and terrifying herself at the time. Once she imagined all the other children at the kibbutz – hundreds and hundreds of them – standing around laughing and scorning her as she lay, paralysed by heat and exhaustion, in their midst. She began to cry, it was so real to her. Her mother came through from the bedroom and sat beside her, stroking her face. She didn't ask her what was the matter; she seemed to know.

'If only you'd get to work, honey,' she said with a deep sigh. 'Your mind is too idle. It doesn't help you to let your-self go like this.'

But Lesley had got to a point where she couldn't help her-self any more. It began to look as if she would begin the new life as weak and unarmoured as a snail without its shell.

There was only one shred of comfort. The founders of Kfar Orde had mostly come from England, which obviously meant that their children would be English-speaking. So she wouldn't have to learn Hebrew. But all the rest was like a great shadow lying over her. And she gave way, and just lay under it, helplessly.

And then Noah's letter came.

It had been simple enough to send letters to him – she wrote and posted them when her parents were out. But get-ting one was more difficult. She had to receive it away from the Centre. And at last she found a way.

There was a little all-sorts shop a short distance from the Centre, run by an old, fat woman from Morocco. She spoke French, so Lesley was able to make some kind of stilted con-tact with her. She made up a story about a boy-friend her parents disapproved of. That was one lie. Then she had to say she was fifteen which, apparently, is old enough in Morocco to be seriously in love. So it was arranged that Noah should send a letter to this shop.

Lesley then dispatched a desperate S.O.S. to Noah, telling

him about the kibbutz plan and begging him to write and tell her why she shouldn't run away from home or kill herself and have done with it. It was a very childish, hysterical letter, written out of the depths of despair, but fortunately Noah was wise enough not to show in his letter back how worried and also exasperated it had made him. He didn't even start talking about the kibbutz straight away, so as not to let her think he gave it so much importance. He referred first to earlier letters he'd had from her.

Dearest Sis,

So you feel 'happily wicked' to be writing to me. I know how you feel. It's a pity we have to deceive them, but I tell myself that my quarrel with them has nothing to do with you and me, and besides, as you won't deny, in the quarrel between *you* and them, I'm on their side!

I'm mad at you for not learning Hebrew. Why can't you see it's necessary? Well, you will, in the end, but it's a shame you've wasted all these weeks by lying in bed in the mornings instead of going to classes. I bet you don't even know what *tipsha* means. (He wrote it in Hebrew lettering.) Well, look it up to know what I think of you about this. (She did. It meant 'silly, fem.')

About the kibbutz. Again, I am all for Dad. It's no good pussy-footing about when you're changing your life. Maybe it'll suit Dad himself, and maybe it won't; but if it doesn't suit *you*, you'll only have yourself to blame. I know a lot about kibbutz life, as it happens, and I can tell you, it might have been made for the likes of you. It's supposed to be the most marvellous life for kids that's ever been dreamed up. The freedom! I envy you, honestly. Thank your lucky stars and jump in with both feet. Forget about Saskatoon and our twelve-room luxury house by the river. Your values have got to change. Twelve rooms, one room, what does it matter if only you've got friends and fun, if you're learning and developing – above all if you're satisfied with yourself? Oh I know I sound like a school-teacher, but believe me, Sis, it's the only sensible advice anyone who loved you could give.

Life here goes on as usual. I work hard at the plant, come home, garden a bit (I'm specializing in gladioli). Then Donna and I usually go out somewhere or stay at home and watch TV. I'm up for promotion at work and I wish I could tell you it gave me as big a kick as everyone thinks it should. A large part of my thoughts and feelings are where you are – not only with you, but with the family, and with *where* you are.

No, there are no signs of you being an aunt yet.

When you're at the kibbutz it will be harder for me to write. But if you find a safe way, let me know. Don't let Dad know about us, and be nice to him. It's going to be much harder on him than he thinks.

> Love from your brother,
> Noah.

Lesley hadn't brought much with her from Canada, apart from a lot of clothes and books. But she had brought her most precious possession, which was her secret box. She had had this ever since her seventh birthday, when Noah had given it to her. He'd made it in carpentry class. It was just an ordinary, biggish wooden box with a hinged lid (Noah had painted a picture on this which had long since worn away, leaving just some mellow smudges of colour) and two metal loops with a padlock.

In it she kept whatever were her current treasures. Of course these had altered and been replaced as the years passed, though there were still a few trinkets, notes and other bits and pieces which dated back to her childhood. Now it was mainly a 'safe' for keeping her diary in. She didn't keep a diary day-to-day, but when she did get an urge to write, she wrote strictly private things which she would have died sooner than let anybody read. Noah's earlier letter was kept here too, and the key of the padlock lived in a large locket that Lesley always wore round her neck.

Her mother of course knew about the box, but respected its private nature.

Noah's new letter now joined the other treasures and secrets. But, in the short time remaining before they said goodbye to the Centre and left for Kibbutz Kfar Orde, it came out again just as often as Lesley had a moment of secure privacy.

And on the day they packed the last of their things and piled them into the kibbutz truck, waiting to bump and bounce them the fifty miles which separated this relatively civilized city from the wilderness, Lesley took a great risk. She removed the letter from the box and carried it in her pocket. Like a talisman to ward off danger and evil spirits.

The kibbutz, Lesley had to admit, was not as ugly as she had expected. She'd previously decided it would be a group of barrack-like buildings set in a dreary waste-land. Instead, her first impression was of a large cluster of trees, many of them tall, exotic palms, under and among which were scattered low white buildings roofed in a cheerful red. A little river ran alongside. Lesley had always taken gardens for granted, and was not unduly surprised to see that every little apartment had its gay plot; what did surprise her was that each plot was different. Some had a patio in front, with tables and chairs set out in rustic invitation; others had rockeries or cactus-gardens; many were shaded with trees. Loving care and individuality were obvious everywhere.

But the buildings were very small, and when they were shown to her parents' rooms, Lesley got a shock. Inside the front door was a very small porch, containing a simple table, two chairs, a sink in a cupboard, and a little fridge like an orange box. Beyond that, a living-room, very simply furnished, and leading off that, a bedroom, just big enough to contain a double bed and a wardrobe. When Lesley looked round for more doors leading to the rest of the apartment, she suddenly realized that this was it – there really was no more.

She glanced at her mother, who was standing in the middle of the living-room, staring round her with dismay only just beneath the surface. Her father, on the other hand, was running his fingers happily along the book-shelves which occupied almost the whole of one wall.

'The man who used to live here was a teacher,' said Ayala, the woman who was showing them the place. 'If you like, we'll take some of the shelves down.'

'I haven't brought many books,' he said slowly. 'But I'm going to begin collecting again. One day,' he added dreamily, 'all these shelves will be full – of books I've had time to really read.'

Lesley turned to the woman, and without trying to keep the sharpness out of her voice asked: 'And where do I sleep?'

'With the other children of your age,' she replied, with a quietness which showed that she sensed Lesley's aggressiveness and disapproved of it. 'When your parents have finished asking all their questions, I'll take you there.'

Lesley's mother looked about her blankly. She couldn't believe in it, the smallness. She'd accepted the Centre because it was only temporary. But this – these little box-like rooms, the tiny shower (no bath!), the non-kitchen, the shabby furniture – this was to be her home. She opened her mouth as if to ask something of the woman, but no question came out. Lesley watched her and felt pity for her. It was a warm, flooding feeling, like the beginning of crying: the first warm feeling she had had for her mother for some time.

Lesley's father said in a firm, happy voice: 'We have no more to ask at the moment, thank you. This is all just great.' He touched the fruit and flowers which had been left on the table, and the chocolate cake shaped like a ring with some Hebrew lettering in white frosting. 'This was a swell idea – a welcome. Something extra. Please thank whoever –'

'It's nothing,' said the woman briskly. She was grey-haired

and not farmerishly dressed at all, more like an office worker, which is what she was. But she had very strong lines on her face. 'Come along then, Lesley.'

Tears sprang to her mother's eyes. 'When will we see you again, baby?'

The woman smiled. 'She can come home as soon as she's seen her living-quarters, if she likes.'

Nevertheless, Lesley felt her mother might clasp her in her arms if she lingered, and she somehow didn't want that to happen. So she waved good-bye quickly and hurried outside. So much, she later thought ruefully, for the nightmare Mongolians. Nothing but her mother's tears had been needed to drive her away into her separate life.

The woman led her along the narrow network of paths without speaking. It was quite a long walk. Lesley asked carelessly, 'What's that river on the other side of the road?'

Ayala looked at her curiously, surprised at her ignorance.

'The Jordan, of course,' she said.

'*The* Jordan?' Lesley couldn't stop herself from asking with a flash of amazement and interest.

'Didn't you look it up on the map before you came?'

'But it's so small ! You could almost jump across it !'

'Well, don't. There are Arabs on the other side.'

'Arabs?' Lesley felt her blood fire up with excitement.

'Yes, Arabs. Jordanian Arabs.' The woman pointed to where the river lay, beyond a row of buildings. On the other side rose pinkish rounded hills, speckled with scrub but otherwise bare and desolate and somehow a little frightening. 'That's Jordan. The river is the boundary between Israel and enemy territory.'

Her father had mentioned that the kibbutz was 'on the border', but she hadn't realized what that meant. She was silent for a moment, digesting her sudden awakened excitement. She wanted to ask if it was dangerous, but she didn't, for fear the woman should suspect her of being afraid, which she wasn't in the least. At last she asked, 'Is there ever any shooting?'

'No, it's quiet enough. They're farmers over there, like us.'

'Can you see them?'

'Of course. Tilling their fields. We could call across to each other, if only we weren't enemies.'

'Couldn't you anyway – to see what happens?'

'Sometimes we do. But they never answer.' There was genuine regret in the woman's voice.

Before Lesley could ask more questions – though quite suddenly she was burning with them – they arrived at a big square beat-up-looking building.

'This is where you'll live.'

Lesley stopped dead and looked at it. The excitement died.

'This?'

'Not quite what you've been used to, perhaps?' said the woman, with just a hint of dryness in her voice.

'No,' said Lesley feelingly. All her resentment returned. The excitement evaporated into thin air, leaving a hollow in her stomach which she instinctively tried to fight with a deep sigh. Then she swallowed. She could hear loud, strident voices coming from inside – *Hebrew voices*. The nearness of the enemy hadn't frightened her as those voices did.

'Do you want me to come in with you?'

The touch of sympathy in Ayala's tone brought out a perverse defiance in Lesley. She suddenly made up her mind to show no weakness of any sort. Standing there with one foot on the steps leading, so to speak, into her new life, she made a lightning but compelling promise to herself.

If she was afraid, she would act brave. If they were mean and unfriendly to her, she would be mean back to them – meaner. If she was lonely, she would hide it. If miserable she'd pretend to be happy.

And if she wanted to cry, she would hold it back no matter what it cost her, until she was quite alone. In this way, she would beat them, and her father too, somehow.

She didn't realize how ironic it was that she was thinking of these young Jews, and not the Arabs across the river, as her enemies.

'No thank you,' she answered Ayala. 'I'll go in alone.'

She braced herself like a soldier going into battle, and walked up the steps.

CHAPTER 8
The New Home

She found herself in a long corridor with doors along it. The doors, which had shutters in their tops, were mostly open, and it was from these rooms that the voices came. The other side of the corridor was a long window, shuttered with venetian blinds, overlooking the lawn outside. There were benches inside under this window, littered with people's belongings. school books, sandals, boxes of trash, a tray with the remains of somebody's lunch on it; a number of framed pictures and some creeping plants hung between the doors. The floor was tiled, and wet, as if it had just been wiped; but there were already the marks of bare feet over it.

Standing half-way along this corridor were two girls and a boy of her own age. They wore faded jeans of different colours, and tee-shirts, one of which had been bleached in circles. One of them was too fat; the other was much too pretty, with long hair.

The pretty one saw her first. She said something in Hebrew to the others, which was probably 'Here she is,' and then called to her, 'Shalom!'

She didn't answer (her mouth was too dry) but stood waiting for them to approach her. As they strolled towards her, her smart tailored linen pants-suit suddenly began to prickle and the brooch on her collar grew so heavy she reached up to touch it. The girls' hair was worn straight and simple, without pins or ribbons. Her own, extra-carefully pin-curled and set for this challenging occasion, burned her head for its fussiness, and her lips felt suddenly greasy as she saw the bare brown skins and natural colouring of the others.

The three of them came up to her. They looked her straight

in the eye, but at the same time she felt they were all – even the boy – taking in every detail of her appearance. Then they began to question her.

'I don't speak Hebrew,' she said with what she hoped was dignity.

They exchanged looks.

'You need to learn,' said the boy slowly.

Her heart gave a lurch of sudden alarm.

'But don't you all speak English?'

'Not so good,' he said with a smile. 'We learn now since two three years. But teacher no good.'

'But your parents are all English!' she said with her voice going shrill with panic.

The boy now laughed openly. 'So what? Parents not teachers.'

She looked at the girls. They were smiling at her in a friendly way, but she seemed to see them winging away into the distance.

'Are all the lessons in Hebrew?'

'What?'

'Your lessons! Are they given in Hebrew?'

The boy consulted the girls. The question, it seemed, was not too difficult to understand, only incredible.

'Of course,' they all answered together. 'All except English lesson,' added the boy with another laugh.

Lesley felt dumbfounded and couldn't find words for what she was feeling. She just stared at them hopelessly.

'I want to see my room,' she said at last.

One of the girls – the fat one – took her by the arm. 'Come.'

She allowed herself to be led into one of the rooms. It was a small square bedroom with four beds in it. Four? Was it possible she was not to have a room of her own? They were all tidily made except one, which was more or less buried under heaps of clothes and shoes and all sorts of apparent rubbish. In that corner, the walls were covered to the ceiling with posters, including a big one of the Beatles, and from the ceiling dangled several model airplanes on threads. The other three corners were less fantastically decorated. Each bed had a shelf over it, and a neat but shabby rug beside it. One shelf was empty.

'This your bed,' said the fat girl, pointing to the one under the empty shelf.

'I sleep here,' said the pretty girl, indicating one of the other beds. 'She sleep there' – the fat girl's bed.

'And this my,' said the boy with pride, and plumped down among the heap of rubbish on the fourth bed.

Lesley's mouth actually fell open and for several seconds she could not utter a word. Her face must have been quite comic, because all three burst into laughter.

'But I can't sleep in a room with a boy!' Lesley almost shouted.

They all went on laughing, and nodded their heads like dummies. With gestures and a few broken words, they tried to tell her that that was how things were done here, and that she would get used to it. She turned her face away, her vow all but broken already as tears of helplessness came into her eyes against her will. But as they noticed she was upset and stopped laughing, she stiffened herself and asked coldly, 'Where do I keep my clothes?'

'What?'

'MY CLOTHES!' She plucked at her clothes with her fingers, great well-springs of frustration rising in her. If they couldn't understand that, what did they understand? But the pretty girl caught her meaning and opened a wardrobe – a very small, old-fashioned one. It already looked almost full, but there was one shelf vacant and by pushing all the loaded hangers to one end, the girl exposed a short length of rail.

'That for you,' she announced.

Incredulity again took possession of Lesley. At home she had had an entire fitted cupboard at her disposal, plus two chests-of-drawers.

'But that's too small! I have three suitcases full of stuff.'

The other girl shrugged expressively. Then she pointed to the linen pants-suit. 'Like this you not need,' she said. Then, with much giggling and consulting the boy for words, she explained: 'Summer – short trousers, shirts, clothes to swimming. Winter – long trousers, sweater, hot coat hang outside. One, two dress or trouser for Shabbat' – Lesley knew this meant Saturday, the Jewish Sabbath – 'they stay in other place. Also work-clothes. Here only clothes for school and go home to parents. This enough place.'

The others rewarded this lengthy speech with loud applause. The boy then pointed to himself and said, 'My name is Ofer. What is your name?' The others laughed. This was obviously a gambit they had had to learn by rote in their unsuccessful English lessons.

'Lesley.'

'My name is Shula,' said the fat one.

'My name is Aviva,' said the pretty one.

'You want see others?'

Lesley wanted nothing less at the moment; she felt overwhelmed, and wanted only to be left alone. But Ofer was already out of the room, and she heard his strident voice calling out in the corridor. There was a noise of answering shouts and the pattering of many feet. Suddenly the little room was crowded with strange faces, all blankly unfamiliar in Lesley's eyes. Impossible to believe that one day soon they would all take on meaning and personality. Names were shouted at her, strange, indecipherable names – only a few like Esther, Ruth and David (pronounced 'Davveed') she recognized. Even a Naomi called herself what sounded like

'Gnomie' which would have made Lesley laugh if she hadn't been past laughing, as she was little and looked rather gnome-like. The others were just sounds and blanks and confusion.

Lesley knew with her mind that they were trying to make her welcome, but the more they tried the more alien she felt. The more she looked at their clothes, the more out of place she felt in her own. The more she thought of living – actually living, day after day and night after night – in this little box, with no space, no privacy, no room to breathe her own breath or silence to think her own thoughts, the more sure she became that Noah and her father were crazy, and that she herself would shortly be crazy too.

CHAPTER 9

A Transformation

She was dismayed to find that her one wish now was to flee back to her parents' little box-flat as quickly as possible. But she set her teeth and wouldn't let herself go. She allowed the crowd of kids to shepherd her about the building which she must now call 'home', and concentrated on keeping her eyebrows down at the size and shabbiness of the shower-rooms (at least there the boys and girls were decently separated!) with the hook on which she would hang her towel and sponge-bag; the roomy but unsmart classroom in the same block, with chipped greenish blackboards and double desks intricately carved with dozens of Hebrew initials; the thread-bare, spiky lawn outside, with a scummy-looking fish-pond they had made themselves; and, eventually, the dining-hall in the middle of the kibbutz.

The children clearly found this big modern building a source of great pride. It was the newest thing in the kibbutz and, Lesley thought, quite the ugliest. Her own home had been luxuriously furnished in the traditional style – brocade upholstery, velvet drapes, richly patterned carpets, paintings, good copies of antique furniture. The kibbutz dining-hall, by contrast, was stark and cold. The scores of tables were covered with Formica, the chairs were plain wood, the walls quite bare except for a weird sort of mural picture made of bits of metal which looked as if they'd been stolen from a machine-shop. There wasn't a bit of colour except the curtains which were a sort of orange.

'Beautiful, not?' Aviva asked her, evidently eager for her praise.

'It's too bare,' Lesley said. Luckily they didn't understand the word, and just assumed she was saying the right thing.

'Too bare' more or less described Lesley's feelings about much in the kibbutz. Bare of decoration, bare of luxury, bare of elegance, bare of comfort. With all the trees and shrubs and flowers it didn't look desolate from outside; but inside it had the barrenness which Lesley had previously expected.

Ofer and two other boys went off to collect her luggage. She had looked forward to the moment when she would unpack all her luscious clothes before an admiring female audience; she now heartily dreaded it. Would they laugh and despise her? Would they be jealous and hate her? The difference, the distance between her and them was already unbridgeably wide; bringing those elegant and totally unsuitable clothes out one by one from her smart touristy suitcases would widen it to the point where they would be practically invisible to each other. When the boys arrived, staggering under the weight of the cases, she chickened out.

'Put them under the bed,' she said. 'I'll unpack later.'

'Now! Now!' chorused the girls. 'We want to see!'

'No.' Frantically she searched her mind for an attractive enough distraction. 'Now you teach me Hebrew.'

They broke into a whoop of approval and began rushing about pointing at objects and naming them in the strange words she had begun to get used to hearing at the Centre. She imitated them easily enough, but she couldn't keep them in her head. It was like with school French. 'I'll never learn!' she thought in sudden terror. 'Oh Noah! Why didn't I listen to you?'

The crowd of kids now began to drift off. It was four p.m., time to visit their parents, rest, do their homework or pursue their hobbies; have 'four o'clock meal' as tea was called. Lesley knew she *should* go home now, but she was somehow afraid to; afraid of her mother's tearfulness, afraid of how she would feel later when she had to come back. Afraid she would chicken out of coming back.

So she stayed in the big building alone.

First she sat for a while and did nothing but stare out of the window. It had a screen on it to keep out the insects, but this was torn in the corners and the room was full of mosquitoes. One shutter was broken and flapped and banged in the afternoon wind. The curtains, once pretty and bright, were limp and faded, and so was her bed-cover. She couldn't help remembering the vivid crisp fabrics at home that she'd chosen herself, her spotless bedroom which was repapered before it was ever allowed to get shabby ... Shelves for her books, the deep-pile cream carpet, the luxurious arm-chair, the abundant space, her own shining bathroom ... Tears were coming. She got up quickly. It wouldn't be breaking her vow to cry now, but she was determined not to be weak.

She pulled out a suitcase and unlocked it. For a moment she looked at the neatly tissued layers of lovely things inside. Then she burrowed down in it, pulled out a few bits of underwear, two towels (too new!), her washing things, and from a second case, her old stuff, her jeans and knock-about shoes and sloppy sweaters. At the bottom she was excited to find two old, old tee-shirts dyed in circles like Aviva's which her mother must have packed – Lesley had certainly not bothered with them. She carefully chose two of her simplest dresses for *Shabbat*. The rest she locked up again and stood the suitcases out in the corridor to be taken away for storage.

Her secret box presented a problem. It had a lock, and she always kept the key in a big silver locket she wore round her neck. But the others, she'd noticed, wore no jewellery other than the occasional Stars of David on fine chains – the locket looked clumsy and ostentatious. She took it off and looked all round for a place to hide it. In her bedroom at home there were a dozen excellent hiding-places; here, you really had to use your ingenuity. The bareness again!

At last she discovered that the mattresses were made of a kind of foam rubber which had little square pockets in it. By making a tiny cut in the bottom of the mattress-cover with her nail-scissors, she was able to drop the locket, with the key inside it, into the pocket. The cut hardly showed and would in any case always be covered by the bedclothes. The box itself she put on her shelf. She thought of under the bed in the corner, but figured sooner or later somebody must see it and it would only make the kids more curious.

The box took up most of the shelf, but she found room for a few of her favourite books. Here she couldn't resist showing off a little, and chose her most 'intellectual' ones for display – a Dickens, Walter de la Mare's poems, Roget's *Thesaurus*, and *Plays Unpleasant* by Bernard Shaw. It was a bit silly, really, because of course these kids wouldn't be able to read the titles, but somehow it gave her back her feeling of superiority which had been oozing away all day.

When that was done she took stock of the contents of her sponge-bag and cut it down to the minimum – soap, face-cloth, teeth things. Her make-up she had put away except for some sun-cream. Now she took these things to the shower-room and had her first shower there. She washed all traces of lipstick off carefully, and washed the curl out of her hair. She combed it straight and put on her old tatty clothes and looked at herself critically in the mirror.

A new Lesley confronted her – a Lesley virtually indistinguishable from an Israeli girl. Her heart misgave as she stared at herself. She no longer looked Canadian. In Canada she would be ashamed to go out looking so – so plain. Yet the fancy clothes, the fancy hair, had *burnt* her – she couldn't have kept on wearing them.

'When in Rome, do as the Romans do,' Noah had said.

Yes, but another time he had advised her, 'To thine own self be true.'

What *was* her real self?

She no longer knew.

CHAPTER 10

Getting Used to Things

It was easy enough to change her appearance. It was not so easy to change herself.

Everything seemed to be against her. The weather made her sleepy; the language made her furious; the work exhausted her; the lessons drove her mad with boredom and frustration. Her surroundings irritated and offended her. The other kids, once the novelty of her arrival had worn off, tended to leave her alone. This was actually because they were embarrassed by their inability to talk to her properly, but Lesley in her insecurity thought they disliked her, and this turned her against them, too.

Only Shula made a serious effort to befriend her, and it was uphill work, because like many girls who have been blessed with naturally slim figures Lesley tended to despise fat people. There were nine girls in the class, and all were more or less pretty except Shula, who was not only fat, but plain. The clothes which made the others look like leggy young colts made Shula look like a baby hippo. Added to this, her skin was spotty and her hair would not grow long and straight and silky, but remained stubbornly in a short frizzy bush.

All this would have made her a very unhappy girl in Saskatoon, but Lesley, watching her curiously for signs of a misery somewhat like her own – the misery of the outsider – found none. Shula was talented. She was a natural comedian and she could also play the flute and the guitar. She was a good student and a good sport, having a go at everything and being the first to laugh at herself if she failed. In other words, she was a *chevraiman*.

But even popular fat people have an affinity with loneliness and sadness. Shula alone sensed that Lesley was wretched under her poised, faintly contemptuous manner. The others had begun to call her '*snobbit*' (the local form of 'stuck-up'), and with good cause: she wouldn't join in the group activities that filled most of their lives; she spent most of her free time reading conspicuously heavy-looking books; she wouldn't show them her things or even try to talk to them about herself. In the lessons, she appeared stupid and dull, and yet she put on the airs of a brilliant student.

As for work, she was frankly hopeless at it. A lot of prestige in a kibbutz, among the young as well as the old, depends upon how well you work. Every kibbutz child does some work around the place from the age of eleven, and by fourteen they are working two hours a day on top of school work. Every day after lessons ended at 1.30, Lesley and her classmates scattered to various parts of the kibbutz to do their stint: some to the kitchen to help prepare supper, some to do farm-work, others to help in the houses where the younger children lived. Lesley was assigned to the kitchen at first, but she hated that so much (and was so bad at it) that they sent her to work in the chicken-houses, collecting eggs and helping distribute the food. But after a big white rooster had attacked her from behind, she refused to go back there, so then they put her in the gardens. She thought she might like that, but she soon changed her mind.

The work there was the hardest of all. It was outside in the sun, fortunately not too hot at this time, and just plain dirty drudgery. The head gardener was a heavy-faced elderly man called Moshe who never smiled, and had a way of popping out from behind a bush just when you were sitting down to have a little break. He wouldn't tolerate slacking in the young; not just because he believed it was bad for them, but for the sake of his gardens. The gardens were his whole life. He spoke just enough English to tell her off for being lazy, but not enough to talk to her properly as they worked together. She knew he'd complained about her being no good and had asked the man in charge of work-lists to give him someone else instead, but the fact was they had nowhere else to put her, so the garden was stuck with her.

Sometimes, though, Shula worked with her. Shula was what they called a 'cork'. She had no regular work-place, but was stuck in wherever she was needed. Unlike Lesley, she was good at every type of work; even the roosters respected her, and Moshe used to point at her with a soil-encrusted finger and say, 'You watch Shula. You work like her. Shula not lazy. Shula's good worker.' Shula would pull a funny face behind his back and shake her head violently, yawning and clowning around, acting lazy and dopey; but the fact was, she worked as if work were her natural element and no effort for her. It made Lesley tired – and deeply envious – just to watch the zest with which she went about the digging and scything and weeding and pruning.

And while she worked, Shula talked. She talked a mixture of Hebrew and the most atrocious English imaginable; but her natural gift for comedy made her garbled conversation so funny that Lesley, half against her will, began to laugh at her, then with her, and then, inevitably, to like her.

Her father was a Cockney who used all sorts of slang and swearing in his English, which he spoke to his wife, not intending his children to understand; but Shula had a quick ear and had picked up more than she was supposed to. It was irresistibly funny to hear her come out with things like: 'I am hating this damn *mikasachat*! I want that it go *kadima*, but it all the time going the hell *achora*!'

The *mikasachat*, or hand motor mower, was the curse of their lives. Moshe and his older assistant could sit on the baby John Deere tractor and sail around the big lawns, cutting them in great swathes while the cut grass sprayed into a

big canvas catcher towed along behind. It was not only effort-
less, but looked the greatest fun.

But Shula and Lesley were not allowed near the precious
tractor. To their lot fell the smaller lawns, full of trees and
tricky corners – and the 'damn *mikasachat*', an ancient
machine which had to be started with a rope like an outboard
motor-boat and which resisted all their efforts to make it
work efficiently.

Lesley was completely incapable of starting it at all, and
only Shula's good meaty right arm had the necessary
strength to pull the starting-cord sharply enough to get the
thing going. Then, pushing it together, they might get a small
patch of lawn cut (the grass was not like in Canada, but
thick-stemmed and resistant) before hitting a submerged
stone and stopping dead. Going downhill it seemed to run
away with them and they'd go flying after it and land in a
heap, while their undisciplined monster vanished into some
prickly bushes.

All these trials drew Lesley and Shula together. Shula was
too easy-going to be critical of Lesley for her inefficiency and
laziness; she took a tolerant view when her work-partner sank
to the ground in the shade for an ill-earned rest every hour or
so, but she herself would carry on. This made Lesley too uncomfortable to rest for long.

It was Shula, too, who rubbed her aching back after an
afternoon's weeding, her fat strong hands kneading the pain
away like magic, while her funny chatter would untie the
knots of tiredness and irritability in Lesley's mind at the
same time.

And it was through Shula that Lesley began to learn Hebrew. It was a painless process compared with the agony of
sitting in lessons not understanding a word. At the end of
the first day of school, she had been close to complete despair.
She wanted to rage and weep. For six hours she had sat, un-

able to grasp a single word! But she had no one to rage at. So she had nothing to do but go out for a long, long walk, and a long, long brood. She started this walk quite positive that she would never go into that classroom again. She finished it in a different frame of mind.

'I won't be beaten!' she thought to herself fiercely. 'They pretend to welcome me, but they don't really want me. They don't expect me to ever get a foothold among them. But I'll get in. I won't be left out!' And to strengthen all this, words of Noah's came back to her:

'Don't ever be a quitter.'

She had quit at the Centre, and how she regretted it now! This was her last chance. She would try. She *would* succeed.

She went every day. She worked as she had never worked – never had to work – before. And being with Shula in the gardens helped. If you see that the motor-mower (whose Hebrew name you have quickly learnt) is going backwards, and someone begins cursing it for *not* going *kadima*, you don't have to be a genius to learn pretty smartly what *kadima* means.

The names of things she learnt automatically, and from listening to the funny way Shula built her English sentences Lesley formed a picture in her mind of how to build a sentence in Hebrew. Pretty soon the lessons began to make some sort of sense. Long blank patches would be interrupted by occasional flashes of light as she heard a word or sentence she understood. And after classes, there was always Shula, who didn't wait to be asked but would come up to her and say:

'I can do stinky old *avodat-bayit* with you?'

They would sit together over the homework and after a bit, Lesley found she could do some of it. And one day, after about a month, she went of her own accord to the teacher who, at the very beginning, had offered to coach her, and asked if she might now take her up on it.

All this sounds as if Lesley were settling down very comfortably, but it wasn't like that. One swallow doesn't make a summer, and one fat friend doesn't make a social life; nor does a victory in one battle over yourself build your character.

Success was the key to it all; and Lesley was not a success in anything – a bitter pill for someone who, until then, had never failed. And she hated the place itself, the smallness, the shabbiness, the crowdedness, the unprivateness. She hated this last most of all.

There was only one time of the day when she could sometimes be alone in the *kitta*, as the big school-living building was called, and that was between the hours of four and seven in the afternoon. That was when the children normally went to their parents' homes. True, they often drifted back early to do homework, practise an instrument, play volleyball or basketball, hold meetings, or go to sleep, so you couldn't be sure even of that time. But on the whole the place was quiet then and you could have a shower by yourself or read or write in your diary or just lie on your bed and brood.

The only thing was that your parents were waiting for you. Lesley was shocked to find how little she actually needed to go to their house after the first couple of weeks. They were there, close by, and she knew she could go and visit them whenever she liked (except during working hours, when she wasn't free anyway) and at first she used to rush home at four o'clock eager to see them and reassure herself that her world hadn't totally disintegrated.

But after a short time she grew uncomfortable in their little bare room. Her father, who was working in the cowsheds (which she'd learnt to call the *refet* even when speaking English), was so deadly tired after work that he could hardly keep awake. And her mother seemed so withdrawn and strange that she made Lesley unhappy.

Lesley was now too occupied with her own problems to be

angry with them any more, and she would have been glad to make up for her bad behaviour by helping them if she could; but she had no idea how to do it. *Their* problems seemed so grown-up, so far away, so un-understandable. When she looked into her mother's face, her mind boggled at the depths of disorientation she could see there. She felt helpless and backed away, as it were, from something too big and complicated for her to tackle.

Once both her mother and father were sleeping the sleep of the totally worn-out when she arrived, and she had the shower-room, the kitchenette and the living-room entirely to herself for nearly two hours – till her mother woke suddenly, jumped off the bed looking guilt-stricken, and began rushing about 'looking after' her. She seemed to feel she'd done something awful in sleeping through most of Lesley's 'home-time', and kept on fussing and apologizing; and Lesley hadn't the heart to tell her that she'd been happier, more relaxed, at home while they were asleep than when they were conscientiously awake and waiting for her with their poor weary eyes propped open and bright, fixed smiles on their faces. A rough-cut cheese sandwich and a cup of her own make of coffee, gobbled while she lay on the floor reading, had been more to her liking than the formal teas laid out on the table which her mother seemed to feel it her duty to make every day.

Of course, Lesley, preoccupied as she was with her own adjustments, had no way of knowing how hard it was being for her parents, too. Her father, who had done no manual work since he was in his teens, now spent his days working in the cow-shed, up to his knees in mud and muck, going through the novel but exhausting process of learning to work the milking machines and handle a large herd of cows. His arms ached from forking the bales of straw, his legs from simply standing on them for eight hours a day; but his heart secretly ached the worst, because he had expected all this to give him some miraculous satisfaction and it didn't, at least not so far.

He didn't understand the cows and yet he pitied them, for their lives seemed so curtailed; the calves were taken away at birth and kept in tiny pens to keep them free of disease; the herd was never allowed to roam the pastures, and often the young bullocks, being fattened for market, seemed to him to be so crowded in their hygienic pens that their existence could not be called living at all. He did not know enough about modern farming methods to dare to criticize, even if he had had the words; but some instinct told him that if we raise animals for food, we owe them a reasonably happy and natural life first. These thoughts whirled in his head while he was working and seemed to increase his tiredness, for he had nobody he could talk to about them.

As for Lesley's mother, she was working in the kitchen of the kibbutz. It was a big modern kitchen, such as you find in a hotel, where all the utensils seem five times as big as normal – like the pots and pans of a giant. It was all new and had every possible labour-saving device, and Mrs Shelby, or Miriam as everyone called her, might have enjoyed it. She had always liked domesticity. There were plenty of English-speaking women working there, the work was not too hard and was varied enough not to be boring.

But one thing grated on her so that she thought she would scream, and that was the complete absence of *kashrut*. 'Kashrut' are the rules of Jewish cooking and house-keeping, set down thousands of years ago and followed by religious Jews ever since. They are very stiff rules, and hard to keep. It's not just a matter of not eating pork or certain types of fish and other meat. It's not even a question of not mixing milk-foods with meat-foods. You have to keep all your meat-dishes separate from your milk-dishes, and not even wash them up together or wipe them with the same dish-towels. Jewish hotels save trouble by having separate kitchens for milk and meat cooking, so there can never be a mix-up.

Miriam of course had only had one kitchen in Saskatoon, but she had two dressers with two lots of dishes (as a matter of fact, she had a third set, a very special and beautiful one kept for the week of Passover in the spring). She was not as punctilious as the very orthodox women are, but she certainly was fairly strict; the laws had been a basic part of her life ever since her own mother had taught her to respect them, and to find herself now in a kitchen with Jewish women who not only disregarded all the rules but, in the case of the younger Israeli women, didn't even know many of them, was more of a shock and an outrage to Lesley's mother than anything else which had happened to her.

At first she felt bound to protest, but people's reactions varied from laughter and shrugs to one more sympathetic older woman who explained: 'We've left all that behind us. Now we have our own country, we feel no need for all those old rules any more. We only needed them when we had no homeland to hold us together.'

'But if it hadn't been for those laws, there wouldn't have been a separate Jewish nation to come back to Israel!' Miriam Shelby cried, deeply offended.

'Certainly. But now their usefulness is at an end. The jug held the wine; but now we've drunk the wine, the jug can be broken.' The older woman smiled. 'You must admit it's all a bit absurd. After all, the law only says: "You shall not seethe a kid in the milk of its mother." It's a far cry from that to using different knives for cutting butter and cutting chicken. Besides,' she added, seeing Miriam's shocked expression, 'to be strictly practical, we've neither the time nor the money to be bothered with it.'

Miriam said no more. There was no more to say. She

didn't even mention it to her husband – she was too afraid that he might not agree with her; he'd been talking so oddly lately, and indeed he had never been as particular as she was about such things. So she felt quite isolated in her beliefs, and every action she took, at work every day, was offensive and scandalous to her. It was the strain of this, more than the work itself, which tired her out and made her want to escape into sleep.

And so Lesley found out how lovely it was to come home to her family and not be made a fuss of. Though she didn't realize it, she was beginning to like the simpler, more informal ways of the kibbutz. But the best part was to sit for two hours without any noise, even of her parents' conversation. In the *kitta* there was nearly always some activity going on to break the silence: a radio blaring, or a record-player; kids shouting back and forth; the thuds and cries of volleyball and other games outside; Ofer practising endlessly on his oboe, or Shula on her guitar.

And in the evenings, there were 'activities'. The weekly committee meetings, when various elected groups settled disputes, talked over personal problems, arranged outings, chose films and thrashed out work-rotas and school problems. There were films once a week, which Lesley would have enjoyed except that all the kids sat in pairs or groups and she often felt left out; there were dances on Friday for the whole high school, but the dancing was not the kind Lesley was used to; it was folk-dancing, which looked wonderful, but she felt strangely reluctant to intrude into the whirling, leaping circles, which was the only way to learn. There were sports galore, and here she might have shone, for she'd been a basketball star at home and her volleyball wasn't bad either; but here they seemed to play so wildly, as if winning or losing were a matter of life and death. She tried a couple of times, but the pace was too fast for her, the style too rough. She took refuge in her usual aloof shake of the head, and stepped to the sidelines once again.

Then there was something they did which was secret, and this of course intrigued her greatly. About once a fortnight, they would all put on bright blue shirts with a thick white lace criss-crossing at the neck-opening, and disappear into the darkness outside, to return two or three hours later, flushed and chattering like starlings. They made a great point of shushing, fingers to lips, whenever she was anywhere about – as if she could understand a word; but this we're-inside-you're-outside attitude pushed her further and further away from them.

True, Shula tried to help.

'You want to know where we go?'

Lesley tossed her head, she wanted to know so badly.

'Is big secret only everybody knows. P'*oolot*. You know what is p'*oola*? When soldiers go out and – she mimed firing a rifle – 'that is a p'*oola*.'

'An attack? Do you all go out and attack someone in your little blue shirts?'

'Not go bang-bang. We go out and do things. It is for the t'*nua*.'

But Lesley didn't know what a t'*nua* was, or a p'*oola* either. She pretended not to be specially interested, but with Shula's help she looked both words up in her dictionary. P'*oola* was an 'action, often military' and t'*nua* was a 'political move-ment'. She was more bewildered than ever.

'What "political movement"?'

'We are called "Young Guards".'

'Is it like Scouts?'

'No!' Shula said scornfully. 'Scouts is not politics.'

'What are your politics?'

'We are *socialistim*,' said Shula.

'But the – the p'*oolot*? The actions?'

'Different things. Sometimes we go out with the little children in the night and teach them. I am a *Madricha*,' she added proudly.

Madricha turned out to be a youth-leader.

'How? What?'

But Shula couldn't explain – or wouldn't. And Lesley felt so hurt and upset about it all that by the time, a few days after this conversation, that Shula came back to her and said, 'Our *madrich* say, you want to come on a *p'oola* with us?' Lesley had turned stubborn and said loftily, 'Oh no thanks, it all sounds rather childish.' Which of course hurt Shula's feelings in turn.

CHAPTER 11

A Strange Encounter

In Saskatoon, the first place Lesley always ran to when she was too happy or unhappy to stand being with people, was the river-bank. She loved water, and was always attracted to it; the land bordering on water – whether it was the sea-shore, the edge of a lake, the lawn beside a swimming-pool or the banks of a river – had a sort of special charm for her. She felt she could be herself more completely when there was water – fresh, sparkling, always the same yet always changing – close beside her.

So it was natural that, at the first opportunity, she had made her way down to the riverside here. Apart from anything else, she was dying to look across and see the Arab farmers and feel the excitement if this strange situation.

But to her great disappointment, as she wandered along through the scrub that bordered the road, looking for a way down, a kibbutznik suddenly appeared, giving her a great fright, and asked what she was doing there.

'I wanted to get down to the river,' she explained, hoping he understood English.

Evidently he did, because he shook his head very firmly, turned her around by the shoulders and gave her a push back along the road towards the kibbutz. 'But why not?' she asked over her shoulder.

He wagged his finger. '*Oy-va-voy!*' he replied, which she knew to mean, 'Don't be naughty or you'll get into trouble.'

'Is it really dangerous?' she persisted, but he didn't answer, just shook his head again and pointed strongly towards the kibbutz.

So she asked Shula, and Shula laughed and said, '*Tipsha*! The river is *gvul* between us and Arabs. We go sometimes but is not really allowed. You want to see the river? Come, I take you.'

She led her up a hill which overlooked the whole kibbutz, and there on the top was a round sort of building with a curved balcony on it overlooking the river and all the countryside beyond it right up to the pinkish hills.

The two girls stood on the balcony and looked at the view. It was very strange to see the green of the kibbutz and its well-watered fields, in contrast to the barrenness of the land on the other side, where there seemed to be just a few small areas of cultivated land curled against the side of the river.

The river itself wound in and out like a silver snake. It twisted and turned so much that in one place you had Jewish land, then the river, then a peninsula of Arab land, then another bit of river, and Jewish land again on the other side.

'Not good farmers,' Shula said. '*Primitivim*. Don't know nothing on *hashka'a*.' Lesley had already found out that that meant watering. 'No tractors too. Like you and me in the garden, only they not even have the damn *mikasachat*!' They laughed. Suddenly she clutched Lesley and pointed. 'Look there!'

Lesley looked, and saw a man, a boy and a donkey slowly coming along a track which led beside the river on the far side. The donkey was heavily laden with sacks. The man, wearing a black gown and white head-dress, walked ahead, and the boy walked behind, occasionally speeding up the donkey with a whack from a long stick. It was a quiet morning, and if you listened carefully, you could hear the smack of the stick a split second after seeing it fall on the donkey's flanks. The donkey's head hung down, and his tail switched continuously at the flies.

As the little procession made its way round the curve of the river and on to the peninsula, the boy caught hold of the donkey's tail and jumped leapfrog-fashion onto its back. The poor little beast grunted with surprise at the extra weight and hurried forward for a few steps before slowing down again. The man looked round, saw the boy mounted, and without hesitating knocked him off again with one sweep of his hand. The boy landed on his feet, and you could faintly hear his laughter and the sudden loud angry voice of the man. Then they continued until they disappeared into a thicket of orange trees, part of a very small grove which occupied a bit of the peninsula.

Shula and Lesley, who had watched this little dumb-show in silence, looked at each other. Lesley's eyes were shining. It was as good as the movies – better. This was real!

'Are they real Arabs?' she couldn't help asking, though she knew it was silly.

'*Betach!*' said Shula, in a tone which could only mean 'Of course!' She didn't seem to think it was anything special. 'The old man, he is the boss of that *pardess*. Is his orange trees,' she explained. 'He is damn poor farmer, many kids, all girls, only one boy. He has no *mazal*,' she said with a laugh.

'How do you know about him?'

'I watch from up here, and my brother, Rami, he work with tractor – down there,' she pointed to the ploughed area on their side of the river. 'He tell me stories about them.'

'Does he talk to them across the river?'

Shula's mouth turned down and she made a gesture which plainly said, 'No percentage in it.' 'One time he saw that old man sit by the river, eat *pitta* for his lunch, and my brother, he was –' She mimed a cigarette.

'Smoking – yes?'

'And he saw that *Arav* watch him, like he want one too, so my brother throw the box over the river. You want to know what the old man do?' Lesley nodded. 'He jumped up and run like hell.'

'But why?'

Shula laughed. 'He think my brother throw to him a bomb.'

'But that's not really funny. It's sad.'

'Sad – yes. Rami also said that.' They stared again at the dark green patch of the orange-grove, waiting for the boy and his father to re-appear. 'One thing funny though. My brother, he saw where the box falled. Next day he look – gone! They came in the night and take it.'

'Why does the boy hit his donkey all the time?'

'All the *Aravim* hit donkeys. *B'ofen automati*. Like breathing.'

'Do you hate the Arabs?'

'I? I not hate nothing. Only the lousy *mikasachat*, and Ofer sometimes when he play his *aboov* when I want to sleep.'

'But they hate us.' It was the first time she'd ever said 'us' meaning 'us Israelis'. It just slipped out, but she had a pang at the disloyalty.

'They fright.'

'They're frightened of us, so they hate us, but we aren't frightened of them, so we don't hate them?'

'*Bidyuk!*' And the way she said that could only mean 'exactly', so that was another word learnt. But she'd learnt more than just words that day.

The building with the view over the river was called the Culture House. It was a theatre and a concert-hall and a cinema and a general meeting-place. Often it was empty during the day, and Lesley liked to go there, to climb up on the balcony and stare out into enemy territory.

'One more river, and that's the river of Jordan –
One more river, just one more river to cross.'

She would hum the Negro Spirituals that mentioned the Jordan as she looked at it; it gave her a strange feeling, like taking part in history. And she could see other interesting things. There were several Arab villages within sight, patches of bleached stone boxes with flat roofs and networks of fields and groves around them, with little thready tracks leading away. It was down one of these that the old Arab and his son and their donkey used to come to work in their grove and because they were the closest, Lesley took more interest in them than in the occasional others she saw, pursuing their lives farther off. They were even more interesting than the Jordanian soldiers that patrolled in jeeps along the river's edge.

Once she borrowed a pair of army field-glasses from Shula's brother Rami. As she trained them on to the tiny approaching figures, her heart began to pound with excitement. There they were, the old man (not so old really, she supposed) in his rusty black garment, like a straight dress, to the ground, his white head-cloth under a sort of 'crown' of black cord; she could even see his broken shoes, scuffing along through the dust. But she didn't look long at him; she was more interested in the little boy, and in the donkey.

When she turned her glasses on the boy, she was amazed to see that, despite his small size, he was by no means as young as she had thought. He was very thin and short-bodied, but he was old-faced, so much so that it was impossible to judge his age exactly, but she guessed he must be as old as herself or even a bit more.

His expression was set and rather sour; the only times he smiled or laughed were when his father was being angry with him, and then it was more defiant and mocking than amused. Oddly enough, this made him even more interesting to Lesley because it seemed so unnatural to her. He was like a being from another world, where all the reactions were twisted – you laughed when you were angry or unhappy, looked grim when you were content, or when nothing special was the matter.

She watched him at his work among the orange trees; she watched him sit by the river eating his lunch which was always the same – an envelope of flat Arab bread full of something, probably *felafel* which Lesley had also learnt to like – chickpea balls with dill pickles and a hot sauce. Sometimes the donkey, whom he kept hobbled, would edge over to him and push at him with its soft grey nose as if begging for a bit of his bread, but he never took any notice of it beyond pushing its head away sharply.

His attitude to his donkey was another incomprehensible thing about him. Lesley had never owned a pet animal because their house at home had been too beautiful to risk a dog or cat spoiling it; but she had always longed for one. Now here was this boy who had a donkey of his own who could have been his companion – clearly wanted to be – and he took no notice of it and in fact ill-treated it quite cruelly. He seemed unable to walk behind it without whacking it all the time, or in front without jerking its head at every step to make it move quicker. While he was working he hobbled it so tightly that it could hardly take a step without stumbling to its knees, and he never bothered to lead it into the shade or down the steep river-bank to drink.

Lesley gave the boy a name. It was Mustapha, the only Arab name she knew. She gave the donkey a name too – Eeyore (which was the only *donkey*'s name she knew) and after that she recorded in her diary the small incidents she had observed on the days when she found time to go up to her eyrie on the Culture House balcony. Immersing herself in the 'small life' of Mustapha and Eeyore was an escape for her from the trials and difficulties of her 'big life' in the kibbutz.

One evening she unlocked her box with more than usual eagerness. It was half-past four, and already getting dark; she had the *kitta* to herself. She knew she must go and see her parents; she was already very late and her mother would be hurt if she delayed much longer, but she *had* to write down the incident she had just seen, and, for the first time, taken part in.

I was watching Eeyore standing by himself at the top of the bank as darkness began to come. Mustapha and his father worked late, and I suppose Eeyore couldn't wait any longer for the drink they MUST give him when he gets home in the evenings, because suddenly he started to try and get down the bank to the river. His poor forefeet were so closely hobbled that he had to make a little sort of jump with them with every forward step, and of course going down that steep slope, he tripped and fell.

My heart came into my mouth as he slipped to his side and slid and rolled down into the edge of the river. He let out a frightened bray, and all at once Mustapha burst out of the trees, waving a stick and shouting at poor Eeyore, who lay helpless in the shallows, kicking his free back legs, trying to get up.

Mustapha skidded down to the water's edge and started to whack Eeyore with his right arm while dragging at his bit of rope halter with his left. But Eeyore couldn't make it with the hobble on. I could just hear Mustapha cursing him as he untied the hobble off one leg and then of course dear, good, willing Eeyore clambered up at once and stood there with a wet patch on his side, hanging his head and looking ashamed of himself. And that stinking Mustapha just started beating him until the sweat was running off him.

It made me sick to see him! I lost my temper suddenly and shouted, 'Let him alone, you pig!' as loud as I could.

Of course I shouted in English, but he heard me and looked all around to see where the shout had come from. I was wearing my white shirt and I waved both arms to attract his attention and shouted again, 'Stop beating him – stop – beating – him!' He saw me! He just stood there, amazed, with the stick half-lifted in his hand. I shook my head at him and made a motion of breaking a stick and throwing it away. I don't suppose he could see me clearly enough to get the message, but at least he'd seen me and heard me, and while I was looking at him he didn't seem to want to beat Eeyore. He didn't know what to do, and we just stood there, with maybe two hundred yards of bright sunny air between us, staring at each other.

Then something else happened. I heard someone calling me from below. I looked down, and there was a kibbutznik, a man, standing at the foot of the steps, looking up at me with a puzzled face.

'Who are you shouting at?' he asked.

'There's an Arab boy across the river, beating his donkey,' I said.

'Did he hear you?'

'Yes. He's looking straight at me this minute.'

'You'd better come down from there.'

'Why?'

'Because you mustn't shout at the Arabs. What's the use? It's none of your business anyway what he does with his donkey.'

I tried to explain, but the man wouldn't listen and told me again to come down and stop being silly. So I did. But I took one last look at Mustapha. He was still standing there perfectly still, as if he was trying to become invisible. Just before I came down, something odd happened to me, and I forgot how angry I'd been and wanted to lift my hand and wave to him – just a friendly, hallo-you sort of wave. But the kibbutznik was watching me and I didn't dare.

CHAPTER 12

A New Friend,
A New Enemy

There was a girl in the class called Esther whom Lesley particularly admired and envied. She was in the same position in her group as Lesley had been in Saskatoon – the acknowledged leader, the most popular and best all-rounder. She was always that bit more daring, that bit more strong-willed and decisive, that bit ahead of the rest. She was also very pretty, and, within the limits of kibbutz fashion (which didn't seem like fashion at all to Lesley at first) very 'with it'. She was the first to have a boy-friend from a higher class, the first to campaign for separate bedrooms for boys and girls, the first to hang a metal mobile from her ceiling and paint a mural on her wall, the first to put false patches on her jeans and the first by a long way to cut the legs right off and fray the cut bit. She was also the first to think of coming to Lesley for help with her English.

She was very blunt about it.

'I want to make friends with visitors,' she explained. 'I want to ask them about England and America. I know you're *snobbit*, but I don't care. My English stinks. You help me and I'll help you.' So much Lesley could now understand. It was the *sabra* manner of approach; she was used to it, she knew they talked to each other like that so she was not offended. She agreed to help Esther, and she did help her, not by doing her homework for her but by explaining and making her understand. For the first time she began to see that there were rules about her own language. When Esther asked, 'But *why* we must say "I have done it" and not "I did it"? Lesley had to think about the reason and formulate a rule. The rule was quite simple and Esther grasped it easily and passed it on to the others. The teacher had not been able to make them see it, but suddenly the whole class understood the Present Perfect tense and began chanting it all over the place, even outside lessons. Their special chant was the nursery-rhyme Lesley taught them as an illustration, and you could hear them singing to each other in the shower:

'Poosy-cat, poosy-cat, where have you been?'
'Ive been to Lon-don to veeseet the Queen!'

And now, for the first time since her novelty-value wore off, Lesley was asked home to somebody's house for tea. Esther's family were founder-members of the kibbutz, but they were not English, they were Czechs, and Lesley had to struggle along with Hebrew if she wanted to be polite. Lesley saw that other parents were more relaxed about the tea-hour than her own. Esther's younger brother and sisters ran in and out, sometimes there, often off somewhere with their friends or lying in the bedroom reading or messing about. Esther's mother laid out a large mixed tea-ish meal on the long coffee-table in front of the sofa and she and Esther's father ate and drank while reading or chatting to each other and the children. The kids picked – a handful of saltsticks went into little Batya's pocket as she dashed in and out again to play; Miron lay on the floor with a plate of cake, reading, and Rachele sat at the desk doing homework and occasionally nibbling a sandwich. Only Esther and Lesley 'sat up' to tea in the rather ceremonial way Lesley did every day in her house with her parents.

Esther's father suddenly put down his newspaper and said, 'I hear you have a friend across the river.'

Lesley almost jumped. Esther turned and stared at her.

'Not a friend,' she said quickly. Then, when the others

seemed to be waiting for more, she added, 'I watch him. That's all.'

'And make signals to him?'

She was quite taken aback, almost alarmed. Signals? Could anyone think they were signals? That sounded like something – sort of military.

'Of course not. Only he knows I'm there, and sometimes I –' She stopped. The room was very quiet. Miron had stopped reading and was gazing at her with wide-eyed interest, and Rachele had turned round at the desk. 'Sometimes,' Lesley said in a small voice, 'I wave.'

'You wave. And does he wave back?'

'No. At least – Once I thought he did, but it turned into scratching his head.'

'Which no doubt needs it,' remarked Esther's father dryly.

'Is this the boy Rami talks about?' asked the mother.

'Yes,' said Lesley. She'd had several conversations with Shula's older brother about the Arabs.

Esther's mother and father exchanged glances, and the father gave a grunt.

'Oh well, it's probably harmless enough,' he muttered. 'For all that . . .'

'What?' asked Lesley.

'I just don't advise you to get too interested in anyone – over there. It's not worthwhile. And besides, you know our soldiers patrol the whole length of the river. I don't know if they'd understand if they ever saw you – waving.'

The subject was dropped, and almost at once Esther beckoned her to say good-bye and come outside.

'You're *meshuggah* – crazy!' she said when they were by themselves. She was looking at Lesley with new eyes, though whether scornful or admiring she couldn't be sure.

'It's nothing! He's just a boy.'

'Don't you know they're enemies?'

'But he's just a *boy*!'

'An Arab boy.'

That evening the whole class was talking about Lesley's boy-friend. Shula came to her in the shower-room while she was brushing her teeth. She was obviously annoyed.

'I'm sorry I took you up there,' she said. 'I not think you were damn silly clot like that.'

'But I haven't *done* anything!' Lesley protested, almost in tears.

Shula said nothing and walked out. When Lesley got back into the bedroom, she was already lying down, her little light off and her back to Lesley's bed. Ofer was sitting up in his bed, cleaning his oboe. Aviva, always the last in, was off at a choir-practice.

Lesley said, 'Ofer – turn your back.'

'Oh ...! I won't look. Anyway,' he noticed, 'you're already in your pyjamas.'

'It's the rule you have to turn your back if I ask you!' Lesley said fiercely.

Ofer sighed heavily and turned to face the wall, still fiddling with his oboe. Lesley stooped quickly and got the locket out of the mattress. She opened it, took out the key, and unlocked her box.

'What have you got in there, anyhow?'

She spun round, but Ofer still had his back dutifully turned to her. He must have heard the lock click.

'My own things.'

'Secrets?'

'So what?'

'Letters from your boy-friend?'

'*Shtok*!' This was the rude way of saying 'Shut up!' Lesley hardly ever said it, but he made her angry with his needling.

She carried her box into the classroom down the corridor. It was empty except for David who was sitting up late struggling with an English composition they were supposed to have written by tomorrow first lesson. He glanced up as she came in, and gave her a brief, hopeless look of appeal. But Lesley was too preoccupied. She settled herself at a corner desk.

'Dearest Noah,

'You see how faithfully I go on writing, even though I don't get letters from you. I wrack my brains how we could arrange something, but it's no use. Dad is finding this life harder than he dreamed, I think, and although he'd die rather than admit it he is very much "pulled" by Saskatoon and the old life. Every day he goes up to the office and looks through the letters before the Kibbutz secretary sorts them into the pigeon-holes. Even if you typed it, he'd want to know who it was from. Sometimes I so long to hear from you that I think I'd be willing to invent and tell lies, but I feel bad enough as it is.

'Now I must tell you more about Mustapha –'

She was interrupted by running steps outside.

'Listen what's happened!' cried Aviva's voice, high with excitement. 'Come and hear!'

At once the building came to life. Kids who were getting ready for bed came running out of their rooms half-dressed – Danny emerged from the showers with a towel round his middle, dripping wet. Others who'd been asleep tumbled out of bed and staggered into the corridor. David dropped his copybook with alacrity and dashed out of the classroom, with Lesley hot on his heels.

They all crowded round Aviva, who was flushed and bright-eyed and bursting with news – not such good news, by the looks of her. She started to pour it out in a rapid flow of Hebrew. Lesley struggled to follow, but after the first seconds got quite lost. She turned to Shula, who was beside her.

'What is it? What's happened?'

'*Aravim* cross the river!'

'What do you *mean*? Their army?'

'No, no! Only some silly twits come to pinch.'

'Were they caught?'

'No. But Aviva see them running away. One carry two hens, one grab stuff from the porch of somebody. Soon we must lock our doors like people in the city!'

'But how did they cross the river?'

Shula shrugged her fat shoulders. 'Walk. Is not deep.'

'What about our soldiers?'

Another shrug. 'Not many around here. Not can to be everywhere. Dark night – no moon. This not the first time.'

'And is that all they ever do? Steal some little things from people's porches or a few hens?'

'That's all. You know what I think? I think it's just young boys. I think it is like a game. I-bet-you-not-brave-enough-to-go. I-*yes*-brave-enough. You-go-then-and-bring-back-something-to-show-you-was-there.'

'We used to play that game in Canada. We called it "Truth or Dare".'

'Safer in Canada. Here you can get dead from it.'

Suddenly Lesley thought of something. She turned to Aviva.

'Which houses did they go to?'

'I don't know. I suppose the ones closest to the river.'

A wave of excitement and alarm washed over Lesley. Her parents' house actually faced the river! Still in her pyjamas she ran out into the darkness.

The kibbutz was well-lit, but still it was a little frightening to be running along like that under a black, starry sky. The bushes that bordered the narrow paths were high and dense enough to hide any number of prowlers ... She shivered as she passed the last 'street-lamp' and had to face a pitch-dark patch of lawn, and she hesitated a moment; but she could see the back windows of her parents' little rooms lit up in streaks through the closed shutters, and she plucked up her nerve and ran across as fast as she could.

As soon as she stepped on to the porch, round the other side, she knew she had been right – something had happened. For a start she could hear that the neighbours were in the main room, all talking at once in shrill voices. There was a jug of milk smashed on the tiles, and Lesley's quick eye could detect some little things missing from the porch – nonsense-things, a soap-stone Eskimo carving of a seal her mother had brought with her, a bright-coloured egg-timer that had hung on the wall. She burst into the room.

'Mom – Daddy – are you all right?'

The room was full of excited people, all shouting and asking questions. The *shomair* – the nightwatchman – was there too, with his *uzi* under his arm, and Lesley noticed an Army officer and an ordinary soldier talking to her father. Her mother came up to her at once and put her arms round her. Lesley felt embarrassed, as if they were all – including herself – over-dramatizing the whole thing. After all – an egg-timer! It seemed suddenly pretty trivial to be making all this fuss about.

But the soldiers apparently didn't think so. They questioned her father about every detail. It seemed they had been fast asleep in bed (Lesley had a sense of astonishment to think of her parents going to bed before her!) when her mother had been woken by some disturbance on the porch, and seen some kind of light out there, like a match. She had thought it must be Lesley, come to fetch something, and had in any case felt too tired to bother, but suddenly there was a crash and something was knocked over in the dark. That woke Lesley's father, who jumped out of bed automatically and rushed out, turning on the light, just in time to see the intruder racing towards the high barbed wire fence on the kibbutz perimeter.

There were bright 'projector' lights all along the fence, and he had been able to watch, helplessly, while the thief slipped under the bottom strand of wire and across the road, to disappear down the bank towards the river.

'Why didn't you call out?' asked the officer.

'I think I did – I remember shouting, "Hey, you there, come back" or something like that, but then somehow I was so absorbed with watching him – he was very small, hardly more than a little boy –'

'What?' asked Lesley suddenly. It was out before she could stop it. Everybody turned to look at her, and she wished heartily she had not drawn attention to herself.

'Do you know anything about this?' the officer asked, fixing her with sharp, suspicious eyes.

'No, how could I? I was in my *kitta* getting ready for bed,' said Lesley innocently.

The interrogation went on. Lesley's mother made tea for everyone, including Lesley and all the neighbours. Nobody else's porch had been robbed, it seemed, and what had been taken from the Shelby's had been so trifling that at first Mrs Shelby couldn't be sure anything was missing. Lesley pointed out the seal and the egg-timer, and the officer made a solemn note of them and their exact measurements and description, and they had just about decided that that was it, when Mr Shelby suddenly said,

'Hey, Miriam – where's Lesley's picture?'

They looked. There had been a snap-shot of Lesley in her bathing-suit tacked to the door-jamb. It was gone.

'What on earth would anyone want *that* for?' said Lesley. 'I looked just awful in it!'

Everybody burst out laughing then. All except the officer, who was still looking at Lesley in that funny way that she didn't care for at all.

CHAPTER 13

A Two-Way View

The next day, after work, Lesley went back to the *kitta* to shower and change. She was burning, absolutely dying to go up to the Culture House balcony and see if Mustapha was visible, but she'd had such a fright the night before that she thought it would be imprudent. There was a volleyball practice going on on the pitch just outside the long corridor window and a culture-committee meeting in the classroom, so there was more noise than usual for the time of day. Aviva was asleep on her bed, tired after their late night. Apart from her, Lesley had her room to herself. She dug out her key, opened her box, took out her diary, and wrote down all that had happened.

At the end, she wrote:

I feel so mixed-up. Could it have been Mustapha? How strange and crazy to think of him on our side of the river! I had the weirdest dream last night. I dreamt I was swimming across, only the river got wider and wider till it was as wide as the Saskatchewan and floating with huge bits of ice like when the ice breaks up in the spring in Saskatoon. [She looked at the last words a moment, then crossed off 'in Saskatoon' and wrote over the top 'at home'.] I *couldn't* get across. It was just terribly dangerous and impossible, and I was so frightened, but having got started I couldn't turn round and swim back either. And suddenly I saw Eeyore swimming alongside me and I found myself riding on his back and I knew I'd get across okay and there was Mustapha waving to me and smiling, as if we were old friends. Then all of a sudden I heard somebody say 'Bang, bang!' and I looked round and there was that officer pointing his gun at me and then I woke up.

She sat and brooded over it for some time. The idea of crossing the river in either direction had never occurred to her since that first day, when Ayala had explained that it was the border and that the people on each side were sworn enemies. But Mustapha had crossed! If it was really him. Was Shula right, and the young boys came across just for a dare, or maybe some kind of initiation test, or ... But any other idea was too crazy. Even if Mustapha *had* wanted to see her, he couldn't have expected to. As for taking her picture, that must have been just an accident. How could he know which was her parents' house?

Lesley locked her diary carefully away and strolled outside. The kibbutz looked rather nice; there'd been some rain, all the lawns were spring-green, and there were wild flowers growing up in every place that Moshe hadn't got around to cultivating. Lesley liked these better than what Moshe called 'real' flowers. She picked a bunch of wild anemones, not many because they were protected and you weren't supposed to pick them at all, to put in her mother's little finger-vase which a neighbour had given her on her recent birthday. Kibbutz people, Lesley had to admit, could be very friendly. The kitchen had made her mother a marvellous cake and given her a bottle of wine to celebrate. She'd been very touched, and for the first time, as people came in to wish her *Mazal Tov* and present her with little, simple, often hand-made gifts, Lesley had noticed her mother's tense anxious expression soften and a real 'old-times' smile light up her tired face. Lesley was surprised to see that she got more kick out of those cheap little presents than out of the grand things she'd always got at home. She'd practically gone crazy over Lesley's, which was a rather messy battik wall-hanging which she'd managed to make under Esther's instruction. It was the first time since Lesley had been a child that she'd given her mother something hand-made.

Reaching the porch-door, Lesley glanced round at the river. There were some trees in the way, but you could still see a bit of it, glinting its snaky way along some distance below. On the other side, directly opposite, was Mustapha's father's orange-grove. And –

Lesley spun completely round, narrowed her eyes against the glare, and stared with her mouth open.

Was it possible? There was Mustapha, a tiny figure in the distance. He was sitting – she could just make him out between the swaying branches of the intervening trees – on the top of the bank, only he appeared to have a mask on the top part of his face, some sort of black band, and – yes! – his hands were up to the sides of his head somehow, as if –

Lesley took off like a startled colt, and ran like the wind to Shula's parents' house. She knocked, panting, at the door.

'Is Rami at home? No, thank you, I won't come in.'

Rami, tall, bronzed from field-work and with hair wet from showering, came out on to the porch. He was at the age when he regarded his sister and her friends as pests, but he was always kind to Lesley, and she secretly much admired him.

'Nu?'

'Can I borrow your binoculars again?'

'What do you want them for?'

'I want to see something.'

'What do you say!' he said sarcastically. He took them from a nail on the wall and handed them to her. 'Here. Let me have them back.'

'Of course! Thanks a lot!'

Then the thing she hadn't wanted to happen, happened. Shula came out.

'I know why you want those,' she said.

'No you don't.'

'I yes do! You're going to look at your boy-friend across the river!' Fortunately she hissed this last so nobody inside the flat could hear.

'I do *not*!'

'You *yes* do. You must to be *careful*.'

Lesley took her arm and pulled her outside. 'Come and see what he's doing.'

But when they got back to the Shelbys' house, and looked through the trees, the opposite bank was empty.

'He was there a minute ago!' said Lesley. 'He was looking at me – watching me – *through binoculars*!'

Shula stared at her with a comic expression of disbelief.

'From where a poor Arab boy get *mishkefet*?'

'I don't know! Listen, Shula. If I tell you something, will you promise and swear you'll never tell?'

'You bet!'

'Cross your heart and hope to die and have to eat a dead pig's eye.'

'WHAT you said?'

'That's how we swear.'

'That is stupid. I swear by the *kavod* of a Young Guard.'

Kavod meant honour.

'All right. Now listen. I think it was *him* who came last night.'

Shula's round face was a study of amazement and incredulity.

'Why you think so?'

'First I just had an idea. But I thought, it's too much of a coincidence that he came *dafka* to my family's house. Only now I think he's been watching me, and look, he can see this house from there, with binoculars he could know which is my house. So supposing he came and took my picture?'

'You mean, he is gone on you?'

'Of *course* not!' Lesley said impatiently. 'He'd just do it for devilment or, like you said, for a dare. Or maybe . . .' She stopped to think. 'Listen, what if they have *p'oolot* too? What if *he* belongs to some movement, like cadets or something, and they sent him across the river to prove he was brave enough to join?'

'From *them* maybe he gets the *mishkefet* – from the terrorists!' Shula's astonishment had turned to alarm.

Lesley knew, of course, about the terrorists. You couldn't live in Israel in that year of 1967 and not know. Their purpose was to creep across the border in small groups or even singly, and plant mines or bombs, preferably where soldiers or army lorries or jeeps would be travelling. Only sometimes they did other things.

Once a little boy was going to a circus in a town not far from the border. Outside one of the tents he found a watermelon. Now, every child in Israel is taught not to pick up strange metal objects, which might be bombs or mines or grenades; but who can teach a poor child not to pick up a water-melon that doesn't seem to belong to anybody? He picked it up and had both hands blown off.

Lesley's teacher had explained that the Arab guerrillas were fanatics. 'They believe that the land of Israel belongs to them and that we Jews took it away by force, so they don't really care whether it's Jewish soldiers or Jewish civilians or even Jewish children who get hurt by the explosives they leave.'

The children of Kibbutz Kfar Orde, like other Israeli children living on the border, had grown up with a strange mixture of respect and contempt for these irregular fighters. They despised them because of their sneaky tactics. But they had to respect them because many of them were, for all that, daring and reckless and determined.

So now, when Shula mentioned them in connection with

Mustapha, Lesley knew quite enough to get an icy trickling feeling down her spine and around the base of her skull. It was well-known that the young Arab boys hero-worshipped their commandos, and often lied about their age to be accepted as runners or helpers. Or even to take part in – p'oolot.

'Listen, silly clot,' Shula hissed. 'You not understand! You think it's all fun and games. That's what all American visitors think –'

'I am not American!' whispered Lesley fiercely. 'And I'm not a visitor!' The last words were out before she'd stopped to think what they meant. If she was not a visitor, was she not a – well, if not a true citizen, at least a permanent resident? Was she not beginning to think of herself as just a little bit Israeli? Certainly being called a 'visitor' made her feel very cross and resentful. Visitors were silly and trivial. They rushed about the place gasping 'Ooo!' and 'Aah!' about the most commonplace things, taking photos from every angle and asking absolutely bone-stupid questions ('Don't you miss your mother?' 'Aren't you scared of the Arabs?') – and sometimes they laughed and said things in the kibbutz were 'cute' or 'quaint'. Everyone was glad when they went away, even though some of them gave money to build new buildings or buy new library books, or a tractor, and it was ungrateful not to be polite to them.

'I *do* understand, anyhow!' Lesley went on in the same undertone. They were still standing outside her parents' house. 'I know how serious it is. I don't care a bit about Mus – that Arab boy, why should I? I was just curious about him. You know how it is, you start watching someone, and it – it just goes on from there.'

'So you not wave to him any more or do more silly things?'

Lesley hesitated only a moment. 'No.'

'Or I must to tell.'

'Okay already!'
'Cross your eye and hope to kill pig?'
Lesley burst into giggles and bent double. Then Shula started to laugh too, and forgot to make her swear.

CHAPTER 14

The Challenge

But even without swearing, Lesley kept her promise. To tell
the honest truth, she was afraid. At first (Shula was right in
a way) the whole situation in Israel with the Arabs had not
seemed quite real to Lesley, but after living there for some
months, she became at least partly an Israeli herself, and
little by little she not only understood it all better, but, more
important, she began to *feel* it. The excitement of the situation was tinged with the healthy warning of fear. She realized that the innocent-seeming act of waving to a boy across
the river was not harmless, if you were not sure what you
were doing.

In any case, as that fateful spring went by, and the weather
grew hot in preparation for Lesley's first summer in the Beit
Sha'an Valley, there was too much else to think about. For
1967 was not just any year. It was a year that was to go
down in history as containing one of the shortest, fiercest,
strangest wars the world has ever seen.

But before that war came, Lesley was fighting, and winning, a little battle of her own. Perhaps it had something to
do with Shula slyly calling Lesley 'an American visitor'.
Perhaps it had to do with a basketball match against an op-
posing team from another kibbutz high-school, in which Aviva sprained her ankle near the beginning and Lesley was
bulldozed into taking her place, with outstanding results.
Mostly it was because as the Hebrew was starting to come a
bit easier she was correspondingly more at ease and her clev-
erness at lessons was beginning to show itself, so that she
was gradually rising to take her proper place in the hier-
archy of the group. This place was not, never could be, at the

top as it had been in her native town; it would be all but impossible for any outsider to rise above the status of people like Aviva-the-beautiful, Ofer-the-good, Esther-the-queen, or Shula-the-clown. Not to mention David-the-athlete, Naomi-the-daredevil, and Danny-the-scholar. But by the time April came, and the kibbutz was looking forward to Passover and making preparations for a wonderful celebration of this Jewish festival of festivals, Lesley found herself on the Passover committee and the Sports committee; she had friends to sit at the weekly film with; she, too, had practices to go to and was getting help with her homework in return for the invaluable help she had given with English.

One night, when the others were getting ready to go out on a *p'oola*, Esther came into her room in her brisk way, without a word of greeting or explanation, and put a parcel on her bed, wrapped in crumpled brown paper.

'What's this?' Lesley asked.

'For you. You mustn't open it till we've all gone.'

Lesley still hated *p'oolot* nights. Since that first time, when Shula came with the invitation from the Madrich (who was a much older boy called Boaz, almost ready for the army) nobody had ever suggested that she should join in, and Lesley had understood that, although for quite the wrong reasons, she'd done right to refuse. The kids hadn't wanted her. Only the Madrich had felt it his duty to invite her. So when they all put on their Movement shirts and went off to who-knew-where, Lesley would always make a point of being at her parents' house, or somehow looking extremely busy and as if even if they all fell on their knees and begged her to accompany them, she wouldn't bother to accept. But after they'd gone, she would always sit gloomily alone, and often write bitter, introverted pages in her diary till they came back, by which time she always tried to be 'asleep'.

Now she looked questioningly at Aviva, Ofer and Shula,

who were getting dressed. She was quite used to sharing a room by now, even with Ofer. There was a rule that when you wanted to undress, the boy turned his back, and the same with the girls when *he* did. There was never any non-sense about this. It was rather like brothers and sisters. Ofer, in fact, was so particular (he was rather shy, really, Lesley had discovered) that one night when he came in late from or-chestra rehearsel, he actually woke them all up to make them turn their backs!

They all had their backs turned to her now. Shula seemed to be trying not to laugh.

'Is it some kind of joke? Will it go off with a bang, or make a smell, or something?' Lesley asked rather bitterly. She was always over-sensitive on *p'oolot* nights.

'*We* don't know what it is,' said Ofer with exaggerated innocence.

'Of course not. How should we?' asked Shula.

Aviva looked at her watch.

'It's time,' she said.

They all called 'Shalom, Leslee!' as they left the room, and soon with much banging of doors and shouting and laugh-ing, they all left the building.

Lesley stared at the parcel. It reminded her of something. Soon she remembered what – it was the Shelby's Store dress-box which her mother had put on her bed in Saskatoon, as a sort of trap which she had duly fallen into. Was this another trap? Their sense of humour was sometimes hard to under-stand. Would Esther let her in for anything awful or humili-ating? Well, she just might ... Lesley was by no means sure of them yet.

On the other hand, if it was some kind of practical joke, wouldn't they have hung around to see the outcome?

Suddenly her curiosity overcame her. She fell on the parcel and ripped the brown paper off.

Inside, brand new and stiffly starched, was a blue Movement shirt.

Not so long ago, she would have hesitated, full of doubts and suspicions. Now she knew better. This was their way of saying something she suddenly knew she had been longing to hear: 'We want you to be one of us.'

In seconds she had stripped off her sweater and slipped the cool stiff blue folds of the shirt over her head. She stood before the little mirror and her hands trembled with excitement as she tied the white lace in just the right kind of sloppy bow. She looked at herself for a moment, and in that moment, a flash of insight told her that she was more proud of this than she had ever been of being 'Lesley-the-Queen' back home. No, not back home. Back in Saskatoon.

She gave herself a great happy grin and dashed outside.

They weren't out there waiting for her, as she'd expected, and for a minute she suffered a sharp pang of anxiety. Could it be a cruel joke after all? But suddenly she noticed a glow in the darkness. It was an arrow in red luminous paint, tacked to a tree. She ran till she found the next arrow, and the next. The arrows were leading her towards the river perimeter of the kibbutz. There was actually an arrow on her parents' house! The next was on the fence. It pointed straight at the ground. Obediently she lay down flat and wriggled underneath, thinking as she did so, with a queer little shiver, that this might have been the very spot where Mustapha had escaped, while her father watched; Mustapha, with her photo perhaps thrust into his shirt, sticking to his sweating chest. She hadn't seen him since the next day, when she'd spotted him watching her through those mystifying field-glasses.

She stood on the road and looked all round. No further arrows ... But down there, near the river, wasn't that the glow of a fire, away to the south? She looked to left and right, but all was quiet, so she slipped across the road and down into the scrub along the top of the river bank.

From there on she behaved like an Indian scout, bending double and creeping through the brush and trees as silently as a ghost. Once she thought she heard a rustle on the very brink of the river, twinkling in the starlight some way below her. She stood as still as one of the trees. She had been forced to learn all this tracking and stalking when she was a Girl Guide in Saskatoon; she had thought it stupid and pointless and had soon given up attending. But now it was valuable, for she remembered how she'd been taught to lay down her foot toe first and slide it in under the rustling leaves and twigs which would snap if you trod on top of them, how to seek out the deeper shadows and 'freeze' in them when anything stirred, turning your face downwards so it wouldn't reflect the light and give you away.

After a while she saw the fire's glow again through the scrub and crept closer and closer to it. Now she could see it clearly, a small campfire burning brightly in a little sloped clearing. There was no one near it, or so she thought at first – but glancing quickly round, she saw a sudden flicker of white, then another, and another, and she realized the wood was alive with tiny white snakes – the snowy laces in the blue shirts! They were moving in on her. She put down her head, and with a sudden spurt of running arrived panting but triumphant at the fireside.

The others burst out of the trees and bushes and fell on her.

'Well done! We didn't see you till the very last moment!'

'We thought maybe you hadn't seen the arrows!'

'We were just going to jump on you when you made your dash!'

They were all laughing and banging her on the back. But she noticed that even in the excitement of the hunt and its ending, they all kept their voices low. And then she noticed something else. The fire, which was very small and neat, built like a pyramid in a dug-out square of ground, was screened on the river side by a double thickness of sacking between two stakes driven into the ground. Looking further, she saw that they had deliberately chosen a place where there was quite thick foliage between the fire and the river, which shielded the firelight still more from possible observers on the far side.

'Is it dangerous here?' she asked, no longer afraid they would think her a coward.

'Oh, only a bit.'

'Are we allowed to be here?'

David shrugged. 'I suppose not really.'

'Is this where you always come?'

They covered their mouths to suppress their laughter.

'Of course not!' giggled Shula. 'We came tonight specially for your initiation.'

'Have I passed?' Lesley asked gaily, sure the answer would be 'yes'.

They all grew rather solemn. 'Not yet. Only the first part. Finding us was just the first test.'

A shiver of excitement and challenge brought goose-flesh out along Lesley's arms. 'What do I have to do?'

They all came and stood closely round her. Danny explained:

'You have three choices. *Aleph*, you can run all the way round the outer edge of the kibbutz, round the perimeter fence. But if you are seen or challenged, you've failed. *Bet*, you can walk along the main road to the next kibbutz, which is three miles away, and report to the Madrich there, and walk back. You have to do it in one and a half hours. *Gimmel* –'

He stopped. He looked round at the others. His face in the firelight was tense and flushed.

'I'm against,' said Shula in a flat voice, suddenly.

There was a murmur of agreement. But several voices, Naomi's among them, were raised against the murmur.

'Why not? We've nearly all done it. There's nothing to it really.'

'Anyway, she doesn't have to choose it.'

'That's right, she has two other alternatives.'

'What is it?' Lesley asked, unable to bear the suspense.

'Well, it won't hurt to tell her,' said David defensively. David was the tallest boy in the class. He was not very clever at lessons, and didn't usually have much to say for himself, but when it came to sport or anything physical and active, he automatically became the leader. Lesley thought that this final possibility, whatever it was, had almost certainly been David's idea.

'So this is it.' They drew in still closer together and his voice dropped to a whisper. 'About a kilometre down-river there's a broken bridge. It's not in use of course, and there's barbed wire at both ends, but you can easily climb up the legs of the bridge if you wade a little way into the water. You mustn't cross right over, of course. But you have to take a piece of chalk and get on to the bridge and crawl halfway across, and in the middle you must make a mark. Then tomorrow morning we can stand on the top of the bank and see if you made it.'

'It has to be big, or we won't see it.'

'You have to be very quiet.'

'And very, very careful,' said Ofer, sounding uneasy.

'And,' said Shula, ever practical, 'you have to roll your trouser-legs right up and take off your shoes so that the *meta-pelet* doesn't see you've been in the water. Or she'll guess.'

It was painfully clear to Lesley that this enterprise she was being challenged to was utterly forbidden. It was something more than a mere prank or it wouldn't matter much if the house-mother, who looked after their clothes and general welfare in the *kitta* 'guessed' she'd been wading.

This woman, whose name was Ada, was the heart and soul of kindness and tolerance, in fact many of the parents thought she was far too lenient. In the three months Lesley had been in the kibbutz, she'd only once seen her really angry. This happened one Friday, when it was the custom for a chocolate ration, half a bar for each child, to be left outside the classroom to be eaten after lessons. Some of the boys helped themselves casually to two half-bars, and when the last children – who happened to include Lesley – strolled out of the lesson, there was none left. These deprived ones naturally made a scandal, but not too seriously – they easily guessed who had done the deed, the usual gutsies who thought of no one but themselves, and were content to set up a howl, chase them around a bit and whack them about the head with whatever weapon came to hand.

But when Ada came to see what the fuss was all about, she acted so shocked and furious that they were all brought up short.

'How can *chaverim* steal from each other?' she had cried, with tears standing in her eyes. 'Tell me, how?' The guilty boys, who'd been laughing and cocking their snooks a minute earlier, now looked startled and ashamed. From then on, Ada left each child's chocolate on his own bed, and there were no repetitions. But afterwards Gadi, one of the villains, remarked ruefully, 'I never knew old Ada had such power over me. She made me feel like a real zero.'

Now the dangerous and forbidden nature of this 'test' was brought home strongly to Lesley, and she stood in the firelit darkness, undecided. It would be terrible to have to face Ada, to hear her 'It hurts my heart' which was her usual reaction when they misbehaved. Not to mention what her father and mother would say if they knew.

She looked downward to the river. It slid by, glinting faintly; the other bank was just a blackness beyond the glimmer, but it was very near. From her perch on the Culture House balcony (before she'd stopped going up there) she had often seen Arab Legionaires patrolling on the far side, or driving along in jeeps ... Of course that was in the daytime. But wouldn't they take even more care at night? And what if even her own side's soldiers should see her? She could imagine how someone like Rami could be very fierce and scathing, and make you feel, in Gadi's words, like a real zero.

On the other hand – of all the three alternatives, clearly this was the one which would win her the most prestige and admiration if she dared to carry it out successfully. It was her chance to prove herself as brave as they were, a chance she might never get again.

She made up her mind.

'Okay,' she said, 'I'll do it.'

'Which? Which?'

'The bridge, of course,' she said as carelessly as she could for a thudding heart.

There was a moment when they all stared at her, a moment that fed her wilting ego as nothing else had since she'd arrived. Then Ofer said, 'If you must, you must. But let's eat first.'

'Eat?'

'Of course! We've brought *naknikiot* to roast, and tins of corn. Boaz said we should give you a feast.' Boaz was the Madrich, and for the first time Lesley realized he was not there.

'Where is Boaz?' she asked, uneasy in her turn. If this older boy had been with them, she would have felt her 'test' couldn't be *really* dangerous or he wouldn't allow it.

'He couldn't make it. He went to the Army yesterday.'

Her heart sank. She wanted to ask if Boaz had okay'd the

tests in advance, but this would smack of backsliding, so she shut her mouth. They built up the fire a bit and sat round toasting the tough, garlicky beef sausages on sticks, much as Lesley used to toast weenies on the riverbank in Saskatoon with her gang. They ate the corn straight out of the tins, passing them round with a single big spoon which they all used. There was *mitz* – orangeade – out of big 'communal' bottles and even rolls, and of course buckets of unshelled peanuts and pretzels which they called *begele*.

While they ate, Shula sat beside her, and as they were finishing their 'feast' leaned towards her and whispered in her ear, 'You don't have to do it if you don't want.'

'Have *you* ever done it?'

'Me? You're making a joke!'

'Has anybody else *not*?'

'Three-quarters of the class hasn't.'

'But Naomi said –'

'Just to push you forward. Naomi did it first, then David. And then most of the boys did it, and finally Esther tried, but she only got as far as climbing on to the bridge, she didn't get to the middle. She said she saw a shadow moving on the other side.' Lesley suppressed a shiver of sudden real terror. 'Are you scared?' asked Shula, who'd felt it. 'If so, do one of the other tests.'

'No. I've said I'll do this one, and I will.'

Shula shrugged. 'All honour,' she said. '*If* you make it.'

CHAPTER 15

The Bridge

It was arranged that Ofer should go with Lesley to show her the bridge, but he was not allowed to wait for her, since the test had to be carried out alone. The others would wait by the fire. The actual climb and crawl to the middle of the bridge, and marking with chalk (which they gave her to put in her shirt-pocket) shouldn't take longer than a few minutes if she was quick and agile, and she should, they reckoned, be back by the fire, drinking *mitz* and relating her adventure, in little over half-an-hour.

She and Ofer set off, her forearm quite bruised from the mighty squeeze of encouragement Shula had given her as she stood up from the safe, cosy circle. Ofer had a torch, but he was unwilling to use it except in an emergency, and of course the actual bridge part had to be done in complete darkness.

As they walked along through the scrub, keeping their heads down, they held a whispered conversation that came and went in short spurts.

'Is there always some kind of test before new people join the Movement?'

'No. There's a special sort of ceremony when we first join, as a group, when we're eleven. But not a test exactly.' He held a branch aside for her with the natural courtesy she had found in many of the boys. They never stood up for women or opened doors or any of the purely formal things; but if you needed help, they gave it automatically, in simple, practical ways, and didn't expect thanks. 'The only "test" we had,' he went on as they picked their way forward, 'was that our Madrich called us unexpectedly out from a very exciting film to go out on our first *p'oola*, The "test" was not to make any fuss or keep him waiting. But of course we knew what it was for, so we came like lambs.'

'So why do I have to pass a test?'

'Well ... you're a stranger, and from abroad. Besides ...' He paused. Then suddenly he grabbed her arm. 'Sh! Be still!'

They froze together in the shadows. Above them, on the road, Lesley could now hear an engine in the distance, and soon they saw the headlights, throwing grotesque shadows as it rounded a bend and chortled by, both lights and noise fading away behind them towards their kibbutz.

'Army jeep,' whispered Ofer. 'Come on.'

'What were you going to say before? About me.'

'Oh,' he said vaguely. 'I don't really remember.'

'Yes you do. You said "Besides". You meant, besides, I wasn't very nice at first and nobody was sure of me.' It took some courage to say this, because although she knew it anyway, she didn't really want to hear it confirmed in so many words.

Luckily Ofer was too kind to hurt her. 'I wasn't going to say that. I don't remember, honestly. Look – there's the bridge.'

Lesley had forgotten to be afraid while she'd been talking to Ofer. Ofer was only a kid, hardly older than herself, but he was kind and he was confident and he was, after all, a boy, and a tall, strong one at that. She felt safe with him. She felt he knew the ropes and that he wouldn't let anything happen to her. But now she followed his pointing finger and saw stretched across the glinting dark river, a great black solid shadow. As she peered, she could make out some kind of broken superstructure which must once have been a hand-rail and below, a tangle of struts causing faint ripples where they entered the water.

Her whole body turned cold and she found herself clutching Ofer's hand.

'Don't you want to?' he whispered kindly.

She shook her head, though whether to say no, she didn't, she'd rather do anything else in the world, or whether to say that his assumption was wrong, was not clear to either of them. Anyway, she was going to do it, that much she knew, though why she must she didn't understand.

'Now listen. You must leave your shoes somewhere where you can be sure of finding them easily – right next to one of the legs of the bridge, I should. You won't need to wade in past your knees, and the bottom's firm. The climb's not hard. Just be careful if you pull yourself up by the rail at the top, it was beginning to feel a bit rotten when I did it and that was before the last rains. When you get on the bridge, be careful not to stand up or you might be silhouetted against the stars. As long as you keep on your belly you're in shadow from both banks. Right in the middle there's a big plank, and that's the one to mark. Make the mark with the length of the chalk, not the tip, so it'll be wide and clear. And as you come back, be careful not to let yourself drop into the water as you climb down, or you'll make a splash.' He gave her a gentle push down the bank. 'Go on. Kol Tuv!'

She started down the bank, and then turned, in two minds whether to heed the pounding of her heart and change her mind at the eleventh hour. 'Ofer!'

He was still standing above her.

'Nu?'

'Wait there for me!'

'I'm not supposed to.'

'Wait for me!'

'Okay.' She started to move again, and just heard him hiss after her, 'I was going to anyway.'

Then the darkness swallowed her and she was quite alone.

The last rainfall had been the day before – a late shower – and the bank was still a little soft and even slippery in places.

Lesley clutched at the stems of plants as she half slid, half clambered down the steep sides. Once she grabbed a thistle and nearly cried out. Then she was right down at the edge of the water.

At once she felt better. It was as if water really did have some magic power over her. She felt – not quite unafraid, but certainly in control of her fear. She took a deep breath and remembered that courageous people were not those who were never afraid, but those who conquered their fear.

The bridge was close at hand, a looming structure looking lopsided and neglected, as if part of it had subsided into the riverbed during its long disuse. She could just make out the rolls of barbed wire at either end. Reaching its deeper shadow she felt still safer. No one could see her underneath here. She sat down on the damp edge of the river in the pitch darkness to take off her shoes and socks.

It was while she was carefully rolling up the legs of her jeans that she heard a sound that made her head snap up and her hair rise up on her neck. She sat for several seconds perfectly still. Had she dreamed it? But no. There it came again! An awful, eerie sound, desolate as a lost soul even by day, perhaps the saddest cry in nature – the braying of a donkey.

She stood up in one jump, peering with all the strength of her eye-muscles into the opposite blackness. Was that something? Yes! Over there, just at the other end of the bridge, down by the water's edge, a vague, almost undetectable movement, accompanied by the faintest scrunching sound – the sound of a donkey's dainty hooves crushing wet stems.

'Eeyore!' whispered Lesley.

Without a moment's further hesitation, she waded into the water. It was far colder than she'd expected, and she gasped as the ripples crept up her legs. The first struts seemed to be farther away than she'd expected, and in fact the water was beyond her knees and almost up to the ridge of her rolled jeans by the time she reached it – the river must be more swollen by the late rains than Ofer had realized. The donkey on the other side brayed once again as if calling to her, as she began to climb.

Her eyes, completely adjusted to the darkness, picked out the joints in the bridge-supports quite easily, and her bare feet seemed to have eyes of their own as they found holds. Almost at once her right hand was groping along the slightly overhanging top surface for some upright grip by which to pull herself the final way up. She grasped a post, tested it, felt it sway in its socket; she felt a pang of fear. If she put her weight on it and it gave way, she would go straight into the river on her back with a splash that would bring any patrol within a kilometre down on her – and she'd heard that some of the soldiers, if they were young and trigger-happy, tended to shoot first and ask questions later.

She tugged at the post again. She couldn't find another – she would have to trust it, but for as short a time as possible. She gave a quick wrench, and the post gave dangerously, but by that time she had her left elbow on the bridge, and in another moment she had heaved herself right on to it.

So far, so good! Using her elbows to pull her along, she crawled forward, commando-fashion. The bridge was horribly unsteady, and in very bad condition. The wooden planks felt soggy and rotten under her hands. Once as she put her weight on her knee to shove herself forward, she felt the board crack and almost give way. Through the warped slats she could make out the Jordan sliding past directly underneath.

The donkey brayed again, a double hee-haw, hee-haw.

Now she'd reached the centre of the bridge. She knew it because the bridge arched and she could sense the planks beginning to slope downwards ahead of her, which meant she'd reached the highest point. She found the wide plank with its smooth, inviting surface. She reached under herself, located the pocket of her shirt, and stuck her fingers in, searching round for the chalk.

It was gone.

She couldn't believe it at first. She almost sat up to look for it better, but remembered in time, and rolled over on to her back instead, fumbling in her pocket from one corner to the other. Somehow or other as she was crawling it must have slipped out. All she could find was a few begele she had popped in there earlier in case she should get hungry on the walk back.

Well, what did it matter? From where he was standing waiting for her, Ofer could surely see enough to be able to report that she had reached the target, even without the proof of the chalk-mark. But somehow Lesley couldn't bring herself to crawl back with her 'mission' only half accomplished.

If she could get a couple of sticks and lay them on the bridge in the form of a cross, wouldn't that do as well? But where –?

The donkey brayed again, forlornly, like an answer.

To be honest, Lesley didn't even now really appreciate the risks. So it wasn't either extreme courage or extreme foolhardiness, only a reckless impulse. She began to crawl forward again.

In a minute she was at the far end of the bridge.

She could see the donkey now, standing alone by the foot of the bridge, looking up at her. Could it possibly be Eeyore? But so far from home? Yet there were no villages any nearer than his. Lesley slid feet-first, backwards, over the edge of the bridge. The rail was stronger here, and it was not at all difficult to lower herself down into the water. She held on to the struts as she felt for the bottom of the river. As she walked slowly and carefully ashore, she saw the donkey stretch out his nose towards her, like a dog smelling at a stranger. She put forward her free hand and touched him. He felt like warm velvet, and his breath was delightful on her wet, cold hand – warmth, companionship, a fellow-creature alive in this cold empty darkness. She stumbled to the bank and put both arms round his soft shaggy neck, burying her face in his stubbly mane.

'Eeyore! Is it really you?' she whispered.

She ran her hand down the inside of his foreleg. Yes, there it was – the hobble-rope knotted round his fetlock, ragged in the middle where it had broken, and here the other frayed end joined to the farther leg.

'Oh, Eeyore – you've run away!'

She took the *begele* out of her pocket and felt his soft lips tickling her palm as he gently accepted it, then listened with delight to the deep, satisfied crunch as he bit it up. She rubbed him up under his jaw and he put his big hard head against her.

'I wish I could take you back with me! Then that rotten Mustapha would never be able to beat you again!'

Just at that moment she heard a soft, low, frantically urgent whistle. She nearly jumped out of her skin. Turning her head, she saw Ofer's dim outline on the far bank. He was waving his arms at her, making great unmistakeable beckoning gestures as if he would like to reach right across and hike her back by force.

She turned and started to wade back into the river.

Eeyore came after her.

She felt his nose butting softly into her back. She heard the soft splash as his forefeet entered the river close behind her.

She turned on him. He had a crude sort of halter rope round his neck, and this she caught hold of and tried to turn his head and urge him to go back. But he was like a rock. She pushed the side of his head with all her might. He wouldn't move. Feeling a turbulent mixture of anxiety and despair, she turned away from him again and, with far less caution than before, began to plough through the deepening water to the first supports.

Eeyore followed with no caution at all.

Now she grew really frightened. The splashing of Eeyore's hooves sounded to her like Niagara Falls – surely everyone for miles must hear it! What had possessed her to cross, to *entice* the poor beast to follow her? As she climbed like greased lightning up the struts and hauled herself frantically on to the bridge, she could hear him braying and splashing below and wished he would drop dead.

But he didn't, needless to say. He stood belly-deep in the stream until he saw her descend again on the other side. Then he plunged into the central channel of the river and began to swim.

In fact he only had to swim a few strokes, the river being narrow and not at all deep at that point. Almost at once he found his footing again, and before Lesley had stumbled ashore on her own side, the donkey had caught up with her and was pushing his dripping chin up against her shoulder.

Ofer had already grabbed her and was shaking her like a cotton duster being shaken out of a window.

'Little idiot! What the four winds did you think you were doing?'

Lesley was frozen with cold and reaction, her teeth were chattering and she was trembling all over. She couldn't speak a word, only weakly try to push Ofer's rough hands away and gain her breath. The second he released her, she slipped down to the ground.

Eeyore nudged her sympathetically.

'Get out of here, you stupid ugly brute!' hissed Ofer, frenziedly trying to shove him back into the river. 'Get back where you belong!' Eeyore wouldn't budge, but stood patient and immovable as a tree, his muzzle resting on the top of Lesley's head.

Ofer gave vent to a fearful burst of swearing, mostly in Arabic, barely under his breath. When he had thus relieved his feelings a little, he reached down and dragged Lesley roughly to her feet.

'Come on! Hurry! Leave him behind!'

They began stumbling up the bank together, Ofer holding tightly to Lesley's arm. Lesley's feet were so numb with cold that she completely failed to notice that she had left her shoes behind. She didn't even feel the thistles or stones underfoot as they scrambled upwards. Soon they found the path, and Ofer recklessly shone his torch so that they might get back to the others the quicker.

Their frightened blood pounded in their ears, so hard that they probably wouldn't have heard the guardsman's rifle that Ofer, at least, was fully expecting, even if it really had gone off right behind them. So they certainly didn't hear the delicate patter of the donkey's little hooves as he came trotting placidly along in their wake.

CHAPTER 16

Homecoming

It seemed a hundred years before Ofer's wavering torchlight coincided with the glowing embers of the camp-fire, and flicked round the huddled figures and frightened faces of the others.

As the two of them burst into the little clearing, the whole group rose up as one man and flung themselves forward as if to envelop them and protect them from harm. At least, that was how it seemed to Lesley, her teeth literally rattling with cold and terror. As she felt their warm bodies gathered about her, and Shula's comfortable fat person clutching her free arm, she had a sense of oneness with them, and her fear, half-paralysing a moment before, dwindled almost to nothing. Now they were all together, with her in their midst as one of them, an outsider no longer, it suddenly seemed to her that nothing really bad could ever happen. This, she realized later, must be the 'group feeling' that she'd been told about but had never understood, the emotion that gives kibbutz children their confidence and security.

'Why were you so long?'

'Why use your torch?'

'Why did you stay with her?'

'What happened?'

And from observant, ever-practical Shula, 'Where the four winds are your *shoes*?'

It was this, really rather trivial detail, that brought the whispered cacophony to sudden silence. Everyone stared downward while Ofer instinctively played his torch on her bare, filthy feet.

'I left them there,' she whispered through dry lips. 'At the – at the bridge.'

The subdued outburst broke out again.

'What for? Are you crazy? What *happened*, tell us!'

Aviva's voice rose a little. 'Come back to the *kitta*. Leslee must go to bed. We can talk there.'

'Make sure the fire's out.'

The boys tramped down the last glows and smothered them with damp earth. Others hastily gathered up all the remains of the food, the rugs and sacks, and Ofer went ahead with the torch as the slow straggling procession started back towards the kibbutz.

Esther came to Lesley.

'Do you want my shoes?'

'No thanks.'

'Your teeth are chattering. Here, you'd better take them.'

She made her put them on. One of the boys threw a blanket over her shoulders and she gratefully wrapped it round herself. Suddenly Danny, the clever one, stopped.

'Someone must go back and get her shoes.'

There was a shrinking silence.

'What's wrong with picking them up in the morning?'

'If anyone found them first . . . they're marked.'

It was true. The shoes, like every item of clothing, were indelibly inked with the name of their owner.

'I'll go,' said Danny, when no one else spoke.

'No,' said Naomi-the-daredevil. 'I'll go.'

Before anyone could stop her, she had grabbed Ofer's torch and gone haring off into the darkness. The boys looked at each other with faint, masculine unease. But in Israel there is equality between the sexes. They let her go, and the procession started forward again.

Suddenly they were all electrified by a scream.

It was echoed irrepressibly by several girls in the group.

Lesley would certainly have been one of them if she hadn't felt half frozen and her emotions numbed by her ordeal. But Shula squealed like a piglet being picked up by its tail, and hid her face in her hands.

Several of the boys turned and started back at a run. One of them, a clumsy good-natured boy called Amnon, tripped and fell. All was confusion, almost panic. Lesley found both Esther and Shula desperately clinging to her. She turned and stared back into the darkness towards the river.

A little figure came flying out of the bush and ran headlong into David and Ofer. It was Naomi, absolutely gibbering with the first real fear she'd ever felt.

'A thing! A thing! A thing!' she gasped. 'God save me! I bumped into a great, grey – thing!'

It was the first even semi-devout mention of God Lesley ever remembered hearing in this Atheist community, and suddenly she began to laugh. It would have turned into hysterics very rapidly if Ofer hadn't seized her and shaken her again.

'*Shtok!*' he hissed fiercely. 'This is all your fault!' He turned to the others. 'It's a cursed donkey she brought back with her from the other side of the river!'

After a moment's incredulous silence, pandemonium broke out, and now it was beyond the ability of even the most prudent of them to keep their voices under control. Some shouted questions, some burst out laughing, some just seemed to be making incoherent noises. Naomi, still so white with her recent terror that her face was ghostly in the dimness, thrust it into Lesley's.

'You – brought – a donkey –' Words failed her.

'You crossed the river?' asked David, his voice rising to a bleat.

'Right to the other side?'

'She's mad, mad completely!'

'You could have been shot!'

'All the ground over there could be mined!'

Lesley had never dreamt of such a thing. She felt icy waves of too-late terror washing over her. 'But,' she stammered, 'Eeyore was standing on the only ground I stood on.'

'Who?'

'Eeyore,' she said faintly. 'There he is.'

They all turned again, and sure enough, reaching out his still-damp nose to explore David's neck was the great, grey Thing himself.

David leapt away with a yell. Shula broke down into shrill, helpless giggles. '*Ma pitom? What next?*' she kept saying hysterically.

Aviva once again took charge.

'Never mind the donkey. Let's go home!'

'But it'll follow us!' said Ofer despairingly. 'It followed her right across the river. It had to *swim*. Do you think it won't walk half a kilometre? The thing's in love with her or something . . . She's put a spell on it!'

'I haven't! I haven't!' Lesley cried. 'I only gave it some begele –'

The tide of hysteria rose higher at this, and several people, Shula among them, simply gave way and sank to the ground, rolling about with uncontrollable laughter.

'She went to Jordan –'

'And stood there, surrounded by enemy guns –'

'And probably in the middle of a mine-field –'

'Feeding some flea-ridden Arab donkey –'

'With *our begele*!'

Even Ofer seemed to lose some of his anger. As for Amnon, the tears were running down his plump cheeks, and he was giving great cow-like moans. Nobody seemed capable of taking a grip on them, and they might never have got home at all, had not a sudden stern grown-up voice from above them suddenly frightened them all back into their wits.

'What's going on there?'

They froze, each holding his position like children playing musical statues. The shout had to be repeated before Aviva found her voice.

'It's only – we're from the kibbutz – having a *p'oola*!' she called back in a husky tone.

'You're making a lot of noise about it,' the soldier's voice returned. 'And it's late. Get along home at once!'

They needed no second telling. In a frantic scuffle they gathered themselves and their possessions together once more and scrambled in scared silence back up to the road. A backward glance showed them the dim outline of the soldier standing, hands on hips, with his *uzi* sten-gun hooked carelessly in the bend of his arm, watching them. In all their minds was a single thought: what if the donkey should emerge on to the road after them? Lesley willed him with all her mind to stay under cover. Maybe what Ofer had said about a spell was true, because he did.

They arrived back at their *kitta* by a special route which avoided the most populous parts of the kibbutz. Ada, their house-mother, didn't sleep in the *kitta*, and the night-watch didn't start checking up that they were all in bed until around 11.30. Incredible as it seemed, it was still only ten to eleven when the last of them got safely inside. Esther did a quick count of heads which reassured them that no one had been left behind.

With one accord they all squeezed into Lesley's bedroom. Lesley clambered straight under the covers, fully dressed, and got Shula to pile more bedclothes over her icy legs.

'You'll make your sheets filthy,' Aviva said.

'I don't care. I'm freezing.'

'Have a hot shower.'

'Later, maybe.'

'Now then,' said Danny, his blue eyes bright and stern

behind his glasses. 'I suggest you tell us what happened.'

Lesley related the whole adventure as best she could in her still-basic Hebrew, and Ofer chipped in his share and amplified the story whenever she fell silent or took a breath. It all came out in rather a confused jumble, because she was trying to defend herself, whereas Ofer was accusing her. But even Lesley had to admit that her side of it sounded pretty thin. She could no longer really remember what had motivated her to go across the bridge. It had something to do with the scenes she had so often watched, of Mustapha whacking poor Eeyore, of Eeyore hobbled and stumbling towards the water, and even further back, of her life-long desire for an animal companion. She had always felt a hot, possessive anger and love about Eeyore; it had always been frustrating to see him being mistreated and not be able to reach him or help him.

But this was something she couldn't explain, and anyway, they wouldn't have understood. Kibbutz children tend to regard animals in the way a farmer regards his cattle and his sheepdog, as part of his farm, or as workers. They kept pet cats or birds sometimes, but they outgrew any actual *love* they might feel for them in childhood. You loved *people*; animals were merely useful. Lesley had already come up against this feeling; she knew it was too deep to allow any real sympathy for her strange behaviour.

In a way she didn't blame them for being angry with her. The realities of life here had taught them, hard and early, what lay on the other side of the river; the relative peace of that border didn't lay their natural, deep-rooted caution to rest. What Lesley had done was beyond daring; it was incredible in its stupidity. Any one of them, even the bravest and the biggest show-off, would as soon have jumped out of an aeroplane without a parachute, or put his hands in a fire, as do what she had done. And for what? For a 'cursed donkey'. It was quite simply beyond them.

It was so far beyond them that they couldn't even be angry with her about it. They shook their heads, one or two of them exchanged looks and made the 'tra-la-la' gesture – one finger corkscrewing at the temple – and then, one by one, they padded away to their own rooms until only her three room-mates were left.

Ofer, who had been standing over her, hands on hips, now looked at her silently for another moment, heaved a tremendous sigh, shook his head in one last gesture of incomprehension, and turned to get undressed. The three girls automatically turned their faces away. Lesley lay facing the wall, still numb with cold and the after-effects of strong emotion; Aviva went off to have a shower; but Shula sat still on Lesley's bed, her hands still slowly, thoughtfully rubbing Lesley's cold legs through the bedclothes.

'What about your shoes?' said Ofer.

'I'll go and get them in the morning,' said Lesley in a flat voice.

'And the donkey?'

She didn't answer. She swallowed hard. A great hard lump had come into her throat. She reached up and switched off her little light.

'Are you going to sleep in your clothes?' asked Shula.

Lesley shook her head and turned her face into the pillow. She knew she was going to have to cry, and cry long and hard, before all the tension built up inside her was released. Shula sensed this, sighed like Ofer and stood up to leave her as much alone as was possible for them.

'You are funny old nut-case,' she said sadly, in English. 'Crazy *legumri*. But I like you. I must be crazy, too.'

CHAPTER 17

Face to Face

Lesley slept badly and woke early, remembering everything even before she was fully awake because her dirty, clumsy clothes made her feel so strange and uncomfortable in bed. She opened her eyes and looked at her watch. It was just on 5.30 and still dark, but it would be light very soon – dawn was already in the sky, and the arrival of the sun is not a leisurely process in the Middle East; there would just be time for her to take a shower and run down to the river for her shoes before the *metapelet* came to wake them up for breakfast and lessons, which she did between 6.30 and 7.

She slipped out of bed, and hurried silently to the shower-rooms which were in the middle of the building. She was anxious not to wake any of the others, but she needn't have worried – they were all exhausted after their exciting evening, and even Ada, an hour or so later, would have to call some of them three times before they so much as stirred.

A hot shower made her feel a lot better. She watched the water washing down her legs, carrying the telltale river mud away. Then she put on clean clothes. She went back to her room and took her saved-up half-bar of chocolate out of her box, glancing at her diary and Noah's letters as she did so. How would she explain all that had happened, to Noah – or even, come to that, to herself in her diary? In the growing, normalizing, daylight, the previous night's adventures seemed like a wild 'cheese-dream' as her mother used to say.

She slipped on a sweater (the mornings were still chilly, though it was the end of April) and her rubber boots and hurried out into the pale morning. The light was pearly pink and grey, and the grass looked milky from the myriad fine drops of condensation. The palm trees shook their tousled giants' heads gently against the lightening sky.

The kibbutz main gates were already open to let the field-workers out on their tractors and platform trucks, but Lesley managed to slip out unseen. In a few minutes she was cutting wet swathes through the dew-soaked brush on the river-bank. She passed the clearing and followed the rough track she and Ofer had used the night before, and soon she was sliding down the bank towards the greyly swirling river.

It seemed incredible that she had forgotten about Eeyore. It was as if, having willed him not to follow her and been 'obeyed', she had just pushed him to the back of her thoughts – he would be such an impossible complication in her life, she simply couldn't bear to think what would happen if he hung around. So that when she suddenly saw him, grazing quietly near the bridge, she got a fright almost as severe as several she'd received the night before.

She stopped dead. Eeyore lifted his head, ghostly in the grey dawn light, and they stared into each other's eyes from a distance of perhaps twenty metres. His long dew-damp ears were pricked, his small jaws slid from side to side as he chewed. His breath showed in a little cloud; his great dark eyes dwelt softly on Lesley. She felt her hand stretch out by itself and he moved like a shadow towards her, making no sound until he was almost up to her, when she could hear his deep resonant breathing.

He dropped his velvet nose into her hand.

'You nuisance!' she whispered. And then, in Hebrew: '*Khamor katan sheli* – my little donkey.' And she took his wet ear in her hand and kissed it.

He butted her gently in the stomach with his nose.

She felt in her jeans' pocket for the chocolate. She fed a piece to him joyfully; he seemed astonished by the strange, delicious taste and tossed his head up and down.

'Wait here,' she whispered.

He turned his head and watched her as she ran to the foot of the bridge. Her shoes were still there, dew-soaked but safe. She stuffed the socks deep into the toes, tied the laces together and slung the shoes over her shoulder. She was just starting back when a movement across the river caught her eye and rooted her to the spot.

It was Mustapha.

He rose up out of the long grass and reeds on the other side and stood looking at her out of his coal-black eyes, one hand on the bridge. If the donkey had looked ghostly, how much more so did this strange figure, who, wet as he was, with his colourless shirt and black hair plastered to his skin, appeared like some river-djinn, risen in eerie silence from the water itself.

The children stood staring at each other, the narrow river all that divided them. Lesley felt dimly that they must stand like that for ever and ever, for how could the first move be made, and by whom? But it was she who made it at last. She raised her hand level with her shoulder in greeting – the same sort of half-wave that she had given once or twice from the balcony of the Culture House. But he didn't answer her salutation. In a rough, low voice, he spoke to her across the Jordan.

'My donkey,' he said in English.

She was amazed. Did the Arab children learn English? True, Lesley's class had to study Arabic, but she knew hardly any. However, she knew the word for 'your' and 'my' and she said them now, shaking her head, pointing to him and saying 'Not your'. Then she pointed to herself. 'My,' she said.

'You thief,' came his clear English reply.

'He came by himself,' she said.

'My donkey. Send him back.'

'Come get him.'

He hesitated. She saw him look at the water, and an irrepressible shiver passed over his thin body. He looked so wet already that she guessed he must have been lying in the grass for much of the night. Trying to pluck up courage to come across, perhaps. Now he glanced upward toward the top of the bank on her side, where the road was, where the soldiers were. He made up his mind, and stepped into the water; but some deep-rooted inhibition stopped him like a glass wall. He could go no farther. He frowned in anger at himself, then looked at her, still frowning deeply with his black brows knitted together, and shook his head.

Lesley stood, irresolute. He was right. Eeyore was his. What was more, Lesley didn't really want him. Well, she did in a way, but what could she do with him, how explain him to people in the kibbutz? And in a flash of intuition, she knew what the donkey must mean to the Arab boy. She had seen his father strike him for the most trivial things. What would he do to him for losing the donkey which was a vital part of their joint livelihood? What might he have done already?

'Did your father beat you?' she asked him.

For answer he turned his shoulder to her and showed her – not his skin, thank heaven, only the black stripes on his shirt, but it was quite enough.

'Father say, not come home without donkey.'

So that was why he looked so wet, dishevelled and exhausted. Lesley's heart shrivelled with pity. For another moment they looked at each other. The sun would soon be up beyond those naked, round hills that loomed over Mustapha's little grey figure – proudly erect, tense with defiance, yet in his dark eyes a desperate, wordless appeal.

'You will not beat the donkey any more.'

He frowned and cocked his head as if he could not hear clearly, yet she knew he had heard.

'You will not beat him any more!' she said in a loud, commanding voice.

After a moment's thought, during which she saw his eyes dart hungrily towards the donkey and back to her, he shrugged his shoulders and moved his head in vague agreement. But it was not good enough.

'Promise!' she said.

She held up her right hand, not loosely as before, but stiffly, in the traditional – in the West – gesture of swearing. The Arab boy looked at her blankly. 'Hold hand like this!' she ordered him. Slowly, uncomprehendingly, he obeyed. 'Now say, "I promise that I will not beat the donkey any more."'

He repeated the words in a flat voice. She suspected he neither knew clearly, nor cared, what they meant. He was merely doing whatever she wanted in order to get the donkey back.

She didn't know what to do. It was getting lighter and lighter. If any adult on either side of the river should happen to see them, the trouble which would follow hardly bore thinking about. Yet she couldn't, she *could not* return Eeyore into Mustapha's untender hands without being *sure*. She would rather keep him on this side and risk every danger.

'Do you believe in God?' she asked him desperately.

He looked still more blank. And now suddenly the sun's first rays seemed to burst over the rim of the eastern hills and struck the top of the bank on the Israeli side. The sky was pale blue and the air was loud with bird and insect noises. The world was coming to life; it was impossible to hope for secrecy for more than a very few minutes longer.

The boy's face contracted into a grimace of urgency.

'Quick! Help me!'

'Do you believe in – in Allah?' Lesley persisted.

'I believe! Send the donkey!'

'Promise in Allah's name that you won't beat him!'

He held up his hand in the stiff, unknown gesture. 'I promise in the name of Allah.' And then he added, prosaically, 'But without to beat him, he not go.'

'Not true. Look!'

Lesley turned and put her hand out towards Eeyore, who was grazing a little up-river where she had left him. She clicked with her tongue to call him. He threw up his head and trotted towards her. She patted him and kissed his nose. She took out the chocolate, broke another square off, and gave it to him.

'What you give him?' called Mustapha's low voice.

'Chocolate.'

'*Chocolate!*'

'But he likes many other things. Carrots, apples, sugar.'

The boy spread his hands and lifted his shoulders. For the first time in her life, Lesley got some inkling of the nature of real poverty.

'Look!' she said. She petted Eeyore, rubbed him under the jaw and hugged his head in her arms. 'Love him a little. That doesn't cost money.'

The boy watched, shook his head in amazement, and then grinned. 'Okay,' he said unexpectedly.

And now Lesley was faced with the problem of how, having agreed to send him back, she was to do it.

She thought a bit, watching the sun come up, and then made up her mind. Quickly she glanced upwards; there was no one in sight. At the same moment, Mustapha on his side glanced all round. Then as if by a signal, they both stepped into the water from opposite banks.

Lesley felt the river creeping up her boots. She held Eeyore lightly by the halter rope. She watched Mustapha wading towards her on his side. When the water was up to the top of her boots, and up to his knees, there were only two yards between them.

Eeyore stood knee-deep in the river, his head up, his ears pricked towards Mustapha. Lesley saw his back vibrate in a long shiver, though whether from the cold water or from unwillingness or fear, she could not tell.

Lesley took the remains of the chocolate out of her pocket and held it out. 'Catch !' she breathed to the boy.

His hands flew up and the chocolate landed between them. He opened his hands slowly and stared into them, as if at some miracle that lay there. Then he held out the piece of chocolate towards the donkey and clicked his tongue.

At the same moment, Lesley let go of the halter. Eeyore hesitated a moment, but instinct was stronger than affection. He lunged forward, swam a few strokes through the deeper water, and in a moment Mustapha had caught hold of his rope and was urging him back to the opposite shore.

Lesley stood still in the river and watched. She had an awful fear that Mustapha would not give any of the chocolate to the donkey. If that happened, she would know that she had delivered him back into the hands of a heartless, dishonourable enemy.

But Mustapha surprised her. As soon as he and the donkey were back on dry land, he peeled the paper off the slab of chocolate, broke it into two equal pieces, and held them both up for Lesley to see. Then he gave one to the donkey, and the other, with a great grin of gleeful relish, he stuffed into his own eager jaws.

She nodded approvingly, and smiled so widely it was almost a laugh. But her smile faded as she watched. The boy was eating the chocolate with closed eyes and a look of rapture on his face so strong it was almost violent, like a spasm. Then it was finished, and he grinned all over his face, looking younger than the youngest kibbutz child in his relief and delight. He caught hold of Eeyore's neck and swung himself on to his back. Then he glanced back at Lesley.

'Thanks!' he called softly.

'For nothing. And don't tie his legs so tight.'

'Okay.'

'Go! Shalom!'

'Salaam! Salaam – Leslee!'

Boy and donkey began trotting along the edge of the water, up-river towards the village. Lesley had to go the same way, so she jogged along on her side, keeping level.

'How do you know my name?'

He grinned again. He looked so different when he grinned, really nice and ordinary, not like a wicked monkey the way he looked at some other times. He reached into his shirt and pulled something out of his belt. He held it over his head and waved it to her.

It was filthy and dog-eared and wet, but she could see – or perhaps it was more of a guess – what it was. Her photo. And, yes, now she remembered, her name and the date had been inked on the back by her orderly-minded mother.

'What's your name?' she asked him in Arabic.

And back across the river, faintly now, for he was getting ahead of her, came back the inevitable and yet astounding reply:

'Mustapha!'

She stopped running.

Of course thousands and thousands of Arabs are called Mustapha. It is commoner among them than John or Tom among us. But still!

Lesley rubbed her eyes. The sun was shining into them and striking sparks of brilliant light off the water and the drops of moisture everywhere. When she looked again, they were gone, boy and donkey, two grey little ghosts vanished with the coming of sunlight.

CHAPTER 18

Crisis

The whole extraordinary episode of Mustapha, Eeyore and the bridge passed over with quite remarkably little trouble or after-effects. The fact was that it was so extraordinary that the kids of the group hardly knew how to feel or talk about it. It was in a way their own fault – they, after all, had sent Lesley off on her forbidden 'mission', which, as they well knew, they should never have done; Boaz would certainly never have dreamt of allowing it. They all felt they had tweaked the very beard of mortal danger, and when they were out of it, they heaved huge sighs of unbelieving relief and tried to put the whole affair behind them as quickly and completely as possible.

All that happened that morning when Lesley got back was that Ofer asked if she had got her shoes, and what had happened to the donkey. She didn't tell him the whole truth. She simply said that she'd seen him on the other side when she'd gone to fetch her shoes. Ofer gave a relieved grunt, and said no more. Shula whispered that she'd had nightmares the whole night and for her part, wouldn't go near the river-bank again for anything in the world. The rest waited tensely for something more to happen – for the soldier to report them or ... Well, they hardly knew what, but it was surely beyond the bounds of hope that there should be *no* repercussions, no kick-back, after such a piece of calculated craziness. They almost felt they deserved some punishment. But nothing happened; and after a week, they relaxed – and if they didn't quite succeed in forgetting it, they certainly never spoke about it, even to each other.

As for Lesley, her life now went into a new phase which

helped her not to brood too much about what had happened. The kids now wholly accepted her. Perhaps they regarded her sometimes a bit warily, for although she was now an insider, she had gained admission, so to speak, by an action which they considered quite beyond the pale. Still, the better her Hebrew got, the deeper she became immersed in the life of the group. School work, sports and other activities took up nearly all her time.

Her parents, at the same time, ceased to be such a worry to her. Her father was getting used to the work and to the life; he had been given more responsibility in the cowsheds, had begun to study dairy management seriously and been sent away by the kibbutz on a course with a view to one day making him the boss of that branch of the farm. He was stronger and healthier physically than he had been for years, and the satisfaction he had craved was beginning, slowly but surely, to come to him.

He was also becoming involved in the social and management side of kibbutz life; his advice was often asked on various technical matters to do with running the farm and the economics of the settlement, and he was beginning to feel that he had something important to contribute for which his 'other life' in Saskatoon had prepared him. So that he had not been wasting his life there; nor was he wasting it here. The two lives fused, each giving meaning to the other. In short, Nat Shelby was beginning to feel sure that, after all he had not made a mistake.

As for Lesley's mother, she knew she would never get over her feeling that the way the kitchen was run, without *kashrut*, was fundamentally wrong and even immoral. So she asked to be transferred to another branch. She didn't feel she was suited to outdoor work (very few older women do work outdoors in the kibbutz) so she was put into the *communa*, where the clothes of all the members are taken care of.

Determined at all costs to succeed at this, she flung herself into the work heart and soul. At first it seemed monotonous sorting, ironing, folding, mending, putting away, endlessly day after day – and not even your own family's clothes but everybody's. However, gradually she began to find a shape and a purpose in it. Many of the clothes were old and worn and shabby, and at first she got no pleasure out of handling them. But as she got to know and like the people in the kibbutz more, it became important to her to make her contribution. If the shirts were old, all the more reason to iron them well; if they were torn, she would mend them beautifully, and fold the finished garment expertly so that it looked like new. It began to annoy her to see how some of the younger women skimped the ironing and didn't check for missing buttons and torn hems and threadbare knees. Sometimes she would stay late to do things again.

It became a matter of pride to her when the women told her that their clothes and their husbands' were coming back looking nice. She got up courage to beg the regular workers not to fold the ironed dresses and put them into the members' shelves, but to leave them hanging up till they were collected so they shouldn't get creased. She made several other suggestions which improved the system.

In this way she made a little niche for herself. It would never, she felt in her secret heart, be the life for her, as Saskatoon had been. Her Hebrew might never be good enough to enable her to take part fully in the social life here – such as it was. But Miriam was, first and foremost, a loving wife. To see Nat at long last beginning to be truly happy, made up to her for a great deal that was lacking in her own life. And this satisfaction began to show itself in her face and manner. She was more relaxed. She had accepted this as her life, to be made the best of. And if she still had deep sources of unhappiness – her son, lost to her for ever; her daughter, slipping away into the life of the kibbutz youth – she hid them successfully, even, quite often, from herself.

And ironically, this change in her brought her an unexpected bonus. For, as she became more at ease, so Lesley became more at ease with her. The daily 'coming home for tea' which – truth to tell – had once been almost a duty for Lesley, now became a pleasure, as it was meant to be. Miriam was no longer so tired, but if she did happen to be napping when Lesley came, she didn't feel guilty, so she didn't fuss. Seeing, and at last accepting, that Lesley was enjoying her life, the life away from her parents, Miriam unselfishly loosed her possessive hold over her and let her go. She made tea for her in a more casual way, so that Lesley felt freer. Thus she enjoyed coming home more, did it oftener, stayed longer; and the Shelbys became a family again.

*

But there was another factor in all this, a powerful outside force which threw not only the Shelbys but all the families in the kibbutz, and the kibbutz itself as one large family, together. This same factor distracted the children's minds from the incident by the river, for shortly after it, things began to happen in the world beyond the kibbutz fence which shrank the whole thing down to the proportions of a childish lark.

Israel was getting ready to fight for her life.

She had already done so twice before – once in 1948, when the British went home and the Jewish leaders declared that Israel was a state. She was promptly attacked from all sides by the Arab armies of Egypt, Syria, Jordan, Lebanon and Iraq. The War of Independence, as it came to be called, lasted for a year, although nobody had thought the Jews could hold out for more than a few weeks; and in the end the Jews won.

The second time was in 1956, but then the war was very short, little more than a series of battles in the Sinai Desert against the Egyptians. Again the Israelis won, and the Egyptians were pushed right back to the Suez Canal. But the Israelis were later persuaded to give Sinai back to Egypt, mostly by the Americans, with whom the Israelis were friendly, and on whom they depended for money and weapons and other supplies. The Americans promised that Israel would be safe if she gave back the land she'd conquered. But once the Israelis had safely withdrawn, the Americans forgot their promise.

Now the Egyptians, after years of harassing Israel across that border in the south, looked seriously as if they meant to attack her properly. There was a United Nations peacekeeping force stationed between the two enemy countries, but on Egyptian territory. The leader of Egypt, President Nasser, told the U.N. to take their peace-keeping soldiers away. Breathlessly, Israel waited to see what would happen. If the U.N. left, that would mean the way was clear for the Egyptians to send their army, with tanks and guns, up into the Sinai Desert right against the border with Israel.

With no delay at all, the United Nations force packed up and left. Israel breathed again – a deep, sharp breath, as a man fills up his lungs in preparation for a great ordeal.

And now every man, woman and child in the country began to feel what was coming. It was not yet time for war. War might still be avoided – there were very few people in Israel who did not hope with all their hearts that it might be possible to avoid it. But they had to be ready.

Lesley looked on, first with interest, then with mounting excitement, finally with – not fear, she was not afraid – but with extreme nervous tension. The first real sign was the rapid disappearance of more and more of the men. Sometimes you'd see them going off in the daytime, singly or in groups as their army numbers were announced on the radio or as khaki-painted trucks and jeeps arrived to collect them. Sometimes you'd wake in the morning to find this one or that one missing. Boaz, Rami and all that crowd of young men – often they were brothers of kids in Lesley's group – had gone early. The young, unmarried women went too. But now the older men began to disappear. The group went into class one morning to find themselves without a teacher.

Soon Lesley's father found himself almost alone in the *refet*, working double shifts and having to learn more about the 'business', as he called it, in a week than he had previously learnt in a month. The kibbutz depended on him for their milk, the cows for their well-being. One night he had to get out of bed at three in the morning, like a doctor, to deliver a calf ...

As for the women, they felt the burden in a special way. First, because their men were going, and going into who-knew-what unimaginable dangers, and they were alone in their houses and in their beds; second, because they not only had to keep the service branches going – feeding, dressing and cleaning the kibbutz – but to the best of their ability they had to do the jobs left vacant by the men.

Miriam worked like two women all morning in the *communa*. Gone the days of careful ironing and mending, except for the uniforms of those going or briefly coming home on leave. Get the stuff washed and rough-dried and the worst holes patched up as quickly as possible; there was no time to be fussy, because as soon as that work was done and a hasty lunch eaten (for the first time she had no time to care that it wasn't kosher) she had to climb on a truck and go out to the fields, or help her husband feed the cows, or do duty in one of the younger children's houses. There were no more afternoon naps, and when Lesley found time to get home at the tea-hour, as often as not she found the place empty –

though Miriam unfailingly managed, sometimes during even the busiest day, to take home something for her to eat.

Lesley and her group were not idle, either. Their ordinary working hours of two a day were expanded indefinitely – nobody watched the clock now. You worked wherever you were put, you worked till the job was done, and no one dreamed of grumbling or shirking. The boys did the jobs of grown men, the girls of women. Lesley found herself thrown in here, there and everywhere – even back with the chickens for a week, and somehow she was too charged up with the intense excitement in the air to give a thought to whether the roosters were planning to attack her. When one did, she kicked him away with her rubber boot, and he flew, squawking with surprise, to a distant perch, and thereafter left her respectfully alone to get on with her work.

The garden was left to go to rack and ruin, for Moshe, it turned out, was an officer in the reserves, and the reserves were all being called up. He put away his tools and put on his uniform with regret but without reluctance. Even for the greatest pacifist – and Israel is full of pacifists, oddly enough – this was no moment to hang back. Nothing less than the existence of Israel, the age-old homeland of the Jewish people, was at stake. There wasn't a Jew in it (except those who are so religious they hardly know what's going on around them) who wasn't throwing the whole weight of his strength and energies behind the national effort. The enemy armies massed for the attack. Really alarming pictures appeared in the papers of rows and rows of Egyptian tanks, and Syrian planes, and Jordanian guns, mustering on the borders.

And still it wasn't war.

One day as the crisis mounted to its inevitable climax, Lesley found a moment to climb the steps to the Culture House balcony. She stood there with her hands on the rail, looking out at the once-peaceful, rural view. She marvelled how she had ever been able to think of the river below her as just another river, dividing her from contact with an Arab boy she wanted to be friends with. Now it might as well have been a wall ten feet thick and twenty high.

There were no signs of farming going on over there. The farmers on that side, she knew, had all run away, or were holed up in their villages. Mustapha's father's orange groves had an indefinable look of neglect. But Lesley felt a secret pleasure in knowing that the last oranges had been picked some weeks before. At least they had got the harvest in.

On the near side, all was bustle and activity. Army trucks and jeeps were everywhere, together with excavators digging trenches and dug-outs and gun emplacements. Little khaki figures hurried purposefully hither and thither. The kibbutz fence was being strengthened, and even as Lesley watched, a government excavator rumbled in through the gates to begin digging a series of zig-zag trenches in the lawns.

Lesley thought of Moshe the gardener, forgot his scoldings and pitied him. Poor man! He would be so grieved. She was grieved too, as she watched the green carpet, so painfully reclaimed and maintained against the dust and stones which nature had intended for this region, being bitten into and scarred by the teeth of the great machines – a work of destruction which might save their lives quite soon, when the bombs started to fall.

*

One of Lesley's jobs was to clean out the four air-raid shelters which the kibbutz had always had, but which had not been in use since they were built – except one, which had been a sort of club for the young people coming out of the army. Now twenty years' dead leaves and dust-drifts and cobwebs had to be cleaned out of the others, ventilation checked and repaired, and, most poignant of all, bunk-beds with little cage-like cot-sides had to be built in for all the babies and toddlers, who would be sleeping down there every night if war came. Shula was working mainly with these toddlers, and Lesley saw her one afternoon bringing her little group of six three-year-olds down into the shelter to play. Lesley was helping the carpenter and she watched Shula settling the little kids on the floor for a story and letting them clamber about on the bunks.

'They think it's a big game,' she whispered to Lesley. 'Their *metapelet* wants them to get used to being down here, so it won't come as a shock when they have to move in.'

'You mean "if".'

'I mean "when".'

'How do you know?'

'Rami's home for a few hours. He says it must come. The soldiers always know. He says there can't *not* be a war now.'

Lesley said nothing. Her mouth had gone suddenly dry.

That night in bed she thought of Noah. If Noah were here, he would be in the army with the others. She wondered how he would look in that rather casual, sloppy, business-like uniform, with an *uzi* hung in the crook of his arm. His face would be burnt brown like Rami's (Rami had been down in the Negev Desert) and he wouldn't be wearing glasses. She was shocked to find herself wanting to see him like that, wishing he were here to play his part as a Jew in all these tremendous events. She should be happy and relieved to think of him safely sitting in his office or in front of the television in his home in Saskatoon, not in any danger; yet she wanted him here, and furthermore, she felt that here was his place, here, ready to fight for Israel and for them all.

Her father had said that no Jew who was not here should be able to sleep easy, even (he seemed to think, though he didn't say so) the ones who were pouring their money into Save-Israel funds so fast that it was a wonder even the millionaires had any left. She supposed her father wasn't talking about Noah when he referred to 'Jews'. But Lesley knew better. She knew Noah was still a Jew at heart. What was he feeling, reading about it, seeing the films on television, hearing the threats the Arabs were making? Many of these were so horrible and blood-thirsty that the children were not supposed to know about them, but they did.

With all the men away, the kibbutz had to get old men from the local town to act as night watchmen. One of these, the one assigned to the children's houses, was a Moroccan immigrant who knew Arabic. He was not a very intelligent or sensitive person, and allowed himself quite easily to be persuaded by the boys to listen with them to Radio Cairo and Radio Damascus and other Arab stations, and translate what was being said. The night when the broadcaster called on the Syrian soldiers to 'pave the road from Damascus to Haifa with the skulls of Jewish children' was the night when Lesley sensibly decided not to listen any more.

To take her mind off the horrors which had begun, despite her best efforts, to fill it, she spent all her spare moments writing in her diary or to Noah.

It was frustrating, writing to Noah, not much better than a diary really, for he never answered, and now more than ever she longed and longed to hear from him. It was like stretching your hand across time and space, feeling the cold winds blowing on it, and waiting in vain for a warm answering hand to take hold of it and grip it tightly.

Darling Noah,

I suppose you must be worrying about us. Please don't. I'm sure the television and all the papers are playing it up more than they should. Here, we don't feel it so much, perhaps because we're in the middle of it. [This was not quite true but she did want to comfort him.] Actually we're on the *edge* and not in the middle! It's quite exciting really. We're expecting front-row seats when the fun starts, but don't worry because we've got lovely safe air-raid shelters and have already done drills to get into them quickly – there's one right next to our classroom with a trench starting outside the door leading right to it. [This was also not quite factual. The shelter was about 100 yards away and the trench leading to it was by no means finished.]

You should see Daddy! We've got a funny father, I must say. When everything was lovely and peaceful, he was miserable. Now when the shooting's about to start, he's as gay as a chipmunk. He's also the best darned cowman in the business. You really should see him lugging the newborn calves around in his arms and milking the whole herd by himself. He talks to them in English and Yiddish, and the local joke is that they're all beginning to moo with a Canadian accent!

As for Mom, she bumps out to the fields in a dirty old cattle-truck and hacks down the bananas like a two-year-old, and believe you me, that's no easy job, I've tried it. You remember how she'd never wear slacks cos she said they were unfeminine? Now she wears a pair of Dad's oldest 'worker-blue' pants hitched up at the waist with an old belt, with one of my tee-shirts and a *kova-tembel* (like a dunce's cap) stuck on top, and I'm here to tell you, she looks *great*.

Yours truly is what's called a 'cork', I fit wherever I'm stuck in. So far I've mucked out chickens, worked in the fields, lugged bananas, cleaned out air-raid shelters, learnt how to carpenter (a bit!), washed ten million dishes in the kitchen (just feature me washing up every night for *three hundred* people) and been left to the mercies of eighteen nine-year-olds for a whole afternoon. That was by far the toughest, they just ate me up! But there's nobody else to do all these things, and I must say I'm not such a lousy worker any more as I used to be. Work seems more natural to me now, somehow. And the crisis helps. You just feel as if you have to do your best – not just *stam*, as we say.

(Yes, my Hebrew is finally improving. I'm quite fluent now, and how right you were, clever old brother – it makes just all the difference.)

In fact, though I hate admitting it, I'm sort of enjoying the crisis in a way. Funny how it brings people together, everyone helping and joking and nobody grousing. Of course if I were grown–up or married or something or if I had someone close to me in the army, I guess I'd feel different.

You know I've been helping the kids in my group with their English. Well, Shula, she's my best friend, has written a poem for our class magazine which I think is just great. Specially considering she's only learning English. I didn't help a bit with this, she did it all herself, and I'm sending it to you so you'll get the feeling of what's going on. It's called 'War', although it's not really war yet, but there's the feeling it's got to come, and so in a way it's as if we were already in it : here it is :

War !
What does that word mean?
I don't understand people.
Why must they fight?
Must we look now into Death's face?
My father, my brother,
And yours, and yours,
We say goodbye to them and wish them luck
As if they were going to an exam.
We smile at them and try to make jokes
And they go away in their new-old clothes.
But we are sending them into the mouth of Death.
We are sending them to be changed
Into killers.
My brother Rami is not a killer.
My father has never hurt anyone.
What will happen?
I'm frightened for my father and my brother !
Aren't you frightened too?
Will we see them again?
Will we know them if we see them?
What is this thing called war?
What will it do to us all?'

When Lesley had sent this off, on the 23rd of May, she had the feeling she shouldn't have sent it. Maybe it would make Noah feel bad – or worse, if he were already feeling bad. But it was too late, and anyway she had too many things to think about to worry about it for long.

CHAPTER 19

The Unexpected Happens

That fateful May drew to a troubled end, but before it did so, Egypt had closed the Straits of Tiran. If you look at the map, you'll see why the Israelis considered this an act of war, because it meant that Israel's ships couldn't get into the Red Sea or use their southern port of Eilat. And then, at the very end of May, something even more sinister happened. King Hussein of Jordan went to Cairo.

King Hussein and President Nasser of Egypt had been abusing each other for years. It had been hard to see how they could ever like or trust each other enough to work together or let their armies work together – this disunity among the Arab leaders was one of Israel's safeguards. But one night most of the kibbutz was sitting, as usual at news-time, in the Culture House in front of their new television, and gasped in unison as they watched the incredible sight of President Nasser actually embracing and kissing King Hussein on both cheeks as if they were brothers. They had just signed an anti-Israel pact.

After the news finished, the crowd of kibbutzniks – mainly women, old people and youngsters – walked out into the darkness. Most of them were silent, as if dazed. Lesley was surely not alone in thinking that this walking out into darkness was a symbol. It was the first symbol she had ever clearly realized for herself.

Instead of going back to the kitta, she went to her parents' house to sit with them. She felt warmly at home there now. The flat had a pleasant, lived-in look, thanks to her mother's ingenuity and effort – and her own, for her battiks were improving and she was getting good at other handicrafts. Lesley always thought the flat looked nicer than others; though basically they were all the same shape and had had about the same amount of money spent on them, her mother's taste showed.

Just now, however, Lesley was too tense and anxious about the war situation to notice anything except that her parents were both there and both seemingly fairly relaxed, which at once had a calming influence on her. Lately they had begun speaking far more openly before her, even discussing their own troubles, which made her trust them and feel that they trusted her – and regarded her as more of a grown-up than they had a few months earlier.

Her father had cleaned up after work and was sitting on the sofa, reading – or trying to read – a Hebrew newspaper. He was frowning; but that might have been the effort of translating. Her mother was making them all a cup of cocoa; she'd just brought some fresh cheese-cake out of the miniature fridge. Lesley kissed them both, and slumped into a chair.

'Did you see the news on TV, honey?' asked her mother from the kitchenette.

'Yeah,' said Lesley grimly. Both her parents looked up. They were less punctilious about listening to every hourly newscast than most of the other kibbutzniks, because of the difficulty of understanding. Wherever you were in the kibbutz you could always tell, without a watch, when it was ten, eleven, twelve or any other o'clock, because from far and near, faint and loud, you heard the news being read on countless radios and transistors.

Now her father asked, 'So what's new?'

'Dear Abdul and dear Hussie were snogging away on the tarmac at Cairo like a pair of love-birds.' Her parents stiffened and exchanged alarmed glances. Lesley repeated something clever that she'd overheard Danny say as they left the Culture House together, 'As they hugged each other you could almost see the daggers they wished they were sticking into each other's backs.'

Her father slapped the paper aside and hastily turned on the radio. Her mother hesitated, then slowly went on pouring out the cocoa. Her hands were steady enough but she bit her lips.

'If those two have buried the hatchet –' muttered Nat.

'They have, for the moment anyway,' said Lesley, feeling proud, in an awful sort of way, to be the first with the news. 'They've signed a pact.'

Nat was trying to get the BBC but it wasn't the right time; reception was always bad at night anyway. Lesley stood by the window, feeling churned-up and restless inside. War itself had begun to seem, in prospect, not so bad as this tense waiting, waiting ... Through the slats of the shutters, closed hours before against the heat of the day, she could feel a refreshing night breeze trying to make its way into the still-stifling room. She started to open the shutters, but her father stopped her.

'I wouldn't, chicken.'

'Oh, why, Daddy? It's so *hot*.'

'We shouldn't show too much light,' said her father.

'Why? There's no blackout yet.'

'Still ... You never know. Anyway, there'll be one soon, so we might as well get used to being stuffy in the evenings.'

Lesley looked at her mother, who was just coming in with the trolley.

'That's true, dear,' she said in a too-bright voice. 'We've just got our order of blackout material into the *communa*. We'll have to spend tomorrow cutting out lengths ...' She turned to her husband. 'You know Rina's been whisked off to the *tson*? She was trained as a shepherd and worked with the sheep for three years when she was younger. Now that Yacov's gone, she's been recruited back to it. Just imagine, handling those great smelly sheep at her age! But it means there's no one left in the children's *communa*, so the few of us will have to try and take that over, too. I just feel grateful that Shimon had that accident to his hand and isn't wanted, or I suppose we'd be working the washing machines as well.'

'Yeah, thank God for a few old guys like me,' said Nat. 'Or you girls would have everything your own way!' He suddenly reached out and squeezed Miriam's hand, and smiled at her with such proud, intimate warmth that Lesley felt she shouldn't be watching. Yet she did watch. She never remembered being so *aware* of how deeply her father and mother loved each other, until they came here. Was it that she was too young and egotistic to notice, or that perhaps they weren't so aware of it themselves, in Saskatoon? These matters seemed to be somehow clearer and simpler here, or perhaps it was the crisis which brought people's feelings for each other into stronger focus.

There was a light knock on the outer door, the one leading on to the porch. Lesley went to see who was there. It was Ayala, the woman from the office who had first shown them round. Lesley knew her quite well now, and liked her a lot. She was rather brusque and no-nonsense, but absolutely dependable. Now she took Lesley mysteriously by the wrist and drew her out into the darkness of the garden.

'Lesley,' she said in a low voice, 'there is someone in the office who wants to see you.'

She sounded very serious, and Lesley's heart began to beat fast. Was it – could it be something to do with Mustapha and that time? But surely that was all safely forgotten!

'Who is it?'

'I'll tell you as we go. Just tell your parents anything, so they won't worry.'

'You mean I'm not to tell them the truth?'

'You can decide later what you want to tell them. I'd just fob them off for the moment.'

Lesley looked at her with growing anxiety. What *could* this be? It was quite bewildering. Ayala was kindly in her abrupt gruff way, but she wouldn't try to cover up for Lesley if she had got into trouble.

'Go on, hurry up.'

Lesley turned back into the flat. Her parents looked up questioningly from their coffee-cups.

'I have to go somewhere,' said Lesley gauchely. 'I'll be back soon.'

'Is anything wrong, honey?'

'No – I don't think so. Be seeing you.'

She ducked out hastily before they could ask more. Ayala was waiting, and together they walked quickly along the paths to the main office block. Lesley noticed that the 'street' lamps had been dimmed to a glow; Ayala carried a torch which she didn't use.

'Is it bad news?' asked Lesley.

'I think you'll think it's just the opposite,' said Ayala.

'Why? What is it? Oh, do tell me !'

'Perhaps I'll let you see for yourself.'

They arrived. There were already blackout curtains on the office windows, and to her surprise Lesley noticed that every pane of glass had a thick 'Union Jack' pattern of brown sticky paper pasted on to it.

'What's that for?' she asked.

'So the glass won't shatter in a blast,' said Ayala shortly. 'Come on.'

There was a lot of unusual noise going on inside the office. As they entered, Lesley was astonished to see a crowd of young men standing or milling around in the outer office. They all carried bits and pieces slung around them – rucksacks, cameras, and so on; other bits of luggage were piled on the floor against the walls. The young men themselves were an extraordinary mixture of types – some were obviously Jewish, but there were a couple who looked quite Scandinavian and there was a coloured boy. They wore an assortment of jeans, jackets with University insignia emblazoned on them or plastered with badges, open-necked shirts and all sorts of funny hats. There were also one or two more conservatively dressed in suits. The general effect was of a group of tourists from different countries; Lesley heard that many of them were talking with American accents. And there was an atmosphere of keyed-up excitement which was greater even than what she'd become used to in the kibbutz.

'What's all this?' Lesley asked Ayala as they pushed their way through to the door of the inner office.

'Volunteers,' said Ayala briefly. 'Haven't you heard? They're flooding in from all over the world. Mostly Jewish of course, but others too, surprisingly enough.'

'But what for? What do they want?'

'To help us. To fight for us.' Ayala gave her a quick, sharp look over her shoulder. 'To die for us, if necessary.' She said 'Excuse me,' to a tall, blond boy leaning against the office door; he jumped aside and pulled it open for her. Again Ayala took Lesley's hand and pulled her through the crush and into the relative emptiness of the Secretary's office.

'Phew!' said Lesley. 'What a –'

And then she saw Noah.

He was sitting quietly on a bench under the window. He rose as she came in and stood there, looking at her.

'Noah. . .?' she asked in a soft, incredulous voice.

'Yep, it's me.'

He looked very pale after the Beit Sha'an Valley tan everyone else had, but his face was more than just untanned, it was really white. He was wearing different clothes from the ones she had seen him in in Saskatoon, more like the casual

tramping gear the men outside were wearing – the volunteers
. . .

She started to tremble and right there in front of the Secretary of the kibbutz and Ayala, she burst into tears. Noah hugged her tightly and she put her arms round his waist, and leant against him.

'Oh Noah – you came –'

'I couldn't *not*, I guess.'

A pang of glad guilt struck her. 'Was it my letter that –'

'Not really. Just sort of put the final kibosh on everything that had been pushing me anyhow.'

'So you're a – a volunteer?'

'If you'll have me.'

Lesley looked through her tears at the kibbutz Secretary. He was a tall, white-haired man with stooped shoulders and a worried look which seemed never to leave his leathery face.

'Your brother's told us the situation,' he said to Lesley. 'It's nothing to do with us really. We're accepting twenty volunteers – the whole batch you saw outside. If you think your parents would agree, we'll accept him just like the others. He came with them; to us, he's a welcome pair of hands, just like any other.'

Lesley turned wide eyes back to Noah's anxious, waiting face.

'But what if – what if they won't?'

'That's for them to decide, don't you think?' said Ayala quietly.

'Of course. But it'll – it'll be such a shock. You don't know! It will be as if he was coming back from the dead!'

'I know,' he said. 'I do know.' He pushed his hand through his tousled hair in a gesture she knew well from the time of his childhood. 'I couldn't not come,' he repeated. 'Won't they understand? You weren't kidding when you said about the media playing it up. From where I sat, it looked as if – as if you didn't stand a chance over here, as if you were all going to be massacred –'

Ayala laid her hand on his arm. 'Don't talk like that here,' she said, gently but yet with an edge of command.

'I'm sorry,' said Noah humbly. 'But you don't know what I've been through. I haven't slept properly for weeks. I couldn't work –'

'What about your job?' interrupted Lesley.

'I quit.'

'Quit your job?'

'I tell you I couldn't concentrate anyway. I was no good to them. They were glad to get rid of me.'

'But they'll take you back afterwards?'

'Afterwards?' Noah looked at her with vacant, bewildered eyes. 'Is there going to be an afterwards?'

'*Dai, kvar!*' the Secretary suddenly snapped. 'Enough already! Of course there's going to be an afterwards! What are you saying, that there'll be no more Israel? There will. We'll beat them because we have a secret weapon.'

Both Lesley and Noah looked at him with wild unreasoning hope.

'A secret weapon? Are you sure?'

'Sure I am sure.'

'What is it?'

'We have no alternative.'

Lesley went limp and gave a shrill, choked laugh. 'Oh, *that* . . .' It was a stock joke from the 1948 war, for goodness' sake . . . 'I thought you meant a real weapon.'

'That's a real weapon,' he said. 'You don't believe me? You'll see.' He sat down, put on his glasses and started attacking some documents on his desk. 'Now go on, take your brother out of here and make some decision. I've got a lot of work to do.'

Lesley and Noah pushed their way out through the crowd of volunteers. Outside they stood in the darkness, their faces lit by the moon. Noah looked even more strained and somehow unearthly out here, really like a phantom. 'The Spirit of Christmas Past,' Lesley spluttered suddenly, remembering Dickens' ghost-story. She put her face against his shoulder. 'That's what you look like.'

'Passover Past, maybe,' said Noah thinly. 'Do quit giggling.'

'What are we going to *do*, Noah? What ARE we going to do?'

'I don't know. I never could plan beyond just – getting here.'

'It's my fault you're here. I willed you to come. I didn't know it, but I did. I willed so hard you probably couldn't help yourself. So I must take responsibility.' She thought for a moment, then said, 'Look. You stay with the others for the time being. I'll go back and ... I don't know what I'll do. Try to prepare the ground a bit, I don't know... Anyway tomorrow they'll see you and somehow it'll resolve itself. It'll have to. It's too silly, they *can't* go on behaving as if – I mean, just because –' Suddenly she remembered to ask, 'What about Donna?'

There was a moonlit silence and Noah turned his face away. 'I left her at home,' he said in a muffled voice.

'How – left her? Not without telling her?'

'Of *course* not! What do you take me for?'

'She let you come?'

'Like Israel, she had no alternative.'

'Didn't she try to stop you?'

'No. Oddly enough. I was surprised how – unsurprised she was. She must have guessed. Maybe she's known all along.'

'You mean, about you – still being Jewish.'

'Yes.'

'Probably the thing she minds most is that you didn't tell her till now.'

'Now quit that, do you hear?'

'What?'

'Being wise about me and her. It gives me the creeps.'

'I'm not wise about anything else, believe me. Although,' she added, 'I think I have grown up a bit since I last saw you.'

'It shows,' he said, squeezing her arm. 'Okay then. I'll stick with the crowd and wait for some word from you.' He gave her a quick kiss. 'Gee, I'm glad to be here! Scared as hell, but it's not as bad as being scared *there*.' He held her away from him and peered into her face with a frown. 'Aren't *you* scared? You don't look scared.'

'No.'

'How come?'

'I don't know, Noah. You feel safe here, in the kibbutz, as if nothing bad could happen as long as you're all together. I can't explain. Maybe you'll understand after a few days.'

'I guess maybe you don't know how bad things are.'

'*Dai, kvar!*' said Lesley, echoing the words and the tone of the Secretary.

'Enough. You're right ... Well, I'm going then.' He looked at her for another minute and then abruptly went into the offices again without looking back.

Lesley felt sorry for him. She remembered Ayala's words: 'They've come ready to die for us.' No doubt that was what Noah was scared of – he thought he'd come to die. Lesley shrugged a little. She wanted to stop him being afraid, but she didn't know how. She guessed it would stop by itself after a short time. Nobody in the kibbutz seemed to be afraid. It was wonderful to see him, but somehow she felt a tiny bit disappointed. She'd supposed he would be so strong and brave, standing like a rock in their defence, and now her woman's feelings told her that she would have to be his rock for a little while at least, until he got used to being an Israeli.

CHAPTER 20

Meeting

However, brave as Lesley might feel about the war situation, she chickened out completely on the Noah front.

Having reached her parents' house full of high hopes and courageous intentions, she stopped dead at the door. She remembered how Mustapha had stopped in the same way at the edge of the river, as if some invisible barrier stood in his way – the barrier of his own deepest fears. Lesley wasn't afraid of her father any more in the ordinary way; he hadn't been angry with her for months and months, and in fact she liked him better now than ever before in her life. But as far as Noah was concerned – that was something else. She knew that telling them he was here would, sooner or later, inevitably mean telling them she'd met him in Saskatoon. Her utter inability to predict her father's reactions to this was what made it impossible for her to go in.

Cursing herself (in Arabic – Arabic swear-words are very satisfying even when you don't know exactly what they mean) for a miserable coward, she grimly made her way back to the *kitta*. It was getting late but the kids were mostly still up, listening to the latest news on the class radio. It was all still about Hussein's Cairo visit, world reactions to the crisis, the troubles the Government was having – 'Talk about lack of unity,' Danny grumbled. 'Put two Jewish politicians together and who needs any Arabs?'

'Why don't they let Dayan take over as Minister for Defence?' said a boy called Baruch, who was by way of being their political expert. 'Then we'd get some action.'

'Don't be such a hawk!' said Shula. 'We don't *want* that kind of action! If Dayan's in charge, we can definitely say goodbye to peace.' Since 'shalom' means 'peace' as well as hallo and goodbye, this came out as 'shalom to shalom'.

'Well, but we have anyway. From the moment they closed the Straits to our ships, war was inevitable.'

'I don't know,' said Ofer. 'The sea-going nations said they'd send a flotilla of ships through as a test. After all, it's supposed to be an international waterway – they've no right to close it.'

'The sea-going nations!' scoffed Baruch. 'America, you mean! A fat lot of good they are with their great big king-sized promises! They'll never do it. They'll just sit back and let us do the fighting, and then either pick up the pieces with big plastic tears running down their faces, or bang us on the back if we win and tell us they were pulling for us all the time.'

They all gazed at him respectfully. Then Esther changed the subject.

'*Chevrai*, have you *seen* the volunteers?' Esther was the oldest in the class, she was fifteen, and beginning to be very interested in boys. It embarrassed Lesley sometimes to hear how she talked about them and sometimes to them. Now she did a little dance which ended with her whirling Lesley round in a circle. 'Thank you, Leslee, for teaching me English,' she said. 'Now I can talk to them, especially that tall *gingie* one. He's from Canada like you. His name is Garry. Ya-va-yay! He is something not normal!' This was the sabras' way of saying somebody or something was super.

'Don't make a fool out of yourself,' said Amnon. 'They're all grown-up men, they won't bother with a baby like you. You'd better stick to us little boys for a while longer.' He wrapped his arm round her neck and pulled her half off her feet, which made her scream and cuff him.

When they were all in bed, Lesley leaned over towards

Shula and whispered, 'My brother's here. He came with the volunteers.'

'What do you say!' exclaimed Shula, fascinated. 'I never knew you had a brother!'

'He married a Catholic girl and my father threw him out of the family.'

'What for?' asked Shula in amazement.

'He – he became a Catholic.' There was a pause. 'He stopped being a Jew.'

Shula couldn't seem to understand. 'How can anyone stop being a Jew? I mean, he is a Jew.'

'Yes. That's what *he* says – now. But he tried to stop being. I mean, he changed his religion.'

'Oh – *religion*,' said Shula in a bored voice. It was a subject about which no kibbutz child could get worked up – it simply had neither meaning nor importance for them. 'But what's all the fuss about? I suppose he only did it to marry his girl. I heard about a girl once who wanted to become a Moslem to marry an Arab. I don't see how anyone could want to, but it wouldn't stop them being Jewish. I mean, if it's only the *religion* –'

'But being Jewish means religion in Canada.'

'Nonsense! If being Jewish means being religious-Jewish, then none of us are Jewish, I suppose. Has your father stopped being a Jew because he doesn't keep the *mitzvot* and all that *shtut* any more?'

'It's not *shtut*! At least,' Lesley added, 'not there. Not anywhere but here.' She stopped and thought. 'What is a Jew, when you stop to think about it? I mean, if you're a Jew because your parents are Jewish, then my brother is still a Jew. But Daddy says he's not, and he can't bear having a son who isn't a Jew. But all Noah did was to change his religion – and that wasn't much of a change because he was never religious anyway since he was about twelve. And I don't think

he ever really believed in Catholicism. And then look at
Daddy, as you said. I expect he still believes in God –'

'Does he really?'

'Yes, why not?' said Lesley defensively. 'I bet some of
the other parents do too, in their hearts.'

'Well, not mine. They say it's all *shtut*.'

'Anyhow, Daddy doesn't practise his religion any more,
or he couldn't live here. He's left all that behind in Canada.
He seems to think living in Israel is religion enough.'

'He's quite right as well!' said Shula stoutly.

'So if he thinks it's religion that makes you a Jew or not
a Jew,' Lesley pursued, 'then he's no more Jewish now than
Noah.' She sat up in bed suddenly. 'Shula! That's it! That's
right, isn't it? How can he argue with that? That's the answer! He may be a bit of a fanatic, but he's fair, and he's
honest. If I put it to him like that, how can he *not* see his
mistake?'

Shula said it was never much use counting on parents, or
any grown-ups come to that, to be reasonable and fair, especially when it came to admitting mistakes. They had their
own notions of fairness and their own funny ways of thinking and working things out. 'If your father was fair, he'd
never have done anything so fantastic as throw your brother
out in the first place.' This seemed to Lesley so true that she
couldn't help losing some of her enthusiasm for her plan;
in any case, it was no easier than before, trying to imagine
herself broaching the subject with her father – or her mother.
Come to think of it, it would be even harder with her
mother, who would inevitably be terribly emotional about
seeing Noah again, especially under these circumstances – giving up everything to come and fight for Israel and them. Any
mother might be forgiven for being emotional about that.
Just before falling asleep, Lesley found herself drowsily wondering how all those other volunteers' mothers had reacted to

their dropping everything and coming here. It must seem even to the most Zionistic of them as mad as hurling yourself into the eye of a typhoon.

The next morning Lesley awoke very early and crept out before the others had stirred. It was already summer in the Valley and the sun was up; there was no dew these mornings because even the nights were quite warm. The kibbutz was wide awake. The tractors, bulldozers and excavators were busy on the earth works. The beauty of the morning was entirely spoilt by the awful roaring and grinding of the machines and the sights of ruined lawns and jagged scars in the ground, more war-like than any weapons – Lesley was quite used to seeing guns and uniforms.

She paused briefly beside a huge pit which was being dug for a new shelter which, Baruch had cheerfully assured them all, would not be ready in time. 'It'll come in useful the way it is now, as a mass grave,' he'd added with grim relish. '*Shtok, kvar!*' all the girls had yelled. Baruch had a very macabre sense of humour. Lesley shivered and hurried on.

She was heading for the cowsheds to see her father who had been at work since four a.m. But on the way she passed the path which led to the *tsrifim* – rather tumble-down wooden huts where the first settlers had lived before permanent housing was built – which were used now to house working visitors or work-parties of youngsters from the towns. There surely the volunteers would have been billeted. She was just going to nip along there and see where Noah was (any excuse not to talk to her father just yet) when she heard the roar of the little garden tractor and saw her father driving it from the *refet*. The cart at the back was loaded with milk-churns; he was bringing the morning milk to the kitchen.

She had a cowardly impulse to duck out of sight, but he'd already seen her and veered the tractor in her direction. She felt her stomach beginning to turn over; she would have to tell him now, and this was not a good moment – he was rushed off his feet and would have no time to digest the news. She should, oh, she should have done it last night! Then he could have slept on it, and in any case it would be *over*.

With the tractor within a few yards of her, she suddenly heard footsteps coming along the path to the *tsrifim*. With an awful feeling of inevitability, she turned her head. Yes, it was Noah! Her father couldn't see him because the path ran off at right angles between high hedges. So father and son approached each other along a collision course which had her at its meeting point.

At the critical moment she stepped back. Her father stopped the tractor and said cheerily, 'What are you doing up so –' And then Noah walked round the corner.

Afterwards Lesley tried to recapture the sensations of that moment. Again a sense of symbolism came to her, for she was standing at an actual and a metaphorical crossroads, and it was there that her beloved father and her beloved brother met for the first time in four long, hard years, during which they had never stopped missing each other and – Lesley suddenly saw it clearly in both their faces – regretting, to some extent and in a mixed-up way, the actions that had parted them.

If Lesley had ever doubted that this was true in her father's case, that moment when Nat Shelby saw his son again put her doubts to rest. Something happened to his face that was quite new in her experience of him. It sagged and grew suddenly old and grey as if the life had been knocked right out of his body. It seemed unnatural that he could still keep sitting there quite upright on the tractor, his hands resting on the wheel and the engine still running like the only live thing on the scene. For Noah, too, was rigid and white in the face as if stricken. Her eyes flashing from one to the other of them,

Lesley's own feeling of involvement – her guilt at the secret meetings, her burden of responsibility – melted away. This was not, she saw now, her business at all. This was something deeper and stronger than she was yet old enough to grasp. She felt the right thing would be for her just to disappear and leave them together, and in fact she did edge backwards into the shadow of the hedge so as to be out of their picture of each other.

Noah made the quickest recovery, because he had been at least partly prepared.

'Hallo, Dad,' he said quietly.

'Hallo, son,' answered their father with some uncertainty, like a question-mark in his voice. And then he seemed to shrink into himself like an old man, and dropped his head between his shoulders, and his hands gripped the wheel of the tractor so hard not only the knuckles but all the fingers went livid with the effort to control the sudden violent trembling that took hold of him. After a moment he threw up his head and said in a voice too loud to be as normal as he wanted, 'What are you doing in this – neck of the woods?'

'Can we talk somewhere, Dad?'

'I can't now,' said this old man whom Lesley couldn't quite recognize. 'I've got work to do.' It was his last effort to escape from the blinding reality of knowing that he couldn't be angry with Noah any longer.

'I've been assigned to work in the cowsheds with you.'

Nat looked bewildered, as if he couldn't grasp what was happening. 'And how – and how did that happen?' he asked, as if this were the most incomprehensible part of the puzzle.

'I asked to be,' said Noah simply.

'Nu,' said Nat bemusedly. 'Nu . . .' He gave his head a shake, like a dog, as if to get the buzzing out of his ears. In a moment it would come real, he would understand, he would *remember* what those four long years had been about. He

would recover his anger, he would ... But before him stood
Noah and he realized suddenly that he had called him
'son', that that was what he truly felt, and that to go on
pretending something else would be a stupid, meaningless lie.

He looked at him, through the mists of receding shock, a
little more carefully, and saw him straight and tall, with his
pale intellectual face and kind eyes like his mother's looking
anxiously from behind his glasses. He saw that he was dressed for work in jeans and his ragged old University sweat-
shirt, and sneakers on his feet.

Nat's eyes rested on his feet because he was ashamed and
afraid to look him in the face again yet. He cleared his throat
and said unsteadily, 'Those shoes are no good to you. You'll
be in muck to the knees. I'd better fix you up with some boots.'
As Lesley watched, a slow, wondering, incredulous smile appeared on Noah's face, and she felt something rising in her
own throat which threatened to burst out in a shout of pure
happiness but she did not let it, because she didn't want to
interrupt them. She watched from her shadow as Noah, still
with that look of wonder on his face, walked forward and
stood beside his father, who, with a great effort, got off the
tractor. She saw her father's eyes come up slowly from the
ground and meet Noah's, and then she saw their hands coming up towards each other.

And then she couldn't watch for another second, she knew
she mustn't and anyway she couldn't bear to. She turned
away in a flash and ran and ran, blinded by happiness and
other tumultuous, powerful feelings, until she came to the
top of the riverbank and there she flung herself down on the
stony, half-scorched, unwelcoming ground, and poured out
her relief and joy, not in tears but in long, trembling waves
of laughter.

CHAPTER 21

Lull Before the Storm

A week can pass like a flash, or it can go on for ever. But this particular week, in some mysterious way, seemed to do both. It hurtled past as far as preparations for war were concerned. These went on night and day, and the work of the kibbutz had to go on too, no matter what might be happening in one's private life; every person of any age capable of work – including Ofer's sister Yocheved who was going to have a baby at any moment – worked almost every hour they were awake, and some hours when, as it seemed to Lesley, they were more than half asleep. When you're working as hard and long as that, time tends to fly, and there's not much time for thought or even for feelings. Certainly as the crisis built to a head and the tension screwed up to breaking-point, Lesley had sense enough to be grateful that she was too busy and too tired to think much, or to feel afraid.

But at home – on the rare occasions when the family managed to get there and see each other – time slowed to a crawl. Five minutes standing in the porch exchanging a few words or silently looking at each other was like time out of time, limitless moments of stillness and deep confused feelings in the rush and tumble of life outside.

Lesley was not there when her father took Noah home for the first time. When she got back, at lunchtime that first day of Noah's being in the kibbutz, she found the three of them; Noah and Nat in their filthy *refet*-clothes and boots, dirt all over the floor – something unheard of, her father always changed at the cowsheds – sitting on the sofa looking worn out with something more exhausting than mere work; while her mother sat in her chair opposite them, staring at them in drained silence. One look at her mother's face told Lesley she had wept until she had no more tears left, and now she looked just empty, but on the smooth, drained face was a look of calm and the pale shadow of a great happiness which was going to burst upon her as soon as she regained strength to feel it.

They all looked round as she came in and her mother lifted her hand as if it were very heavy and held it out to her. She came and took it and they all just looked at each other, except that Miriam looked only at Lesley, and then Lesley saw that there were some tears left after all because her mother began to cry again, weakly, and held her hand very tightly and said in a choked voice, 'Thank you, darling, thank you.'

'What for, Mom?'

'Noah's told us. He – it wouldn't have happened except for you.'

Lesley looked quickly at her father. Her mouth came open.

'You're not angry with me?'

Her father shook his head and smiled a little, a smile with a lot of pain left in it. Her mother held her round the waist and pressed her face against her.

'No, dear, no ! How could we be angry now?'

Lesley said nothing. She knew only a bit of the credit belonged to her. The crisis had done most of it, their own buried feelings had done the rest. She had only been the – well, the trigger.

But it was a long time before things began to be natural between them. Too much anger, too much misunderstanding, too many gaps had to be bridged and talked through and overcome. And it was hard to talk. Polite chat was impossible, and words were hard to find for the deep-rooted things from the past that had to be discussed; so there were silences, and it was these silences that made the time pass so slowly.

Lesley saw that it was agony for her father and mother –

agony to be with Noah because they longed to be close to him and didn't know how to bridge these gaps; agony not to be with him, and there were long hours when the demands of work and the crisis kept them apart.

Noah was soon taken out of the *refet* and put to other work – work that infuriated him because it seemed to have nothing to do with war. For two days he actually had to serve as lifeguard at the swimming-pool. It may sound odd that swimming went on, but the kibbutzniks tried to keep things as normal as possible especially for the children, and swimming was an essential part of their lives in that boiling weather. But for Noah, who had come to fight for his family, spending the days lounging by the side of the pool with a whistle round his neck getting a beautiful tropical tan was so great an anti-climax that he could hardly stand it.

'Couldn't they use me, Dad?' he kept asking. 'They're building shelters here! Drainage, ventilation – this is my field for Pete's sake!' Nat went to the Secretariat and suggested that Noah be put to work on the shelters, but it was no use – the kibbutz was not responsible for building the shelters, the Government was doing it, and the designs were fixed at some much higher level. They let him help with the manual work, digging, installation of pipes, cementing the huge grey concrete blocks ... It was better than the swimming pool, but it was not enough.

'Couldn't I join the army? I know how to shoot!' But the kibbutzniks only smiled tolerantly. Foreign nationals were not allowed to join up. Besides, 'knowing how to shoot' is not quite enough to be a member of the world's most highly-trained and efficient fighting force. Noah's frustration added to the tension at home.

And then, early on the 5th of June, it happened.

There'd been a sort of little lull – well not exactly, but a pause like a drawn breath the day before. On the Monday morning Lesley was sweeping out her bedroom. She could hear a radio droning faintly from the classroom. It would be English first lesson again this morning – since their class-teacher had been called up, they seemed to have English practically all the time, which meant Lesley hardly ever went to lessons and had to help Ada with the housework instead. This was maddening, just when she'd been beginning to make great headway with her studies ... She was grumbling to herself about it, to take her mind off the boringness of sweeping the extraordinary amount of sand and bits of junk out from under Ofer's bed, when she felt something strange, like the shock-wave from an explosion before you hear it. It was so real it sent a shiver down her back and made her straighten up. A second later she heard a frenzied whoop from the class-room.

She rushed out of the bedroom into the corridor. The whoop had died, and been replaced by an acute, listening silence, dominated by the voice on the radio. She ran to the classroom. The group round the radio, which was on the teacher's desk in front of the blackboard, looked like a foot-ball scrum – all backs and behinds, no heads. She cried out, 'What is it, has it started?' Nearly everyone said, 'Sh!' but Shula's and Ofer's heads came out of the scrum and their faces were respectively red and white. 'Yes!' said Ofer. 'It's begun!' said Shula. She disentangled herself from the group and rushed at Lesley, clutching her. Her round face was funny-looking. Lesley couldn't decide whether she was more scared or excited.

'The lousy damn war has begun!' she whispered. 'Do you wish you were in Skaskasoon?' She never had learnt to pro-nounce it properly.

'No!' Lesley almost shouted.

'Nut-case,' said Shula. 'Come and listen. I translate.'

Lesley listened. The Egyptians had moved their troops forward, right up to the Sinai border, and the Israelis had met them in a head-on battle which was raging – hundreds of miles to the south – at this very moment. Shula's red face turned pale and she put her fingernails between her clenched teeth. Usually when she bit her nails Lesley pulled her hand away; but she knew she was thinking of Rami, and if gnawing her nails helped her to bear that, then who was Lesley to try to stop her? Many of the others lost the first feeling of excitement – relief, almost, at the break-up of tension – as they began to realize the implications for their fathers and brothers. Lesley saw Ofer turn and hurry away. She guessed where he was going. His mother would be working, his father was far away. His sister Yocheved, her young husband also 'somewhere in the south', was in a state of pitiable anxiety already, what with her baby due at any moment. The announcement that the war had begun must have upset her dreadfully.

One by one the kids started to drift or hurry away – to be with their parents or to find some work to do. But suddenly there was a bang as the outside door closed sharply, and the voice of their unsuccessful, but nevertheless formidable, English teacher resounded through the building.

'What's going on here? Where do you all think you're going? Don't you know you've got an English lesson?'

A babel of voices began to bring her up to date on the situation, but she interrupted on a high note of authority.

'But children! CHILDREN! I know all that. It makes no difference to our class schedule. Now come along – into the classroom. Get out your *New Horizons* and open to page 83!'

A groan went up from a dozen throats, but she was adamant. A moment later she stalked into the classroom, with most of the class trailing reluctantly after her. A wave of loud, uninhibited grousing went round as they settled down.

'What a stupid idea!'

'Who wants to learn today?'

'To all the winds with English at a time like this!'

Nevertheless, in a few minutes they were all bent over their texts, and the war and its terrors necessarily took a back seat in their minds for the length of the lesson. For the first time the English teacher invited Lesley to join in. 'I need a little help today,' was the way she put it. Lesley sat at the front and gave definitions of new words and answered questions on grammar which were too hard for the others. She thought at the time that the teacher was being unreasonable, that the lesson was irrelevant and ridiculous. Thinking back on it, though, she took a different view.

CHAPTER 22

War Diary

June 5th: War's begun! Learnt English in morning. Couldn't concentrate! She let us stop every hour to hear the news. Heavy fighting in the desert ... Shula's simply sick with worry about Rami. Is he there? David's father is; he's an officer. So's 'Brosh', Yocheved's husband. She went into hospital this afternoon to have her baby. No news yet. Baruch says it's good she's having it now, all the hospitals will be full of wounded in a few days.

Listened to Radio Cairo this morning, broadcasting in Hebrew – horribly funny! Their Hebrew was full of funny mistakes which even I had to laugh at, like saying 'our soldiers are advancing on all *bras*' (*khasiot*) instead of 'on all *fronts*' (*khasitot*). They said Haifa and Tel Aviv had been completely wiped out, but of course we knew they hadn't. Why do they tell such lies? On the other hand, our radio must be lying too, because *they* said our Air Force has destroyed the whole Egyptian Air Force on the ground. That must be nonsense – just too good to be true! It would mean we hadn't even had to kill their pilots. But if it isn't true, why haven't they bombed anywhere? Of course maybe they have and we haven't heard, but surely we would have, if ... One does long to believe one's own radio is telling the truth. We've got to expect some bad news. I'd rather *know* than feel I was being lied to. (Danny said that, but it's true.)

Worked all afternoon in Gan Yud with Shula. The little kids are terribly keyed-up. They can't grasp what's happening, but Shula says they sense the atmosphere, which is electric. Practised taking them down the shelter, 'putting them to bed' ... They loved it!

I hope the Jordanians don't join in the fighting. I bet the Lebanese won't, so why should Jordan? Baruch says they probably have already, that King Hussein won't be able to keep out of it because of the pact.

June 6th: Still absolutely quiet here – it's uncanny. But there's fighting going on practically everywhere else. The Jordanians *have* joined in. I'm sad about it. Danny says they're the best fighters of any of the Arabs. There's something pretty fierce going on around Jerusalem. Daddy said, with a wild kind of light in his eyes, 'If only we could get the Old City back!' What's so important is the Western Wall of the old Temple. It's our holiest place, and the only Jews who've been able to go there since 1948 have been Western tourists . . . I guess this doesn't mean much to the young Israelis who'll have to fight for it. It would be great to be able to visit it some day – if anything's left of it. Baruch says we'll have to pull the City down stone by stone to take it away from the Arab Legion.

It's terrible to think of the fighting that's going on so close to us while we lie here so quietly with things going on almost normally – except for the blackout, and the fact that practically everyone's worried sick about somebody. Farther north the Syrians are shelling the valley settlements. They always have, but now it's a real barrage. Sometimes I imagine I can hear the rumbling on gusts of wind. There's a rumour they're attacking on the ground, too – trying to reach Kibbutz Dan. All the boys are fretting because nothing exciting is happening here and all the girls (except Naomi!) think they're crazy not to be grateful.

Yocheved's had a boy. Ofer's thrilled. She's going to call him Shalom, which means 'peace'. How awful having a baby when your husband's in a battle!

No news of any of our soldiers yet, but they must be

fighting wonderfully. The Egyptians are being pushed back on all fronts – I mean, on all bras! (That's our current joke, everyone keeps saying it.) Oh! How could I forget to mention it first? It was TRUE about our knocking out all their planes – we must really have a secret weapon! Esther's cousin's a pilot, he must have taken part in that operation. She's so proud of him. We're all terribly excited absolutely every minute. We can't believe it's all real – but of course, as Baruch keeps reminding us, things can easily turn against us.

June 7th: Terrible news today. Baruch's brother Avri's been wounded. We don't know how badly. His family live next door to Mom and Dad. His poor mother's nearly crazy ... He's been sent to the hospital in Beersheba. It's far away but they've both gone straight off there; we won't know more till they come back.

Our local hospital's sent Yocheved and her baby home. Baruch was right; they're clearing all the maternity and other non-serious cases out to make room for the wounded from the Jordanian front, which is very, very hot. We've taken a lot of the big bulge of land on the West Bank of the Jordan, just below us. I'm sure I can hear noises now when the wind blows from the south. There's a rumour that we've captured Ramallah and Jenin, two big towns there. But most of the attention is on the battle for Jerusalem ... By tonight it may have fallen to us!

(Later) Danny's father came along to the *kitta* and gave us a talk about the situation. He's in the reserve but they haven't called him up yet because he's got a bad back, and anyway we have to have *some* men at home. He says, whatever else we do, we've *got* to take the Heights of Golan. The Syrians are dug in all along there and have been shelling those kibbutzim right underneath them for years. Our planes are bombing them now, and Danny's father says that now we've taken Sharm El Sheikh (that's where the Egyptians stopped our ships getting into the Gulf of Akaba, which is what the war really started about) a lot of our men will come up from the desert and attack the Heights. It will be terribly hard to capture them; it means the infantry climbing right up a practically sheer cliff under the bunkers, straight into the Syrian guns.

The Syrians have been the worst about saying what they were going to do to us ... I sort of hate them when I think about that, and about how they've never left our settlements in peace, all these years. I don't hate the Egyptians. I feel sorry for them in a way, I mean the way they're screaming lies at us over the radio is kind of pathetic. Nobody could hate the Lebanese, they're not doing anything to us anyway. As for the Jordanians, of course I don't hate them. I even like their little king, and as for the people – well, when I think of them I just see Mustapha riding away on Eeyore. Of course I know they're not all like him, but even if half of them were that poor ... I'd feel like fighting the world if I'd lost my land and were as poor as him. I bet Eeyore never tasted chocolate again, or Mustapha either ... I wonder where he is? And if he hates me? Baruch says Arab kids are taught to hate us in school. The way they learn their maths for instance is 'If there are ten Jews and you kill three, how many are left?'

We've heard from a lot of our men. Something wonderful happens here. When the soldiers pass through a town, lots of people come out to cheer them and give them little presents of chocolate and soft drinks. In return, the soldiers give them pieces of paper with their names and home phone numbers scribbled on them. The person who gets the number goes off and phones the soldier's home to say, 'I've just seen him and he's okay and sends his love.' I've seen lots of mothers getting these messages in the middle of their work. I just hope those kind people know what it's meant. I saw one mother – Rina, who's gone back to the sheep – do a funny clumsy dance with a great big dirty sheep in her arms when her message came. Others just burst into tears of relief. I do wonder if that sort of thing happens in every country during a war, or if it's just here.

June 8th: We went to bed early last night because the excitement makes us all tired, and woke up this morning to the most wonderful news. We've taken the Old City! The whole country is going mad with joy! They say we've reached the Suez Canal as well, which means we've got the whole of Sinai and we don't have to be afraid any more of those awful rockets the Egyptians had there, ready to blow up our cities. The way it's all going so well and so *quickly* is making the Egyptians say the Americans and British are helping us – ha ha! Fat chance. Anyway, as Moshe Dayan said, we don't want any other country's soldiers to die for us. We can manage by ourselves.

Shula told me a secret. She prayed last night, 'Please God take care of Rami.' She says she knows there's no one to hear, but she had to do something. Her father's home. He was wounded when his tank ran over a mine, but it's not serious, so that's one less to worry about. But it's awful about Avri. He's lost his foot ... Can't write about it, can't think about it. All Baruch can say is, 'If only that's the worst ...'

June 9th: The worst day so far, though the war is going so well nobody can quite believe it. We *have* reached the Canal – our soldiers actually went swimming in it – we've taken the whole of the West Bank, and now only the Syrians have to be finished with.

But something dreadful has happened. We heard about it this morning. Even now I can't get it into my head. Danny's father came and called Ofer out of the lesson. He didn't come back, but after a while someone came in and told the rest of us. Yocheved's husband, 'Brosh' as he's called (it means a cedar tree, because he was so tall), has been killed.

We were just stunned. We all knew him. He worked with the sheep and everyone thought a lot of him. He was Works Manager too, so there's no one in the kibbutz who didn't talk to him just a few days ago. Shula and Aviva and some of the others couldn't stop crying, but I could only cry when I saw Ofer. He looked so broken up . . . He'd been crying too, I think. I went to him and put my arms round him. It's not done among us really, but I couldn't help myself. Most of the others couldn't look at him. He loved Brosh almost as much as his real brother, Adam. (There's a rumour Adam's at the Heights . . . If anything happened to him ! No, I won't even think about it.)

A military escort brought Brosh back to the kibbutz in the afternoon. The whole kibbutz went to the funeral, except a few people who had to look after the youngest children. It was just awful, but so moving I could hardly stand it. All us kids walked together, wearing our Movement shirts and carrying the wreath we'd made, out to the cemetery which is way out in the fields. Yocheved didn't come, of course, but Ofer's parents did, and Brosh's mother. I couldn't keep from looking at her. You couldn't imagine how she must be feeling. You felt you shouldn't look, but you had to. She wore an ordinary *Shabbat* dress with no sleeves (it's horribly hot) and her sun-glasses, and Ofer's father stood close to her at the graveside and held her arm. Ofer stood on the other side of her. He looked so tall and straight, my heart gave a queer sort of lurch when I looked at him. She looked as if she'd fall down if they let go of her. A lot of people cried the whole time, but she didn't – she just kind of leant forward as they took the coffin off the back of the open army truck and lowered into the grave.

Then different people spoke about him and an Army rabbi

droned something (you could feel people didn't want to listen to him) and then came the worst part – the escort fired a salute into the air and everybody jumped because it was like hearing the shots that killed him.

Then Ofer's father came forward and shovelled some earth into the grave and Ofer had to hold Brosh's mother's arm by himself, and when she heard the earth falling on the coffin she seemed to shrink into herself. But she kept standing upright and she didn't make a sound, though there were a lot of groans and Ofer's mother gave a sort of gasping cry, the saddest sound I've ever heard in my life.

Ofer came to put in the next spadeful, standing there all alone on the mound of earth. I can't describe how I felt when I saw him standing there against the sky. He gave a sob and I sobbed too, at the same moment. Then our men, those that are still at home, came in turn and helped fill up the grave. Then three girls in uniform from Brosh's regiment came forward with a wreath, and afterwards everyone who'd brought flowers came and laid them on his grave. We did, too. The earth looked so *raw*, somehow; most of the earth here is so light coloured and dry, the grave looked like a thick scar. I couldn't believe Brosh was lying dead underneath, that we'd never see him again.

I had to help Shula home. She just couldn't see for crying. She's lying with her back to me now, in bed, still crying. I know it's partly because she's more and more frightened about Rami, even though he's in Jerusalem and the fighting there is practically over. Oh, how could I ever have been so stupid and unfeeling as to want Noah to fight? I'm so glad and thankful every day that I can see him and touch him and know he's safe! *He's* going crazy, of course, wanting to go, but I'm not such a fool as I was. Brosh has made me realize there's nothing glamorous about war. Poor, poor Yocheved! Poor little Shalom! I'm starting to cry again, I must put the light off – I mustn't wake Ofer, he's worn out ... Amnon has just put his head in with the latest news. The Syrians are nearly beaten ! If only nobody else of ours is killed or hurt ...

June 10th: It's midnight. The war is over ! Just six days, and we've beaten them all. Every Arab country who was fighting us has agreed to a cease-fire, even Syria. It's like a dream, or a miracle.

In spite of all the worry and strain, and Brosh, and Avri, there's a fantastic feeling of triumph and – well you could almost call it exultation. How could we have won at all, let alone in six days? There's one old man, Abba Asher, who's Aviva's grandfather, who keeps saying to anyone who'll listen that it's the hand of God. Lots of the old people – the parents' parents – are still religious of course. There's sometimes talk of building a little synagogue for them, even though the kibbutz doesn't believe. But it's funny. Shula's father, who's probably the most violent atheist of all, actually had tears in his eyes when the news came through that we'd taken the Old City of Jerusalem, and over the radio came the sound of the *shofar* being blown beside the Wailing Wall for the first time in twenty years. Shula told me she'd laughed at him and asked what a few old stones mattered to him, but that he'd turned on her quite angrily and told her to keep quiet about things she didn't understand. Daddy was overjoyed. He says it's the greatest thing that's happened to the Jewish people for a thousand years apart from the founding of Israel, and that I was to remember this day all my life, that I was lucky to be alive for it. I thought he meant, lucky not to have been killed, but later I decided he meant, lucky to be living at this period of history. Strange, one never thinks that one's own time will be history one day.

Now I suppose everything will get back to normal, and seem rather dull. I still can't believe I've been through my first war! (And my last, please God – gosh, am I getting religious too?) Soon all the boys will be back and school will start again and ... ho-hum! But then there are so many exciting things to look forward to. I expect we'll go on trips to see Old Jerusalem and Golan and Hebron and all the other places – maybe even to the Suez Canal! We'll have to go quickly before the Arabs make peace and we give it all back to them. All except Jerusalem, of course. We'll never give that back, Daddy says – never.

The kids all sat up talking very late about all that's happened and all that's going to happen. They persuaded me to read them this journal and I read it all (I mean all the part about the War) except the bit about Ofer. I felt myself blushing when I skipped over that bit and Esther noticed and asked me afterwards what I missed out, but I wouldn't tell her of course. I do like Ofer, even though he is only two months older than me.

Then we talked about how wonderful it will be to have peace at last, not to be afraid any more and for our boys not to have to go and fight. Ofer says he simply can't imagine himself fighting, but then he can't imagine his brother Adam fighting either. Adam is the most gentle, peaceful young man, all he cares about is his archaeology and his cows (he's Daddy's boss in the refet). And his music ... Ofer says just the *noise* of battle must have been agony for Adam, his ears are so sensitive he jumps if you shout near him.

Baruch listened to us all talking about peace and finally came out with what you'd expect: 'What makes you all so sure they'll know they're beaten?' We all hooted at him. How could they not know they're beaten after this?

I had some private thoughts. First I thought that Noah will go back now, and that will be awful, even though not so awful as before – at least we'll all keep in touch. But I know he doesn't want to go, even though the war was an anti-climax for him and he felt the kibbutz didn't use the volunteers as much as it should have. (The fact is we managed pretty well without them in the end, and only the fringe-jobs were left for them.) The other thought I had is that when peace comes, they'll mend 'my' bridge and take away the barbed wire and I'll be able to walk across it and visit Mustapha and Eeyore. It'll be great! Danny told us that when there's peace, Jordan won't be so poor any more because we can work together with them, send experts to help with their farming and industry, and anyway none of our countries will be spending all our money on defence any more so we'll all be richer. And we'll be able to visit Cairo and Damascus and Amman and Beirut! Oh, how wonderful everything's going to be!

CHAPTER 23

Aftermath

It was actually only when it was all over that Lesley, and many other people, allowed themselves to realize fully the deadly danger they had stood in.

Noah had unwarily let himself use the word 'massacre', and Lesley had let it glance off her mind the way soldiers in olden times used to turn arrows off their shields. But after the war was won, she looked at the word. She heard that the rabbis of Tel Aviv had gone out at night and blessed the park areas which they feared might have to be used as cemeteries for thousands killed in air-raids. In fact, not a single bomb fell on any Israeli city.

The soldiers coming back from the newly-conquered territories, especially the Syrian Heights, brought back, as souvenirs, pamphlets and magazines which the enemy armies had been given to read. On their covers were cartoons of huge handsome Arab soldiers driving wretched, ugly, snivelling little Jews into the Mediterranean and striding across a map of Israel with hob-nailed boots. There were others even worse … The boys joked about them, but they made Lesley's blood run cold in her veins. How narrowly they had been saved from horrors that even now she dared not think about !

Sometimes she looked at a map of the region and reflected on the eight-mile-wide waist that Israel had had, the piffling distances between the borders and desert and the centres of population, and, most of all, between their own kibbutz and the Arabs across the river, and shook her head in wonder. Maybe old Abba Asher had not been so far wrong in calling their deliverance a miracle.

But 'miracle' is an easy and misleading word. 'Miracles

don't really come from God,' Shula said solemnly. Rami was safe – but he was one of the lucky ones. 'Miracles!' she went on. 'You have to buy them. They are very, very expensive.' And she burst into tears.

In a kibbutz, you don't only cry for your own family. Shula was crying for Brosh, and for Amnon's brother Yuval who had died after the 'impossible' assault up the almost sheer Heights of Golan into the Syrian guns; and, perhaps even more than for the others because it seemed somehow so unlikely, for their old boss, Moshe the gardener. He would never scold them any more. He had been shot by a sniper in the Old City, as the victorious Israelis fought their way towards the Wall.

Rami told them how the Israeli officers, including Moshe, had decided not to shell over the city walls. It would have broken the Jordanian resistance, perhaps; but it might also have destroyed the Holy Places – not only Jewish, but Muslim and Christian. Perhaps Moshe would have returned, to fret over his ruined lawns and one day to restore them, if the Israelis had been prepared to risk the Mosque of Omar and the Holy Sepulchre, the Via Dolorosa where Christ walked to Calvary, and the last precious Wall of their own sacred Temple.

He described how the older men, the officers and army rabbis, plain soldiers like himself till they stood by the Wall at last, had suddenly begun hitting their heads on the stones and rocking and praying and crying and holding up their hands ... 'I felt like laughing at first. It seemed so peculiar! And it sounded as if we'd lost instead of winning. But then I saw all my own *chevra*, standing there filthy and sweaty and bloodstained with their guns still in their hands, and when the old fellow blew the ram's-horn some of them began to cry too – the young ones, I mean. I almost felt like crying myself. We'd lost so many men getting to it, and now here it was, and in a way it was just big stones. It made me angry. I'd seen Moshe fall an hour before, and I thought: Are all those stones worth one finger of his hands that could make things grow? I bet his wife doesn't think so. But I don't know. I saw those faces ... I just didn't know. Maybe they were.'

Others had their stories to tell too, and they found eager listeners. But some like Ofer's brother Adam wouldn't talk about it.

'Don't ask me,' he said to his family. 'War just makes me sick. I've got to forget it.'

And he went back to the *refet* and hardly talked to anybody about anything for weeks. But just once, when he and Ofer were alone, he suddenly said: 'Try not to be in the front line if your turn comes. There's plenty that's useful to do in the rear. Nothing's worth having to kill people for.'

And when Ofer, who was burning with enthusiasm for his brother and the whole Israeli army, asked in a shocked voice if saving the country wasn't worth it, Adam replied in a voice full of bitterness and anger: 'Maybe if you're brought up to hate your enemy. Maybe if you're taught to be tough. I just couldn't hate enough, I suppose. It's the kibbutz's fault, really. They teach us to be human beings and to respect life, and not to hate, and then we're expected to turn round when we're twenty and be ruthless killers.'

After this conversation, Ofer lay awake night after night, arguing it out in his mind. Lesley would force herself to stay awake for hours, to give him someone to talk to.

'He's right. Even now I don't hate them. Even seeing Yocheved crying doesn't make me *hate* them. Just think of putting a bullet into a man, seeing him lying there, knowing you've ended him! Maybe they should teach us to hate, the way the Arabs are taught to hate us.'

But surely there would be no need for 'his turn' ever to come? All through the long, hot months, there was hope and jubilation in the air. Now at last, without doubt, the Arabs must sit down round a table and talk to the Israelis face to face, settle everything, make peace. The refugees would be compensated or taken back, the prisoners-of-war would all be sent home. The borders would be opened – peace, wonderful, longed-for, dreamed-of peace would surely come!

But it didn't. And slowly, slowly, that feeling of joy and triumph died. The conquered territory stayed conquered, and the Israelis found out that conquest can have a bitter taste for the victors as well.

Shula wrote another English poem, a companion-piece to her pre-war one, which summed up a lot of people's feelings when it appeared in the kibbutz magazine:

Afterwards

War...
What that really meant
I never knew...
I don't even know it now.
I never felt a bullet in my body,
And I hope I never will.
I'd never heard the ugly sound of weapons,
Nor feared that someone won't come back.
But what I felt, I can't forget:
Israel is one family, caring for her every son.
I saw the people all so friendly;
No one hated each other, but hated
Something worth hating: the War!
I knew Israel's family well:
The women: waiting, hoping, rushing to every place,
At night alone in a big bed.
No sleep,
But thinking, waiting, hoping.
The children: With confusion, something strange was
  happening.
They knew later, if not then.

Why Mummy loved more, why everyone was so sweet to
  you . . .
I hardly knew the men : serious hard,
Fighting for Israel's family,
Cheering everybody up,
And needing it for themselves.
But I knew the boys, the girls – myself :
Grown in one night, helping the women, smiling
To the men, and laughing with the children.
At night, no light, only candles . . .
Writing to a soldier-father, a long, long letter
With jokes . . .
I knew the Israel family well.
But not the meaning of War.

At home, things were still not quite smooth, but just being
together had bridged some of the gaps. Especially being together during the war. As Lesley confided to Shula, war was
like a kind of black magic. It made some people disappear
from the earth, it changed others for ever – and then
just sometimes, it worked good spells, like bringing people
together or healing old wounds.

It had certainly cemented Lesley to her group, made her
one of them without any lingering doubts or reservations.
Thinking about the doubts there *had* been, Lesley always remembered Mustapha and Eeyore, wondering about them –
where they were, how they had fared in the war. She felt glad
that Mustapha was too young to fight; but not only soldiers
had suffered in those six days.

Despite all the outside worries, it was a lovely summer for
Lesley – perhaps the happiest of her life till then. Though she
liked school, it was naturally lovely not to have to learn.
Working instead was a bore in a way – it was the chickens
again – but it was soon over; she began at five-thirty and that
meant that by ten in the morning she could be up at the
pool. All the gang came up there as they finished work, and

they would lie around on the lawns chatting idly, staring up at the hot blue sky, listening to the joyous racket around them, and plunging into the electric blue water when they felt too hot. She was chestnut-brown and her swimming and diving improved marvellously; she felt and looked wonderful.

Up there at the pool was where she really got to know her brother again. The parents didn't come up in the mornings; they could be alone there and talk as much as they liked. What they mostly talked about was Noah's future.

He wrote regularly to his wife, Donna – something their parents had no idea of. And she wrote back, but less regularly, and the tone of her letters was strained. Lesley was hardly surprised.

'What do you want of her, Noah? First of all you leave her, and put her through awful worry. Then when the war's over and you could come back, you don't.' She waited, but he didn't say anything. 'Why *don't* you go back, Noah?' she asked timidly at last.

'Do you want me to?' he asked quickly.

'Of course not ! How can you ask? But –'

'But you think I should. Is that it?'

'Well, she's your wife, after all,' she muttered into the grass.

'And I love her,' he said with unexpected fierceness. Lesley had never been sure on this point.

'So what do you want to do?'

'I want to live in Israel. Not in a kibbutz, though. There's not enough scope. I'm an engineer. I'm not a farmer, or a life-guard, or mucker-out of cowsheds, and I never could be.'

'But what about Donna?'

Noah shrugged moodily and sighed. 'What I'd like best, of course, is if she'd come here. But she wouldn't.'

'Have you asked her?'

'Sure,' he said, but he didn't sound sure.

'Really asked her, Noah? So she knows you mean it?'

And Noah burst out: 'I don't know if I mean it or not! Our life together's been based on a lie, a pretence. You don't know how I felt, going to church with her and all that. I hate thinking about it! I know it's not her fault, but it's all mixed up with her, somehow ... I can't explain. I haven't felt whole for years. I'm still not whole, because I'm only part of myself without her ... The whole mess is because I tried to be what I'm not. Even love can't make that all right.'

Noah hadn't found the courage to tell their parents that he wasn't finally separated from Donna. They just took it for granted he was in Israel for keeps. Lesley heard her mother say to her father once, 'Thank heaven there are no children to worry about!' Often Lesley would see her mother watching Noah with an expression almost of rapture. Noah's return, it seemed to Lesley, had more than made up to her for the things she'd left behind in Saskatoon. Her father was even more deeply satisfied, for he was now completely absorbed in his work, which, Lesley knew, makes all the difference to a man.

If it had not been for this feeling of Noah's decision, and breaking it to the parents, hanging over them all like a poised rock that must soon fall, Lesley would have been entirely happy.

And then suddenly one afternoon Noah appeared in the doorway of Lesley's room in the *kitta* with a white face and a cable in his hand.

'Sis, come outside, will you?'

She had been resting on her bed, but she jumped up at once and together they went out into the burning afternoon heat. The fierce sunlight made her screw up her eyes and some indistinct alarm gave her an inner wincing sensation too. They went and sat under the big tree which shaded part of the lawn. Noah put the cable into her hands, and she read:

'Expecting our baby in December please come home. Donna.'

'Oh, Noah . . . my gosh!'

She wanted to hug him but one look at his face showed her it was no time for congratulations.

'What'll you do?'

'Go, of course. What else?' His thin, sensitive face was like a lake with a wind blowing over it – the skin rippled and his expression changed so rapidly that she couldn't tell what he was feeling.

'Are you at least a little bit glad?'

'Sure. No, not really . . . Hell, I don't know!'

'But Noah –'

'Look, it was bad enough before. But now I've seen *here*, I – Of course I want a kid. We always wanted one. Specially if it's a boy. But I want to raise it *here*. I want it to be a whole Jew, like I never was . . .'

'It can never be that – with a Catholic mother.'

'Oh, that wouldn't matter so much if only it could be an Israeli. That's what I mean by a proper Jew. It's how and where you grow up, not what race your folks are, that matters.'

'Maybe you're right about that. But she'd never –'

'Yeah, I know it.'

'You're sure?'

He fiddled with a stem of the tough, prickly grass for a moment and said dismally, 'I don't see how I could ask her to.'

'A woman's supposed to go wherever her husband wants to go.'

'Ah, c'mon, sis! That notion of women as men's goods and chattels went out with the Victorians. Anyway, how could we live together if one of us was miserable?'

'You have till now.'

'Yeah, and look how it didn't work!'

They sat in silence for a while. Noah gazed out across the fields.

'And then there's the little matter of how I'm going to break it to Mom and Dad.'

'I was just thinking of that.'

'What a mess! God help us, what a lousy mess!'

'We'll go together.'

They told their parents the news that day when they all foregathered at tea-time. Lesley had been dreading it all day with a horror such as she might have felt if they were all going to undergo major operations. In the event, her parents listened with astonishing calm; the outburst of grief, opposition or anger she had expected never came. But this didn't mean that her mother and father didn't have very strong feelings about it.

When the first shock was over their father said:

'Well, son, if that's the way it is, you'll have to go, of course. It's a terrible blow to us, I don't need to tell you. But new life is the great exception-maker. Everything and everybody else comes second to it. You must go back to your responsibilities.' He glanced at his wife. Miriam was sitting quite straight in her chair staring ahead of her. She looked like a wax figure. 'Isn't that right, sweetheart?' Nat asked her, very gently.

'Yes,' she said.

'Mom –' began Noah.

'No,' she said quickly. 'Don't say anything. Go as quickly as you can if you want to be kind to me. As quickly as you can,' she repeated.

'Mom, I'm going to try to come back. With Donna and the baby.'

'Don't give me hope,' she said. 'It's sometimes easier without it.'

CHAPTER 24

Birthday Outing

As the end of August approached, Lesley began looking forward to her fifteenth birthday.

It was to be a very exciting day, because it so happened that on it, her class was making a tour of the newly-captured part of the West Bank, climaxing with the Old City of Jerusalem. Lesley decided to pretend that this marvellous outing had been specially arranged as her birthday treat. With this in view, she gave hardly a thought to the splendours of her fourteenth birthday in Saskatoon, with its grand party and rich presents.

It was her good luck, she felt, that the class trip to the Heights of Golan was over. That had been more like a journey through Hell than a birthday treat.

Bleak, scorched, war-scarred; miles and miles of hot barren road with nothing worth looking at; stops every now and then to scramble about in fearsome warrens of trenches and concrete bunkers, through the gun-slits of which you could look down on to the green valley and the tiny toy-like kibbutzim, with their fishponds like dolls-house mirrors – much as the Syrian gunners must have looked through their sights.

Hardly a sign of farming up there, nor any civilian dwelling – only deserted barracks, black ruins, weed and scrub-covered land; a country given over to war.

In the midst of it all, they'd found what must once have been a field, with some tomatoes growing half-wild on their weed-choked, broken stalks. They'd all picked some and eaten them, hot and squashy as they were, but their colour and texture, even their salty-sweet taste, made Lesley feel sick and she threw hers away.

The group had grown quieter and quieter and hadn't re-
covered their normal spirits until, after hours of bumping
along in the back of the lorry, they'd descended again into
the green richness of Israeli fields, and were able to plunge
into the Sea of Galilee for a swim. There they shouted and
screamed and played wildly, feeling the dust and the indefinable hopeless sadness of hatred and defeat, picked up in the air
of the Heights from the departed Syrians, wash off them in
their own well-loved lake.

But this time would be different. Now they'd see the fam-
ous old towns of Hebron and Nablus, the scenes of battles in
which some of their own men had taken part. And at the end
of the outing – Jerusalem the Golden !

Lesley had received her first, and perhaps best, birthday present the day before. It had put her into such a wonderful
mood, she felt she could hardly fail to enjoy every moment
of her birthday, no matter what it brought. It was a letter
from Noah, containing the news they had all been secretly
praying for.

Dear folks (and especially you, Les, to whom I wish the very
best of birthdays) –

I won't beat about the bush, because I know the news I have
will make you all happy (at least, I hope so!). Donna and I have
talked without stopping for two weeks, and we have decided to
emigrate to Israel – together.

This is not a decision I have forced on her. Women are very
strange creatures ! It seems she has known all along how unhappy
I've been, and has only been waiting for me to talk to her
straight. She's a Catholic and she can no more stop being one than
I was able to stop being Jewish. But we're married and we love
each other, and although we don't underrate the difficulties
we're facing, we want to try to make a go of it, with each of us
sticking to what we really are.

Donna says that as I've lived her life for three years, it's only
fair she should give mine a whirl. She wanted the baby to be

born in Canada, and I want him/her to be born in Israel, and that we *couldn't* resolve, so we tossed for it in the end, and Israel and I won! She's accepted it, and we're selling up here and coming over in about a month's time.

I'm going to get work as a civil engineer. I have a very uneasy feeling that if real peace doesn't come before September, then it won't come for a long time. There might be more trouble. If so, air-raid shelters on a big scale will have to be built, and I'm just the man to build them. If not ... there's always plenty of building going on in Israel. We'll make out.

We won't be living in the kibbutz, but we won't be far from it either. We'll see plenty of each other. You're going to get to know Donna. She's going to be the mother of your grandchild, and surely it's an old Jewish tradition that All Gets Forgiven under those circumstances!

Early on the morning of her birthday, Lesley woke up to find a tray on the table beside her bed. On it were eighteen little plastic bags full of sweets, chewing-gum, nuts and beg-ele. Each bag had the name of one of the group on it. Lesley knew of this custom, among the younger children: birthdays began with the child giving each member of his group a little present, which his parents had left in the night. But at her age? She picked up the envelope which stood in front of the bags.

Darling daughter,

You missed out on all the fun of being a kibbutz child when you were little. We've decided to give you *Saciot* just this once before you have completely grown-up.

We hope this birthday marks the end of your settling-in period, the beginning of true belonging. We are infinitely proud of you and of the way you've adjusted to our new life. Forgive us if we hurt you or failed to be understanding. We love you so much. We only hope you know, now, that everything that's happened this past year has happened in a framework of that love.

    Mazal tov, dearest,

        from Mom and Daddy.

Her present from them was underneath all the *saciot*, and she only discovered it after she'd given them all out, amid shouts of ironic delight and much fooling around, pretending to be toddlers (Shula disappeared and came back with a towel wrapped round her nappy-fashion, sucking a lollypop from her *sacit*, and Ammon and Gadi had a peanut-throwing battle). Lesley looked at the flat package, wondering how many years it was since her parents had given her anything for her birthday other than expensive clothes. When she was nine, she thought, and had wanted new figure-skates . . . and then there was a ping-pong table one year, but that wasn't a birthday . . . She held the package, hoping with all her heart that it would be nothing expensive, nothing that would embarrass her before the others. But she need not have worried.

It was a glorious record of the *Hair* music, something the whole gang could enjoy, something they'd been dying for. When the others saw it, there was a moment's silence, then a concerted whoop of joy.

'Look what she's got !'

'What parents !'

'Eze yofi!'

'Fantasti!'

'Lo normali!'

But there was no time to play it then. Ada was calling them to get dressed quickly and get out to the lorry which was waiting to take them on the big trip.

They wore their coolest clothes: shorts, little striped 'vests' with scooped-out backs and necks, idiot-hats pulled well down to shade the face, and *kafkafim*, rubber sandals with just a strap between the toes. They were all burnt brown by now, and for her part Lesley had never looked or felt healthier. She had hated the heat in Canada, but here, where you had to be active no matter how hot it was, she had actually learnt to enjoy sweating. It was pleasing to feel the cooling touch of a breeze on one's wet flesh.

Once, when she was working in the gardens (there was a new gardener now, a young man called Reuven) she had stopped to wipe her face with her hat. She'd stood looking down at the dark wet mark on the faded cotton; and at that moment the punctual morning wind sprang up and pushed cool fingers through her shirt on to her damp back. She took a deep breath and suddenly she jumped up in the air as high as she could and let out a wild shout as she flung her hat towards the sky.

Shula had come running. 'What's with you? What happened?'

'Nothing. I love it here, that's all. I just love it here!'

'Nut-case,' grumbled Shula, stumping back to her pruning. 'I thought you saw a snake.'

Now they all scrambled on to the back of a big lorry. It had four rows of hard, narrow bench-seats inside, and canvas sides which could be rolled up. You had to decide, as you went along, whether it was more important to get a cool breeze blowing in, together with all the dust, or whether it was preferable to die of heat and suffocation but keep the air clean. There were always two opinions about this and it always led to a shouting-match. The cool-air people usually won.

Ofer, Amnon and Baruch were already rolling up the canvas on their side. Ada, the house-mother, appeared with box-loads of food and was greeted by a mighty cheer. They were already munching their pre-breakfast of bread and sour cucumber. Churns of cold drink were stored up near the cabin.

They grew impatient to start, and soon they were giving the tardy driver the slow hand-clap to make him hurry. He came strolling out from the back of the kitchen, eating a sandwich, and got an ironic cheer. Five minutes later they were on their way.

It was not a long journey. They followed the river south, and soon found themselves driving through what had, until very recently, been Jordanian territory.

One could see the difference – no kibbutzim here of course, with their characteristic long white buildings and red roofs all slanting the same way amid their trees and lawns; no huge fields and great blocks of fruit trees, no communal outbuildings and cowsheds. Here were the little jumbled villages made of natural stone or adobe, with just a few fig-trees in the small yards where poultry ran loose and a cow or two were housed in individual sheds, often made of mud or corrugated iron.

The plots of land were small, like patchwork quilts, the furrows running in every direction; even the vineyards were broken up into plots, divided by rough walls made by piling up the stones cleared from the fields. There was no modern irrigation here, but big white wells like windowless houses. You saw a few tractors, but mainly it was donkeys, a few horses and even the occasional camel. Lesley knew that a lot of the ploughing was still done by hand with the ancient biblical type of hand-cut wooden plough. There was something very beautiful about this land and the villages.

Little saucer-eyed dirty children ran out to watch them pass – and were often dragged indoors again by frightened-looking mothers in long full dresses with white muslin shawls over their heads. The war with its primitive terrors was not yet over for them.

And there were still signs of it if you looked carefully. Here and there was a house that stood empty and lifeless, but not yet neglected – as if the households had only just fled. And as they travelled deeper into Samaria they saw more obvious signs – burnt-out trucks still standing by the roadside, a freshly-ruined house . . . But for the most part, Lesley was glad to see that the fields were in good heart with people working in them and most of the villages seemed to be carrying on normally. There were remarkably few troops to be seen, which was also a good sign, though of course there were road-checks for vehicles entering and leaving the new territories.

The first town they stopped at was Jenin, and here Boaz, who was with them, told them about the campaign there which he'd taken part in. Boaz was a phlegmatic sort of person; the war didn't seem to have bothered him as it had some others. To him it was a job which he was proud that they'd done well. He told a funny-awful story about how he'd had to winkle snipers out of houses one by one with his patrol. At one house where they thought shooting had been coming from, they kicked down the door and burst in. He caught sight of a movement on one side of the room and spun round, his *uzi* already firing like mad at the movement. Then he stopped in confusion and all his men started to laugh. He'd been shooting a big mirror to pieces! It was his own reflection he'd seen moving.

The town had a strange 'feel' about it. They went for a walk in a group and looked at the shops and stalls, but they stuck to each other like a swarm of bees and there were no stragglers. Nobody bought anything, although to Lesley's astonishment there were dozens of street-traders smiling and bowing, obviously only too anxious to sell to them. A little boy of about eight ran up to them with a tray of pencils crying in Hebrew, '*Hacol b'lira! Hacol b'lira!*' – 'One lira each!' They grinned sheepishly at him and shook their heads.

'A lira for a pencil? What a cheek!' whispered David, but Shula said, 'That's probably all the Hebrew they know.'

Lesley thought it queer that these people were so friendly and willing to do business with them, but Boaz said cynically, 'Typically Arab. Hatred's forgotten when they smell money. There's bound to be thousands of Israelis flocking through these little towns wanting souvenirs to take home. Look at those faces! No, the hatred isn't really forgotten, just pushed behind the come-and-buy smiles until we've gone.'

Lesley wished he wouldn't talk like that. She felt sorry for the Arabs. How awful it must be to have been defeated, and have the conquerors wandering about your town, staring at you! She didn't blame them. But still, Boaz was right about one thing. You could feel the hatred and bitterness, still there, flowing over and around you in waves. She was glad to get back on the lorry and move off into the country-side again.

As they drove along Ada began to hand round food in little packages. There were thick egg sandwiches and pickles and chunks of cold roast chicken, wrapped in greaseproof paper. They were all hungry and thirsty and the driver had to stop while they all took turns to dip into the churns and fill the paper cups with cold delicious *mitz limon*. Some of the boys jumped off the back of the truck to look around, and there was a general plea to be allowed to picnic by the roadside, but Boaz wouldn't agree.

'But there's no one around except those field-workers over there,' objected Amnon.

'You can't trust them,' said Boaz. 'None of them. Come on, *chevrai*, move!'

Reluctantly the boys scrambled back. The truck was about to start. Suddenly Ada let out a cry. They all jumped, thinking from the tone of it that something awful had happened.

'Amnon! Yossi! Gadi!' Her voice was like pistol shots. Her arm came up and she pointed down at the ground behind the truck with a finger that trembled. 'Get out at once and pick up those papers!'

They looked blankly at her, at the food-papers left crumpled up on the verge, and finally at each other. 'What's with you?' grumbled Gadi. 'It's only rubbish. I thought we'd *done* something.'

'You have done something, you little pigs!' The children gasped. Ada never called them names. 'Where do you think you are? Make a pigsty of your own place if you like, it's only your poor parents or me who'll have to clear up after you. I won't agree to you leaving your filth all over other people's land! Isn't it enough we've beaten them? Boaz, tell them!'

Boaz looked sheepish. Clearly he didn't think it was so awful to leave rubbish by the roadside, but Ada was formidable in this mood of rare anger. He stuck his hands into his pockets to cover his awkwardness, and gave a brief nod to the boys.

'Better pick it up, *chevrai*,' he muttered.

Very reluctantly, Amnon and Yossi climbed down again and picked up their balls of paper, tossing them rebelliously into the back of the truck. Gadi stayed where he was, a look of mulishness settling on his large, red face.

'Are *they* so clean?' he asked.

'That's not the point!' said Ada. 'This place is *theirs*!'

'Not any more,' said Boaz unexpectedly.

Ada gave him a look of astonishment and – almost – dislike. The whole group was abruptly stiff with tension and antagonism. Suddenly they all burst into argument.

'That's right, we won it. It's ours now, we can do what we like!'

'No we can't. We'll be giving it back soon, when there's peace.'

'*If*, you mean! Anyway we won't give this part back.'

'Of course we will! It's not ours! It's these people's. Think how you'd feel if –'

'I don't have to think how I'd feel! I felt plenty when they were threatening to destroy us.'

'Anyway it doesn't matter if we give it back in the end. We don't have to go throwing litter over it. That's a shame anywhere.'

'Yes, we should behave properly and not as if we didn't respect them.'

'I don't respect them!' Amnon shouted. 'Murderers!' He was thinking of his brother and this silenced everyone for a moment.

'As for "behaving properly" as you call it,' said Baruch, 'I just ask myself how "properly" they'd be behaving if *they'd* won. Never mind a bit of litter – *we'd* be the litter – our corpses.'

'He's right!'

'They'd have killed the lot of us!'

'Why do we have to be so particular?'

And with that, first Amnon and Yossi, and then one or two more, and finally about half the class, caught up their lunch-papers, screwed them up and started flinging them out all over the road and the ditch. Some flew right into the vine-yard on the other side of it. For a few moments the air was full of flying balls of paper like a fantastic midsummer snow-storm.

Hardly any of the girls, except Naomi who always said she was half a boy anyway, threw theirs, but most of the boys did. Ofer picked up his as if he had half a mind to throw it, but Lesley caught his arm. He looked down at her, looked round him in confusion and indecision, and then turned away into the back of the truck. But he didn't throw.

After this orgy of littering, there was a sudden silence. They all stood in the truck not knowing what to do or say. Looking out you could see the papers scattered everywhere, and all the boys, and especially Boaz, must have felt how bad it looked and been ashamed. But they were much too stub-born to do anything about it.

'Nu,' said Boaz at last, stirring uneasily. 'Let's go.'

'Please wait a moment.'

It was Ada. Very quietly, she pushed through the crowd of children standing between the long benches. Those she brushed past felt how she trembled and moved aside for her. She climbed backwards down the ladder and without a word began picking up the paper.

They watched her in paralysed silence.

All at once, Ofer nudged Lesley, and pointed with his head towards the vineyard. The Arab workers had stopped picking grapes and were standing in a tight group, looking at them. As Ada, oblivious, crossed the dry ditch and entered the rows of low vines to pick off the two balls of paper which had been caught in the leaves, Lesley was horrified to see the group start moving rather quickly towards them. The leader was a big Arab in a white kefiya who might have been Mustapha's father. His dark face was darker still from the angry scowl on it. His fists were doubled up and the others, both men and women, about ten of them altogether, came striding along behind him. He had something in his hand that glittered in the sharp sunlight . . .

He suddenly barked something in a deep, nasal voice, and waved his fist. At the same moment Lesley screamed out: 'Ada! Come back!' Boaz's head came up like a stag's and he leapt off the tail-board, jumped the ditch and grabbed Ada, pushing her behind him. She got such a fright that all the papers she'd been holding spilled on to the ground again.

'Get back in the truck!' Boaz ordered her – and it was an order. He stood facing the oncoming Arabs to cover, as it were, her retreat. But she didn't retreat at once. Her hands now trembling visibly, she picked up all the papers again, but she kept dropping them, and finally Lesley couldn't stand it another second. She jumped down and ran to help her, picking up the balls so fast they were just blurs, and then almost dragging Ada back across the ditch, her heart simply pounding with some unnameable fear.

Boaz and the leading Arab were shouting at each other, in Hebrew and Arabic. Neither understood the other, but what each was saying was clear to the children. The Arab was telling them to leave them alone and move off, and Boaz was trying to explain that they were only tidying up and were going to go at once, but he was being very aggressive about it, not polite at all. The Arab's voice rose higher and higher, and suddenly he raised his hand menacingly.

'Look out, he's got a gun!' cried Lesley, just like in a film. But Baruch said, 'Don't be silly, it's only clippers.' And Lesley looked and sure enough she saw a pair of grape-cutters in his hand. But even those could wound Boaz if the Arab so far forgot caution as to strike or stab him with them. The children watched breathlessly – how could Boaz get out of it? Should they get out and back him up? But just as they thought the tension would explode, a quiet voice spoke from the cabin in front of the truck.

'*Dai, kvar,*' said the voice of the driver. 'Enough. Get back to work, all of you. Boaz, let's go.'

The big Arab looked towards him and slowly lowered his hand. Grumbling, he backed off, the others behind him backing too. Boaz, after one glance at the driver, turned and walked calmly back to the truck.

Danny, who'd been craning through the open side, drew his head back in.

'What happened?' asked several hushed voices as the truck jerked forward.

'He's got a rifle in the cabin,' he replied in an awed whisper. 'I could just see the muzzle sticking out over the window-sill.'

They all found seats and huddled into them, sitting close together. Lesley sat next to Ada, who was shaking all over.

Ada still had hold of Lesley's hand, and with her other hand she clutched some of the paper balls. Her face was sweating. Lesley thought her perhaps the bravest woman she had ever personally known. It never came into her head that she had been quite brave herself, until Shula leant over and whispered, 'Heroine!' in a sort of half-joking way, but with real admiration in her eyes. The boys were all looking mulish and defiant, a sure sign they were feeling very small inside.

There was very little talking until their next stop, which was Tubas. This was the town where all the people had flocked into the streets to welcome the Israelis – or so the Israelis thought as they entered the town in their tanks and half-tracks and saw the flag and heard the cheers. But the flags disappeared and the cheers faded into horrified silence when the townspeople saw who they were. They had been told the Iraqis were coming!

In Tubas it was market day. The town was alive with bustling trade, and there were a few Israeli soldiers lounging about looking bored, so the group decided they might be bold enough to go a little farther from the truck and perhaps even buy something to take home. There wasn't much worth buying, to be sure. There were stalls full of junk which mostly seemed to have been made in Hong Kong, little tinny toys and every sort of plastic monstrosity. But finally they found a shop that sold Hebron glass, and several of them bought beads and medallions and little vases in yellow, peacock blue or green. The shop-keeper seemed genuinely friendly and insisted on bringing out coffee for them and as he spoke a little English they were able to exchange a few pleasantries. Their recent alarm began to fade.

They had broken up into smaller groups. Lesley's group, which included Ofer, Shula and Esther, strolled along the main street (which they'd been told not to leave) watching the bright bustle of the market. Lesley was thinking how strange it all was, all these people who, such a short time ago, had been their enemies, and who were now smiling and beckoning to them, the age-old craving for trade and profit pushing enmity aside. Jews were like that too, Lesley thought; they loved to buy and sell and do business and make money. Boaz had no right to sneer at the Arabs for it. (Maybe the war *had* changed him, after all. He never used to be so sarcastic and cynical.) It was a good thing, anyway, surely. Trading was obviously better than fighting, better for everybody. And if they still held some hatred and resentment in their hearts, well, was it surprising? Could there be a better cure for it than doing business, which the Jews enjoyed as much as themselves?

'Hacol b'lira! Hacol b'lira!'

The cry was familiar to them already, and they grinned at each other. 'More pencils?' asked Lesley, craning to see where the voice was coming from.

'No, it's nuts this time – look – almonds! He's over there. Let's get some.'

Lesley followed Ofer's pointing finger and saw the street-seller, a thin boy half-turned away from them, with a tray of small paper pokes of shelled almonds hung round his neck.

'Hacol b'lira!'

'A lira a *nut*, no doubt!' murmured Esther as they pushed their way towards him.

Just at that moment, the boy turned his black head towards them and Lesley stopped in her tracks, staring in disbelief. For his part, as he saw her the street-cry stuck between his lips and broke off in the middle.

'Mustapha!'

CHAPTER 25

Mustapha Grows Up

He did not reply, only stared. It was Mustapha – Mustapha three months older in time, three years in experience.

Before, he had been a fourteen-year-old boy, his body thin and small through overwork and under-feeding in his childhood, his eyes narrow and dark with depths of hard knowledge of hard-driven people and their ways of survival.

But now many new things had happened. His father, whom he disliked and feared, had, at the onset of war, taken him and one of his older sisters and fled to the home of his brother, Mustapha's uncle, who lived in Tubas. It was a foolish thing to do, but Mustapha's father was not a clever man, and just then he was a frightened one as well, which decreased his power to think clearly and imagine what might happen. All he knew was that Tubas was a lot farther from the Israeli border than their own little village; therefore it seemed safer, although it was on the West Bank of the river. He would have done better to keep that sluggish, narrow, vital stream between him and the enemy.

It was typical of the man that he left his wife and five small daughters behind in the village, without a qualm. They were women and hardly counted. He took his eldest daughter with him because he had some fondness for her as his first-born, but chiefly so as to have some female to look after him in his brother's house, and not have to depend on *his* women.

When the soldiers marched into the town, the two brothers were among those who poured out of their barricaded houses to cheer the 'Iraqis' – and fled back into them pell-mell when they saw who they really were. They cowered indoors, expecting the worst of worsts, and only days later, when food was running short, did they send their womenfolk venturing out to see if the market was functioning and if the enemy had moved on. They found that the notables of the town had long since surrendered.

Mustapha had watched all this with his wise little monkey-face blank, his narrow, observant eyes unreadable. Only once, to his sister, did he open his mouth.

'Our father is a fool and a coward!'

She recoiled with shock at this disrespect.

'How can you speak so? Our father is our father!'

'You are only a girl. I am a man and I can see what is true. He curses our army, but what did *he* do? If only I were old enough! How I would fight them! How I would kill, kill, kill them and drive them back into the sea!'

He pounded the tiled floor with his fist, bruising the side of his hand and making the little loose bits of cement jump. His sister watched him with a blank, black look, like his own, but with a little feminine slyness in it.

'Would you kill also the girl whose picture you keep in your shirt?'

Mustapha's head flew up, and the next minute he was on his feet and flying at her, but she was a big, strong girl and she pushed him away with one flat blow of her hand.

'Don't talk so much of killing till you get some strength into your body, little brother!' she sneered, hands on hips over him as he sprawled on the floor.

'Pig's daughter, I will kill *you*!' he shouted and came at her again, but she quickly dodged from the room and locked the door behind her, taunting him through it: 'Will you? Come and try, little donkey, I will ride you to market!'

His sister would not have dared treat him like that in front of their father, but he was out at the café drinking coffee and smoking his *narghila* as usual, and Mustapha was left with nothing to do but kick the door till his toes ached and then go out to the yard and console himself with his donkey.

Once he would have gone out and beaten it to relieve his feelings, but things were different now. Ever since his encounter with Lesley by the river, he had taken a different attitude to the donkey. Seeing Lesley petting it had been a revelation to him. To be friends with an animal! To give it titbits of food, to pat it and talk to it – well, until that time he would as soon have thought of patting and talking to his father's plough.

But the truth was, the boy was lonely, lonelier than he knew. He had some friends in the village, but they all had to work as hard as himself, and there was little time for playing or talking together. And he had no brothers. Sisters could be useful or they could be spiteful; they could never be companions or equals.

But the beast was different. It was a living creature who spent all the day with him, it was warm and soft and it responded to his touch and his voice, without ever being sly or cruel or indifferent like so many other creatures around him.

He felt foolish when he first began to stroke and talk to the donkey, and made very sure nobody saw him. But later he grew so fond if it that he no longer cared who knew of it, and when his sisters teased him he simply ignored them. His mother alone understood and was kind, giving him little bits of left-over carrot tops, or cabbage-leaves, or sometimes even apple-cores to give his animal. To watch his father beating it now made him feel sick with frustration and anger – and shame, for he hated to be reminded that he had once illused it himself.

Now he sat in the dirty straw by the donkey's feet and it put its grey nose down to be rubbed. Mustapha's feelings were so powerful that he would have cried, if he had not long ago got over crying.

'Pigs, sons of pigs and daughters of pigs!' he ground out between his teeth. Then he said a lot of much worse things, about the Israelis, about his father and his sister, things which can't be written down but which expressed his feelings and made him feel a bit better. The donkey nibbled his ear with its rubbery lips, and he couldn't help laughing because it tickled. 'Donkey, donkey, donkey ...' he said in a different, sing-song voice, and lay down on his back between the donkey's legs. 'When I am grown I shall join Al Fatah. Properly, not just doing odd jobs so they'll lend me the binoculars. I shall learn to fight like ten lions. I shall be the bravest fighter of them all. I shall not have to cross the river to lay my mines and plant my bombs. I can do it right here, for here is the enemy, strolling around the town, sitting in the cafés and buying in the shops ... And our people serve them and smile, but only because we know we shall kill them all one day ...'

He wished he could be sure that this was true – both parts; that they would kill their enemies and get back their pride, and also that the Arab tradesmen truly hated the Israelis in their hearts and were only smiling at the thought of revenge. But it was hard to go on believing this when he had to listen to his father and uncle, gloating between customers at his uncle's grocery shop:

'Business has never been better! These Jews know how to buy.'

'Especially the American tourists. Wait until their holiday in September! The war has done us no harm in the way of trade, at least. If only there's no more trouble! Things should be allowed to settle back to normal, to give us all a chance to make some real money.'

They even smiled at the soldiers. It was as if, by entering the shop with money in his pockets, any creature could become a friend and an equal in the eyes of Mustapha's father and uncle. Mustapha himself was forced to go into the streets of the market and peddle his little packets of nuts to anyone willing to buy – and those nuts were something that even the poorest Israeli could afford. He sold many more to them than to the townspeople. But that did not mean he had to smile at them. When they bought, he stared into their eyes with a blank look which just masked his hatred. He would not let his hands touch theirs, even to take money from them. He obliged them to put their dirty coins on to his tray and take the nuts without his help. It was the only gesture of rebellion left open to him, but it made him feel a little less ashamed, a little less defeated.

And now here he was, his body pushed and jostled by the market crowd, staring into the eyes of the girl Lesley who, though he never would admit it, had somehow changed his life. She was the exception in all his thoughts, in every way. She was a Jew, and yet he did not hate her. She was a girl, yet he did not despise her. Her photograph which he had stolen had lived so long next to his body that her face on it was just a blur, but in his mind it was still clear, as it had been the last time he had seen her waving to him across the river – and this was exceptional too, for he had tried to blot the past out of his mind and live only from day to day. He hated to think of life in the village, of his mother abandoned. He hated the thought of the nightmare he had lived through when he'd lost the donkey and had lain all night, trembling with terror more than with cold and damp, among the reeds by the bridge, the donkey in his sight, like a grey ghost on the other side of the River of Death – tantalizing, unreachable without a courage he could not muster in himself, not a second time, not all alone ... He loathed remembering it.

But the part that came with the morning, the meeting knee-deep in the Jordan the sublime taste of the chocolate, the recovery of the animal and the birth of love in him – for the donkey, and for who knew what else? – these things lingered in his mind and heart. He often dreamt of them.

Now the other Jewish children were looking at him, at Lesley, at each other.

'You *know* him?'

'Who is he?'

'I know,' said the fat one. 'He's him! The one from across the river!'

Mustapha did not know what to do. He wanted to speak to Lesley, but he didn't see how to do it. His eyes seldom betrayed him; he had learnt to keep them blank, to hide his thoughts. But now an expression of appeal came into them. And Lesley responded at once.

She turned to the others.

'Yes, it's him,' she said boldly. 'I want to talk to him. It's okay. You go and wait over there. I won't go out of sight.'

Too astonished to protest, the group moved to the other side of the crowded street, and watched them from the distance. Lesley turned back to Mustapha and walked slowly up to him.

CHAPTER 26

The Most
Important People

'Shalom.'

'Salaam.'

They looked at each other, awakened, happy, embarrassed. Then she put out her right hand and he took it and shook it and they half-laughed. Her hand was not soft like a little girl's nor hard like a woman's (all the grown girls and women he knew had hard, calloused hands) but something in between. It was very warm, and her grip was firm. Lesley, on her side, thought his hand felt somewhat too cool and limp, and she gripped harder than she usually did to encourage him to grip back, for she sensed his shyness and uncertainty. The strength in her hand challenged the man in him, and he suddenly pressed hers almost convulsively before letting go.

'How is your peace?' she asked in Hebrew, and he replied:

'My peace is good. And yours?'

'Also good.'

They spoke stiffly, but their eyes were shining. They were each strangely thrilled to see the other. Their meeting seemed to both uncanny, an event not to be dreamed of, not really part of normality.

'What are you doing here?' asked Lesley.

The boy shrugged and indicated the tray with hidden shame. 'What you see – selling. You want nuts?' He took a bag and offered it to her. 'Without money. I give you. Take.'

She took them and thanked him and ate one, and offered one to him. 'Are they yours?'

'My uncle's.'

'Won't he care?'

'He not know.'

They grinned. Then he asked her what she was doing in Tubas.

'I'm on a trip with my class.'

'You like our country?' he asked, with just a hint of irony.

She flushed and said, 'Yes, very much. I like the villages. Why did you leave your village?'

She at once noticed his withdrawn expression and knew she had touched him on the raw. He answered with his old roughness:

'That is my business.'

'I'm sorry.'

After a moment, feeling ashamed, he added, 'It was the war.'

'I understand.'

'I live now with my father and my uncle in this town.' He didn't consider his sister worth mentioning.

'It goes well with you?'

'Not bad.'

'And Eeyore?' she asked eagerly, without thinking.

'What?'

'Oh ...' She giggled, and a smile twitched his tough mouth at the sight. 'Eeyore – that's what I used to call your donkey. Hee-haw – Eeyore – it's a donkey's name from a book.'

'He's okay.'

'Did you keep your promise?'

'Yes.'

'You don't beat him, ever?'

'Only when he is bad,' he said, to keep his pride, for he couldn't let her know how completely he had obeyed her.

'You shouldn't beat him at all! He doesn't mean to be bad.'

'He is lazy and no good,' he said sternly, but then he smiled. 'But I like him – sometimes.'

'You have him with you here?'

'Yes, of course.'

'But this is your work now – the nuts?' He nodded. 'So why do you need him?'

'He carries things. He carries us. We would be nothings without a donkey,' he said. 'My father rode him here, all the way from our village, with all our stuff on his back too. He never gets tired.'

'I thought you said he was lazy and no good.'

'Oh, that is only sometimes.'

'I think you love him now.'

'Of course not. He's just an animal.'

They stood for a while saying nothing. Lesley waved lightly to Ofer, who was craning his neck to watch her.

'You can't go back to your village now?' Lesley asked suddenly.

'No.'

'Would you like –' she began, then hesitated. The war was over. Surely there would be proper peace soon, and yet ... Would the kibbutz allow ...? What would her friends think of her? But she finished her sentence. 'Would you like to visit the kibbutz?'

'What?'

'My – village. Where I live. You can see your village from there.'

He stared at her. He was trying to come to grips with the idea of seeing his village like that, from the Jewish side of the river. To visiting that hated place which, had it not been for Lesley, he would long have dreamt of destroying. He wouldn't mind destroying it anyway, if he could just be sure she wouldn't be there at the time.

'No!'

'Why not? Why are you angry?' He turned his head away. His eyes had a curious burning in them. 'Mustapha ... I understand how you feel about – us. About the war and everything, but –'

'No you don't. You can't understand.'

'But we're not enemies, are we? You and I?'

He looked round at her slowly. His eyes were lustrous like black olives, and just as bitter, but they softened as they looked at her.

'Perhaps no. But I am enemy to all your people, except only you.'

'Don't talk like that!'

'You want lies? That is the truth. You must know it.'

'But the war's over!'

'It is not over. It is not begun.'

She gazed at him with a deep sensation of horror swelling inside her. 'But Mustapha, it can't be like that! Don't you see that it can't go on and on? There's been so much fighting, so many people are dead. How can you want to go on? Let it stop, let it stop and let's have peace!'

'You can say that. You can talk of peace. You – won,' he said with great difficulty. 'But when you lose, it is different. Then you can't talk about stopping. You must talk about fighting and you must fight, until you lose your –' He groped desperately for the English word.

'Till you lose your life?' Lesley cried.

'No, no! Till you don't have to feel –' He curled his hand into a hard claw and made a savage gesture towards his chest as if some beast were tearing at him. And Lesley understood.

'Ashamed.'

'Yes, *yes*! Till you are not ashamed – any more.'

'Oh, Mustapha! Then there'll be no end to it – ever. Because someone must always lose.'

'It will not be us. Not at the end.'

'You will fight? You, yourself?'

'I will fight and fight and fight, till there is not a Jew left.'

She touched the furious fist which was clenched, trembling with violent passion, against the side of the tray.

'I'm a Jew too. You won't kill me?'

'I don't know,' he said despairingly. 'Perhaps. If I shell your village and the shell kills you, I am sorry. But you are only one person and I am only one person. We are not important.'

Lesley felt, indistinctly but strongly, that this was not merely wrong but perhaps the greatest untruth – the gravest false statement – she had ever heard in her life. But she was too overwhelmed by the conviction that he was wrong to be able to find the words to say so to him.

'That's not right,' was all she could manage, but in a voice that shook with feeling. 'That's not right! I know it's not!'

'It must be right,' Mustapha said stolidly, staring into the distance. 'My father,' he added suddenly, 'he thinks he is important. If you think you are important, you behave like –' He stopped. He had seen Ofer and her other friends, impatient and anxious, beginning to cross the street towards them. Mustapha turned back to Lesley with a deep frown.

'Your friends come,' he said.

'But won't we –'

'No. What use is it? Goodbye.'

'Mustapha!'

'I said goodbye!'

He began to move away from her, then stopped and made a quick, sudden movement of his hand into his shirt. It was so sharp that it actually scared her for a moment, a moment that she felt ashamed of when she thought of it later. He pushed a crumpled, fuzzy piece of paper into her hand.

'I don't want this any more.'

Then he was gone, pushing his tray ahead of him through the crowd. For several moments she was able to follow his black head until it disappeared round the edge of a stall selling water-melons. She stared at the place, her mind in confusion. Then she looked down to see what he had given her, though she'd guessed already and dreaded to be sure.

In her hand, dog-eared, worn and soiled, was her photograph. Yet the creases were new, and had been made by his hand only a moment ago. Till that impulse of enmity, that had made him crumple it and thrust it at her, it had been kept smooth, and the other damage had been caused by much handling.

She held it and stared at it with a hollow sense of loss. It was more than the loss of her strange friend, or the exchange of a friend for an enemy. It was something like the loss of hope. For if she and Mustapha were enemies, what chance was there of their countries ever making peace?

The others burst to her side through the crowd.

'Well? What did he say?'

'How long you were talking!'

'What happened? What did he give you?'

Lesley tried to pull herself together. 'Just some nuts. Here – have some.'

'But what did he say?'

'Oh – just some *shtuyot*. It doesn't matter. Come on. Let's get back to the others.'

Ofer, Esther and another boy led the way back to the truck, but Shula walked behind with Lesley.

She peered up into her face. Lesley turned away her head.

'What you crying?' Shula whispered in English.

'I'm not!' said Lesley fiercely.

'It wasn't just *shtuyot*, was it?'

'It was, it was! He's an idiot, he can't understand anything! Oh –' Her voice pitched up shrilly. 'Do let's stop talking about him!'

Shula tried to hold her arm, but she jerked away. However, when they were settled in the truck she leant forward.

'I'm sorry,' she said very quietly. Shula nodded and screwed her nose up.

The truck racketed along on the road to Jerusalem. The children all sang the latest pop song which, oddly, was also a sort of hymn which had come out of the war: 'Jerusalem of Gold! Of copper and light! For all your songs, I'll be the violin . . .' After a while Lesley sang with the others.

In the Old City they went straight to the Wall. The religious authorities had already made separate sections for men and for women. To the kibbutz children, this was at once a joke and an outrage. But if you wanted to approach the Wall, there was nothing for it but to obey the new rules. The boys had to cover their heads. Some of them laughed and cat-called, but elderly people who were praying there looked so shocked that the boys were silenced.

Lesley was more interested in the place itself. Rami had said the Wall was in a narrow alley, but this had changed. The Israelis had begun to clear a wide area in front of the Wall, bulldozing whole streets aside so that an open square could be created. The Wall itself now loomed up monolithically; each stone was so huge that it seemed a miracle it could ever have been laid upon another. And between these vast blocks were crevices. Into these cracks, old Jews piously slipped bits of paper with prayers written on them, according to age-old tradition.

Lesley watched them, the old men with their broad-brimmed hats and beards and side-ringlets on the far side of the barrier, 'davening' as her father called it – rocking as they intoned their prayers; and on her side, the old women, swathed in shawls which covered all their hair. (What must it be like, thought Lesley, to be an orthodox Jewess, and have to shave your head when you married?) Of course there were plenty of young people too, and modern clothes; the tourists, especially Americans, were there in their hundreds, and the noise was fantastic. There were peddlers selling things, and when Lesley went close to them, she saw to her amazement that they were Arabs, selling souvenir medals of Moshe Dayan and other Israeli heroes! She felt bewildered. It seemed so undignified. Yet the way some of the Israelis were behaving at the Wall offended her too. She didn't have any special feeling for the sacredness of those ancient stones, though the very size of them impressed her; but men like Moshe had died here, and men like her father looked on it as a great symbol of Jewish history and continuity. It was no place for idle chatter and buying souvenirs. You had to respect it. She was glad Ofer hadn't cat-called.

She stood back from the Wall for some time, just watching the scene and thinking, puzzling it all out. The bulldozers had stopped work, but the edge of the cleared part was piled high with broken bricks and masonry. People had lived here; perhaps the very spot she was standing on had been somebody's living-room. It made her feel very uncomfortable. She looked again at the Arabs selling the medallions, at others, just beyond the square, with ice-cream stands and stalls for coffee or iced drinks ... Were they accepting the Israelis, or just making use of them – insulting them? How helpless they must feel, to come to this so quickly! Since talking to Mustapha, she no longer felt it was a good sign that trade had sprung up while the soldiers were still to be seen on guard everywhere.

She sighed heavily. Her heart was bruised, somehow.

When the others came and they all walked through the old market together, something she would ordinarily have revelled in for it was like scenes from the Arabian Nights, she was too depressed to look properly at the myriad delights that tempted the eye on every side of the half-lit, narrow alleys. Jewellery, rugs, sheepskin coats, delicious food, leather, glass, old pottery and metalwork of all kinds slipped past the tails of her eyes in a kind of exotic blur, while the others dashed in all directions with cries of excitement and Ada and Boaz kept having to round up the stragglers like sheepdogs.

All the time her hand was in the pocket of her shorts, the fingers curled round the crumpled photograph lightly but tensely, as if tenderly protecting it. In the lorry she had had a strong impulse to throw it angrily away. But this had passed.

All too soon, for the others at least, it was time to start for home. They had seen the Wall, had coffee and bought souvenirs in the market, stood under the great crenellated towers of the Damascus Gate, touched, with something like awe, the sun-whitened stones of King David's Tower and seen – most beautiful of all, perhaps – the exquisite Mosque of Omar.

Now they were very tired, and it was suddenly almost too much effort to drag their weary feet back to where they had left the truck, outside the City walls beside the Dome of the Rock. It was already twilight . . .

Suddenly Shula noticed that Lesley was missing.

She at once started a hue and cry. 'Lesley's gone! What could have happened? Perhaps she's been kidnapped!'

Ada, who had spent the better part of the day in a state of terror that something like this would happen, went white as chalk and clutched Boaz and the driver with either hand.

'Go! Go and find her! Where were we when she was last seen with us?'

'In the Mosque!' said several voices.

The two men dashed back through the gate of the City.

Ada ordered the others to get into the truck, and forbade
anyone to get out or wander off anywhere. A few pleaded
for ice-creams from a nearby kiosk, but Ada was too agitated
to take the slightest further risk.

'I knew we couldn't get through the day without *something*!' she kept moaning, wringing her hands. 'Oh where
is she? Where *can* she have got to?'

A moment later, Ofer, lingering on the tail-board of the
lorry, gave a shout and pointed to the gate. It was Lesley,
running towards them through the strange, mystic, sun-
echoing, glowing half-light of the Jerusalem evening. Her
feet were noiseless as they flew over the cobbles, and her face
had a queer limpid look of tranquillity.

Ada chewed her to pieces, standing there by the back of
the truck railing at her while she hung her head and did not
try to explain. Then Ada cuffed her behind and sent her up
into the truck. It was almost dark in there, and while Ada
fussed outside about how they could let the men know she
was found, Lesley squeezed in at the end of a bench next to
Ofer and gazed out over the hills, where a last touch of red-
gold sunlight was still to be seen burning on the far crests.

'Jerusalem of gold, of copper and light –' she sang softly
to herself.

'Where did you go?' hissed Shula in her ear, leaning forward from her place opposite.

'Back to the Wall. I had something to do there.'

'What, though?'

But Lesley didn't reply. Her pocket was empty now. The
long-cherished and finally rejected photograph was lodged
in a chink as high as she could reach, pushed far in and
wedged there with a little stone. On the back of it, under the
now unreadable notes written so long ago by her mother,
was added a brief prayer, written with a stump of pencil she
had borrowed from a stranger :

'Shalom b'eneynu ubeyn ameynu.'

'Peace betwen us and between our peoples.'

God *might* be there, and He *might* listen. You never knew. Of course it was superstition really, she supposed. But anything which gave you back a little hope when you'd nearly lost it, is as good as a miracle ...

The two men were found and the journey home started. The light faded through pale gilt to pearl to the platinum-silvered blackness of a moonlit summer night. Lesley gazed out at it through the square dark frame at the back of the lurching truck. The lights of men and of God twinkled face-to-face across limitless black spaces. The mysteries of war and peace, friend and enemy, love and hatred, were swamped for the time being in that vast black star-sandwiched emptiness. Lesley allowed her heart an hour's peace, and was so rapt in it that she did not even notice at first that Ofer was holding her hand.

And Mustapha? Mustapha sat in the straw and leant his thin back against the thin ribs of the donkey and let the poison of his hatred wash out of him, a burning, bitter salt tide of tears. It was so long since he had last cried that he had forgotten the taste. He didn't understand himself why he cried or why he was suffering. He felt as if peeling the photo away from his side had uncovered a wound which was bleeding. He wanted it back. He wanted it back! It had been like a talisman, and now he had thrown it away he felt unsure, unsafe. He no longer knew what he was or what he would be. He had said that he was of no importance, that *she* was of no importance, and she had denied the truth of it, and he believed *her* and not himself.

He didn't in the least know why, but his tears, his awful sense of loss, told him that he and that girl he would never see again were the two most important people in the world.

Glossary

of main Hebrew (and Yiddish) words used in this story

abba – father, daddy
aboov – oboe
alph – first letter of Hebrew alphabet
Arav – Arab (Plural, Aravim)
avodat-bayit – homework
begele – salt biscuits twisted into '8' shape
bet – second letter of the alphabet
betach – of course
bidiyuk – exactly
b'ofen automati – automatically
chaver (usually spelt this way in English, but pronounced
    'khavair') – friend, comrade (Plural, chaverim)
chevra – your own group or crowd of friends
chevrai – kids, friends, company, 'gang'
chevraiman – an all-rounder, a good sport
chutzpah – cheek
chutzpahdik – cheeky
communa – clothes-store in a kibbutz; place where ironing,
    mending etc. are done
dafka – unlikely, the opposite of what one expects
dai ! – enough !
eze yofi ! – how lovely !
fantasti – fantastic, wonderful
gimmel – third letter of the alphabet
'gingie' – red-haired person
gvul – border
hacol – all, everything
hacol b'lira ! – everything for a pound !
hashka'a – irrigation, watering of crops
kafkafim – Japanese sandals
kashrut – laws of Jewish housekeeping, cooking and diet

katan – little

kavod – honour

kfar – village

khamor – donkey

khasiot – brassieres

khasitot – war-fronts

kibbutznik – person who lives in a kibbutz

kitta – class; the building in a kibbutz where a whole group of children live

kol tuv ! – good luck !

kosher – like 'kashrut'

kova-tembel – a soft, pointed hat, like a dunce's cap, much worn in Israel

kvar – already

legumri – completely

limon – lemon

lira – an Israeli pound (£1 equals 8 lira, about)

lo normali ! – not normal ! super !

madrich – youth leader

ma pitom? – slang expression, meaning 'What are you talking about? What next? Is it possible?'

mazal – luck

mensch – a real man

meshuggah – mad, crazy

metapelet – children's nurse, house-mother of a kibbutz children's house

mikasachat – lawn-mower

mishkefet – field-glasses

mitz – fruit-squash

mitzvot – religious duties

naknikiot – sausages

nu? – slang for 'well? so?'

oy-va-voy ! – expression of warning, usually to a naughty child

pitta – flat Arab bread

p'oola – an action (Plural: p'oolot)

primitivim – primitive people

rabbi – religious teacher, Jewish priest

refet – cowshed, dairy, herd

Sabra – a person born in Israel. Taken from the name of a sweet, but prickly, cactus-fruit

sacit – a little bag (Plural : saciot)

sheli – my, mine

shmaltz – sickly sentiment

shmatter – rag

shofar – ram's-horn, traditionally blown to call Jews to prayer

shomair – guard, night watchman

shtok ! – shut up !

shtut, shtuyot – rubbish ! nonsense !

snobbit – (slang) a snob, snooty, stuck-up

socialistim – socialists

stam – untranslatable slang expression, 'ordinary' 'just' 'merely' – opposite to 'special' 'extraordinary'

tamid – always, for ever

tembel – idiot

tipsha – silly (for a girl)

t'nua – a movement, sometimes a political movement

tson – sheep, sheepfold, flock

tsrif – hut

uzi – sub-machine gun used by Israeli soldiers